KV-374-955

Angela Dracup was born and educated in Bradford and read psychology at Sheffield and Manchester Universities. She is a chartered psychologist and works with education authorities to assess the needs of children with learning and behavioural problems. She is married with one daughter and lives in Harrogate, North Yorkshire.

THE BURDEN OF DOUBT

When consultant anaesthetist Moira Farrell is found stabbed to death, shock reverberates amongst her medical colleagues. Worse follows amid rumours regarding her clinical director's incompetence. Had Moira been silenced forever to prevent her from blowing the whistle on him? But then a petty criminal who had worked as a gardener for Moira comes under suspicion. DCI Ed Swift must unravel the tangled threads of the murder whilst his own daughter, unaccountably, has run into trouble with the police. Then, unexpectedly, Swift's investigation flushes out a killer with all the motivation for the murder. Will justice now be done?

Books by Angela Dracup
Published by The House of Ulverscroft:

ANGELA DRACUP

THE BURDEN OF DOUBT

Complete and Unabridged

ULVERSCROFT
Leicester

First published in Great Britain in 2007 by
Robert Hale Limited
London

First Large Print Edition
published 2008
by arrangement with
Robert Hale Limited
London

British Library CIP Data

Dracup, Angela
  The burden of doubt.—Large print ed.—
Ulverscroft large print series: crime
  1. Swift, Ed (Fictitious character)—Fiction
  2. Police—England—Yorkshire—Fiction
  3. Detective and mystery stories 4. Large type books
  I. Title
  823.9′14 [F]

  ISBN 978–1–84782–438–7

Published by
F. A. Thorpe (Publishing)
Anstey, Leicestershire

Set by Words & Graphics Ltd.
Anstey, Leicestershire
Printed and bound in Great Britain by
T. J. International Ltd., Padstow, Cornwall

1

The little white van pulled to a halt. It was 8.45 a.m. on a dismal January morning and the van's cheery pink *Merry Maids* logo was barely discernible in the gloom. Spots of freezing rain had started to smear the windscreen. The occupants of the van, who at this point were neither maids nor merry, yawned as they swung themselves out of the van on to the wide gravel drive.

'No lights on,' Pat, the driver, remarked, glancing towards the house before walking around to the back of the van to pull open the doors and reach inside for the bag containing the *Merry Maids* overalls and the firm's standard issue of pink rubber gloves.

Her companion, Meg, nipped the end of her cigarette and placed the dead results in the breast pocket of her pink overall. 'Brass monkey weather,' she observed, shuffling around to the back door of the house, clutching her padded jacket around her.

Pat selected a key from the fat bunch she carried in her handbag. Most clients were prepared to hand out house keys: the firm prided themselves on the integrity of their staff. And the staff, in their turn, knew that if anything went missing from the houses they cleaned in the clients' absence, they would be the first ones under suspicion. As the key touched the lock Pat prepared to exert the pressure required to slot it into the snug gap. But at the touch of the key the door began to open and Pat found herself stumbling to stop her weight falling forward. 'Door's open!' she exclaimed. Walking forward, with Meg following cautiously at her heels, she called, 'Mrs Farrell?' The words echoed, high and anxiety-tinged, into the large hallway.

Three mornings a week, at 8.30 or thereabouts, Pat and Meg would greet Mrs Farrell and sometimes Professor Patel in the kitchen, before proceeding to the walk-in cloakroom under the stairs where they would remove their coats and then climb the stairs to the first floor and spend an hour wiping, polishing and vacuuming, before returning to the ground floor, snatching a coffee — and a cigarette if the coast was clear — then repeating the same dirt-busting procedure in the kitchen and reception rooms.

This morning they tiptoed cautiously over across the wood floor, the one they polished each week with a mixture of beeswax and vinegar. The curtains on both the ground floor and landings were closed. Pat stopped, resting her hand on the dark wood newel post, atop of which was a large, ornately carved acorn. The acorn required regular applications of almond oil and a fair bit of elbow grease to make it shine. And it was indeed shining away now in the gleam of the electric lights which were all on.

'I'm getting a bad feeling about this,' Meg muttered, hanging back.

Pat raised her chin and walked forward steadily up the stairs and on to the wide landing. Together they made a tour of the main guest room and its starkly white art deco bathroom suite. On one of the beds the covers had been thrown back, revealing the crumpled white sheets beneath.

'Looks like they've had guests this weekend,' Meg remarked.

'That's not like them; they seem to like to keep themselves to themselves.' Pat was surveying the room with hands on hips. 'Funny isn't it,' she mused, 'how most rich folks spend their time having company or jazzing off all over the world? They seem to need a lot of entertainment.'

Meg was not one to muse on the generalities of human behaviour. 'We'll be needing to strip these sheets off later and put them in the wash,' she said.

There were creaking sounds as the central

heating warmed the wooden floors. A draught of cold air stole up the staircase. The two women eyed each other nervously.

Pat went back on to the landing, calling out again, 'Mrs Farrell? Hello, hello.'

They looked in the master suite, in the his and hers dressing areas, in the master bathroom.

Nothing.

'Oh dear,' Pat exclaimed in a stage whisper.

Returning downstairs they went into the sitting-room.

'Dear God Almighty!' Meg bent double, gasping with shock and revulsion.

Pat stared in frozen horror. Talk about blood on the carpet. And on the furniture. And all over Mrs Farrell's white Indian rug. She found herself automatically considering the best way to clean up, and flushed at the crass inappropriateness of the thought.

It was now a few minutes past nine. The sky had darkened and a mean wind drove small daggers of freezing rain against the windows.

By this time the two maids were very far from merriment.

★ ★ ★

Ed Swift looked down at his watch. 9.55 a.m. The speaker had been on his feet for less than half an hour and already time had slowed to a crawl. His voice was a dull monotone, he made no use of visual aids or humour and his subject was that of statistical reliability in psychometric testing.

Swift straightened his spine against the back of his chair and made an effort to dredge up some interest. Still another fifty minutes to go before the morning coffee break. He took a glance at the conference delegates sitting on the row beside him. Their body language suggested they were as bored as he was. Weren't the best speakers usually put on first? Surely sponsors and organizers preferred to avoid a mass walkout after lunch. If things carried on like this the place would be empty after the coffee pots had dried up.

Glancing towards the windows he saw that the hesitant sleet of an hour ago had now turned to snow. Flakes as big as rose petals were tumbling out of a grey, glowering Yorkshire sky. Already the lawns flanking the hotel hosting the conference were coated in pristine white.

He became aware of a door at the back of the room opening, of hurried footsteps making their way to the front of the audience. It was one of the conference assistants, a young woman in a tightly fitting navy suit and black stiletto heels. She went up to the speaker, silently claiming his attention. He looked visibly annoyed and pointedly finished his long sentence before allowing her to communicate with him in whispered phrases. Frowning he stepped back from the microphone and the woman moved forward to speak.

'If Detective Chief Inspector Swift is here could he please go to the organizer's desk in the lobby.' She paused, clearing her throat. 'As soon as possible. There's an urgent phone call for him.'

Swift's heart lurched. Reason told him this would be a work call, but his emotions automatically leapt into action, hurling a picture of his daughter into his mind, taunting him with visions of some horrible road accident, or some unidentified distress or menace which might be threatening her. His reaction was founded on his long experience in the police force; a knowledge of how tragedy could come out of the blue and alter people's lives at a single stroke.

He got to his feet and edged along the row, schooling himself to be calm and unhurried. There were one or two curious glances from other delegates wondering what could be so important as to justify interrupting a speaker in the middle of a lecture. The conference assistant met him in the aisle and led the way through the exit door and into the lobby. 'This way, sir,' she said, moving to the organizer's office and pointing to the telephone whose handset was resting on the desk beside it, indicating that the caller had been holding.

He picked it up. 'Ed Swift.'

'Ed. Damian here. There's been an incident at a house on the north-west side of Ilkley. A suspicious death.' He began to give details.

Swift listened, envisaging the newly appointed Superintendent Damian Finch orbiting his office, the phone clamped fiercely against his ear as he projected himself into the investigation ahead.

Relief swept through him: it was work.

★ ★ ★

In the bedroom of her small flat overlooking Five Rise Locks in the small town suburb of Bingley, a few miles north of Bradford, Detective Constable Laura Ferguson snapped awake as her radio, which was tuned to Classic FM, sprang into action and began playing her a fragment of Beethoven's Symphony Number Eight.

Her mind was switching itself on like a row of street lamps steadily picking out the details which had faded into the dusk of a winter afternoon. From the gloom of a winter morning the dark head of a man infiltrated her field of vision. Oh hell!

She'd been at a party in one of the other flats in the block. He'd chatted her up. He was quirky and funny and flattering, and way too sexy to resist. She'd brought him home and taken him to bed. Just like that.

Well, to be fair she had met him twice before some weeks ago at the estate agency which had handled the purchase of her flat. He had been a very persuasive salesman and she had taken quite a fancy to him right from the start, she supposed. All strictly business, of course.

But to let him pick her up at a party. To take him home and into her bed, and then to let him stay on. And then stay the night. She would blame the plentiful intake of wine on both their parts. Because if it hadn't been for that she could think of no excuse whatsoever.

She sat up, pulled on her blue towelling robe which lay crumpled on the floor like an abandoned slut, and parted the curtains. The world outside was snugly carpeted in white, the only relief being the contrasting black gleam of the canal. Snow was falling steadily, vanishing as it hit the cold white surface of the lying snow or dissolved into the canal.

She tiptoed to her wardrobe, glancing at

the bed and praying its occupant wouldn't wake up. Not just yet. Not until she was on the point of leaving when she would issue him firm instructions to shut the door behind him when he left.

Showered and dressed she switched on the kettle to make coffee and rooted in the biscuit tin for something to sustain her on the drive out to the station. He stole up behind her and the first she knew of his awakening was the feel of his arms around her waist and the touch of his mouth on the back of her neck.

'Don't even think of shooting me a line about coming back to bed,' she told him. 'I've got to go to work.'

'Och, lassie, you're a wee tease,' he said, squeezing her tighter and mimicking her Scottish lilt to perfection. 'And it's only just gone seven.'

'I'm a wee bonehead for letting a slippery shite like ye have your wicked way wi' me,' she responded tartly. 'Away with ye!'

'I've no clothes on!'

She squirmed out of his grasp. Reluctantly abandoning thoughts of coffee, she began to collect up her things. 'Well, get them on,' she snapped. 'Help yourself to coffee if you must. Then go. And be sure to drop the latch.'

'Never fear, you can always trust an estate agent to behave well in an empty house.

That's my job.' He offered a stunningly seductive wink.

'Aah!' She stalked to the door.

'You're the loveliest girl I've ever met,' he said, with a wry smile.

'For pity's sake!' She slipped around the door.

'And the cruellest,' he said without rancour, as she closed it behind her.

★ ★ ★

An hour and a half later in the CID room at the station Laura and her colleague Constable Doug Wilson were ploughing through their backlog of paperwork.

Laura laid down her pen, gazing out of the window at the snow which was falling in giddy swirls. She wondered if Saul had left the flat and hoped he'd remembered to lock the door. And then she thought of her mother's face if she knew her daughter had had a one night stand with a man she hardly knew. And then she felt a lurch of horror as she tried desperately to remember if Saul had used a condom. Stabs of molten alarm sped through her nerves. Yes, he had, she was sure of it. But, of course, condoms were by no means one hundred per cent reliable. Her heart rate was now running at an alarming high. What about the morning after pill? Could she slip out to a pharmacy and get one? The idea swamped her with guilt. She had long since rejected the Catholic faith in which her parents had brought her up, but the idea of killing potential life still held a pull. She simply couldn't do it. Oh hell! She lifted her head and took a few deep breaths. Banishing the dilemma, and Saul, from her mind she went back to the paperwork with a small sigh.

Doug looked up and smiled as he watched her. 'Fretting at the bit?' he suggested.

'Uh-huh. I could do with some action.'

'I remember the feeling,' he said. 'When I was young and eager and longing to be at the cutting edge. But now, I don't mind a spell of keeping my bum on the seat and letting the old brain have a bit of a rest. Not to mention the nerves. There'll be trouble and agitation before long. Always is.'

Right on cue the phone on Doug's desk trilled. He straightened his back as he heard the new super's voice. For Doug, Damian Finch was a New Age police person: crisp, correct and decisive. And pretty clever if the framed first class degree from Oxford sitting on his shelves was to be believed. Doug listened as he spoke. 'I see, sir. Yes, I can come straight away.' He listened again. 'Yes, sir, Constable Ferguson is here too.'

Laura's head snapped around to look at him.

'We're commanded to join the big boss in his office for a preliminary briefing,' he told her. 'I took the liberty of suggesting that you were free.'

'As a bird,' she said, jumping to her feet and slipping her arms into her black jacket.

They walked together along the corridor, Laura trying to stop herself breaking into a trot. Doug looked down at her and raised an eyebrow. 'Told you so.'

★　★　★

An hour later the assembled team sat in Detective Chief Superintendent Finch's office, sipping the ground coffee he kept constantly simmering in his room. Swift glanced around, marvelling at the way in which Finch had transformed the cluttered den of the former superintendent, Tom Lister, into a place of brightness and order which proclaimed a dedicated organizer's touch. Banished were the piles of tottering paperwork on the desk, the little cluster of family photographs and the little tin ashtray which had once brimmed over with cigarette ends. In their place were a pen stand, a notebook and a state of the art laptop. On the shelves to the side of the desk were neatly stacked police manuals, books on criminal law and Finch's university degree certificates. A large potted palm sat in one corner of the room, its shiny leaves forming an artistic tracery against the background of the pure white walls. Above was a hand-painted reproduction of Da Vinci's *Mona Lisa* keeping watch over the room with her steady disturbing gaze and her inscrutable smile.

As Detective Chief Superintendent in the Homicide and Major Enquiry team Damian Finch was responsible for the work of three stations on the north-west side of Bradford. Swift knew that his workload was heavy, and that he was required to spend a good deal of his time in meetings, where the discussion of budgets and finance would no doubt form the lion's share of the agenda. He guessed him to be in his early fifties, but already his hair was greying at the temples and beneath his coolly professional exterior he sensed an air of harassment.

Resuming his place behind his desk, Finch placed his china mug beside the laptop and began to speak, his delivery slowly and carefully enunciated as though the acuity of the hearing and comprehension of his subordinates might be in doubt. 'The body of

13

a woman has been found in the sitting-room of her house. She's suffered stab wounds. The uniform response team believe she's Mrs Moira Farrell, a consultant anaesthetist at the Wharfedale Hospital. Her husband is a professor at the Leeds Medical school. Orthopaedics.'

'High-powered duo,' Doug volunteered in his gentle measured tones.

Finch didn't like to be interrupted. He shot the ageing constable a sharp glance look, decided he was harmless and pressed on. 'We're going to be under the spotlight,' he said. 'I would draw your attention to a case last year in south division where a regrettable mistake was made in charging the wrong suspect, a well-respected doctor.'

Swift recalled the case well. A keen, newly appointed DI had built a powerful case against a sixty-year-old GP on the verge of retirement, accusing her of unlawfully 'assisting' the death of a seventy-year-old man who had left his entire estate to her. The case had gone to court, where the defence lawyer had pulled a previously ignored rabbit out of the hat, namely an embittered stepchild who had got wind of the will change and promptly set about taking revenge by murdering the old man himself and cleverly setting up the doctor as he did so. The rabbit had been transfixed in the glare of the defence lawyer's piercing spotlight. The case had collapsed.

The lawyers in the Crown Prosecution Service had been furious to have ended up with egg on their faces. And after the hounded doctor had cracked under the strain and died of a stroke, the medical fraternity had been up in arms.

He could appreciate Finch's concern. If you were superintendent you had to take due account of the status of the victim, and you had little choice but to regard those of high or sensitive status (whether that was social, racial or financial) as having priority over the rest. Which was one of the reasons why he, himself, had no wish to climb any further up the police status ladder.

'Has Professor Farrell been informed?' Swift enquired.

'We haven't been able to contact him.' Finch paused. 'His secretary said he was attending a conference in Lancaster. We've checked on it and it appears he's arrived and registered but he couldn't immediately be located. And, by the way, his name's Patel — I gather Moira Farrell worked under her maiden name.'

There was a short silence as each member of the team made their own evaluation of the reasons for a woman declining to take her husband's name.

'We'll follow up and make contact with Patel,' Swift told his boss. 'Are there any children to inform?'

Finch shook his head. 'No children as far as I'm aware, but Moira Farrell's mother lives locally. She's been informed by uniform but I'd like her seen as soon as possible.'

Swift set about draining the last of his coffee, already steeling himself for the inevitable visit to the crime scene.

'I'm ready to authorize as much manpower as you need on this one,' Finch told Swift, his tone crisp. 'I haven't had an unsolved murder case in three years.'

*　*　*

'It was either beautifully judged, or a lucky strike.' Tanya Blake, pathologist, sat back on her heels and observed the corpse with an expression which mingled professional conjecture with a hefty dash of human sympathy for a life cut short. 'A direct hit to the carotid artery. Just one hit, as far as I can tell.' She paused. 'That's all it takes, of course.'

Swift nodded. He had every confidence in Blake's judgement. She had invariably got things right on the other cases they had worked on together. Not only was she young, bright, and well on top of her chosen work,

16

she had that streak of intuition that made her a valuable member of the investigative team.

He looked down at the dead woman sitting in a chair, the front of her body slumped against her writing desk and lapped in a great pool of blood. He imagined the 'hit', one plunge into the white skin of the neck, a great plume of fresh, warm blood arcing out into the air. A myriad droplets speckling the atmosphere like summer drizzle.

As Tanya worked, a police cameraman was capturing every angle of the body on film. Swift sometimes wondered what that job must be like, constantly recording scenes of carnage. Maybe police photographers comforted themselves with dreams of being future film-makers, biding their time whilst waiting for the call from Hollywood.

'From the look of her she was a healthy woman in her prime,' Blake commented. 'But then, you never know what you'll find until you get your corpse on the slab.' All this was said in matter-of-fact tones with a lacing of black humour, prompting Swift to wonder if there was any truth in the general view held by the police that pathologists truly appreciated sectioning up dead bodies. Looking around he noticed one or two smudgy marks at the edge of the shiny red pool. They didn't look too promising, but maybe forensics could work their magic and get something useful from them.

'Any sign of the weapon?' he asked Tanya.

'Not so far.'

'What might it have been?'

'Something slim and pointed, I'd say. A very sharp skewer maybe, or precision scissors. There were probably both of those kind of items available in the house. Plenty of kitchens harbour potentially vicious weapons. And, as a doctor, she'd have access to any number of lethal instruments.' Blake gestured towards the battered Gladstone bag she always carried with her.

'At home?' Swift asked, raising an eyebrow.

'Items from work sometimes find their way home from time to time,' Blake observed, with a dry smile. 'And usually return to where they belong.' She reached out a hand and touched a strand of the dead woman's hair. It was long, thick and black with a springy, natural-looking curl to it. 'A very striking woman,' she murmured. 'At least she would have been when she was alive. Which would have been between five and six hours ago.'

'Right, so she was killed around six this morning?'

'That's what the temperature reading suggests.' Blake tilted her head, allowing a shiny streak of hair to fall over one cheek.

'Looks like your killer's an early bird.'
'Or a very late night owl.'

*   *   *

Laura was sitting in the kitchen, talking with one of the women who had discovered Moira Farrell's body. The woman had given her name as Pat Bainbridge. She was forty-nine years old and had been working for the *Merry Maids* domestic cleaning agency for six years.

Her partner, Meg Miller, had complained of nausea and dizziness after seeing the crime scene and had temporarily retired to the conservatory to lie down on the sofa. But Pat seemed more stoical, her manner conveying a mixture of shock at the murder of her employer and a despairing glumness at the increasingly wicked ways of an unsatisfactory world. Laura had made her a mug of strong coffee and expressed sympathetic acceptance of her wish to smoke.

While Pat lit up a new cigarette, Laura reviewed the notes she had made so far, reminding herself that according to Pat the cleaning team had found the house door open when they arrived. That nothing in the house seemed to have been disturbed as far as Pat could tell. That Mrs Farrell had seemed her usual self on the last occasion they had seen her on the previous Friday.

'So you and your partner, Meg, visit twice a week to clean the house,' Laura said.

'Three times. Monday, Wednesday, Friday.' Pat drew on her cigarette. Her hand was still shaking with distress.

'And how long do you stay?'

'Three hours.'

'At each session?'

'Yes.'

'That's eighteen hours altogether,' Laura stated.

'Uh-huh. It's a big house,' Pat said, as though needing to defend the time she and her partner spent in the Farrell household. 'And in addition to the cleaning we change the beds and do all the laundry and ironing.' She ran a hand through her mahogany-tinted hair and tapped ash into a screw-top lid she had produced from her bag to serve as an ashtray. 'And we do all the clearing up, an' all,' she said, nodding towards the kitchen sink which was crammed with dirty plates and crockery.

How the other half live, Laura thought, conjuring up a picture of her mother who refused to have a dishwasher and diligently washed the pots and cutlery before polishing them to gleaming brilliance with a tea cloth.

'Oh, yeah,' Pat said. 'We do most of what

needs to be done. She's a busy woman, Mrs Farrell.' She balanced the glowing end of her cigarette on the edge of the tray and rested her chin into her hand. 'Was,' she said, with heavy regret.

'I get the impression you admired her,' Laura commented.

Pat considered. 'Yes, I did. She worked hard — and she was a decent sort.'

'A good employer?'

'Yeah, no side to her, no airs and graces.' Pat considered. 'Always made sure there was coffee and biscuits on hand. Said we had to sit down and have a proper break. Some women just bring you a glass of fruit juice or whatever while you're cleaning the lav.'

'Really.' Laura's curiosity was aroused, not yet being familiar with the world of the rich and their servants. She never ceased to be grateful that she'd joined the police and got herself the opportunity to see the world. Not in the geographical sense like sailors joining the navy, but in the human and social sense. In the police you had an entrée into the houses of all kinds of people you'd probably never meet face to face in a social setting.

'Oh yeah. Some employers are the pits. But Mrs Farrell was like . . . well, interested in us — as people, not just the poor beggars who push the vacuum.' Pat picked up her cigarette

21

and pulled on it with a thoughtful expression.

Laura waited.

'I can't think anyone would want to kill her. Just can't imagine it. It must have been one of these nutcases roaming around, targeting women on their own. They're always telling you crime isn't on the increase, but it must be. There've been so many stories of pensioners and vulnerable folks living alone set about by young thugs, or people let out from places for the mentally ill. And it's happening locally, you know. I don't watch *Look North* any more, it sickens me what goes on. Scares me too.' Pat let out a sigh and shot Laura a glance of faint challenge.

Laura gave a non-committal nod. 'But Mrs Farrell wasn't on her own, was she? I mean she was living here with her husband.'

Pat frowned. 'Yes. But he obviously wasn't around this morning, was he?'

'Do we know that?'

'Well, no. I suppose we don't. But he was often here when we arrived for work. They seemed to be an OK couple together. I mean you never really know how people are in private, do you? But Mrs Farrell and Professor Patel seemed to rub along all right as far as I could tell.' She looked at the quietly attentive detective constable. 'God! I'm jabbering on, aren't I? And you're just

22

waiting for me to spill the beans.'

'What beans, Mrs Bainbridge?'

Pat went so far as to produce a smile, albeit a grim one. 'None.' She pressed her lips together as though buttoning them up.

There was the sound of sighing and rustling beyond in the conservatory. A few moments later Pat's partner Meg reappeared in the kitchen. She was a small, skinny woman with wispy fair hair. She sat down unsteadily on a chair with the air of someone who has just woken from a drugged sleep.

'Are you feeling better?' Laura enquired.

Meg grimaced. 'To tell the truth, no. Pretty rough, in fact.' She glanced towards the hallway. 'Is she still in there? Mrs Farrell?'

Laura nodded in confirmation.

Meg looked at her partner, her face grim with tragedy. 'I'm giving my notice in after this. I'll never be able to walk into another place without wondering . . . what I'm going to see.' She wrapped her arms around her chest and made an alarming retching noise.

Laura jumped up and filled a glass with water at the sink. 'Here.'

Meg took a sip. The liquid refreshment seemed to bring a new alertness. 'Are me and Pat suspects?' she shot at Laura.

'We'll need your help in answering some further questions, Mrs Miller,' Laura said.

Meg scowled. 'It's bad news, isn't it, when you find a body? Talk about being in the wrong place at the wrong time.'

Pat placed a hand on her partner's arm. 'Look, love, we both know we didn't kill Mrs Farrell. We were just the ones who found her. And the police are talking to us to find out as much as they can. We're witnesses, I suppose.' She glanced at Laura, a light of importance in her eyes.

'Well, I'm not up to talking to anyone at the moment,' Meg said. 'I'm going to ring my husband and ask him to come and pick me up.'

'We'll take you home, Mrs Miller,' Laura said with gentle firmness. 'When DCI Swift has had a chance to speak to you.'

Meg rounded on her partner. 'See! They *are* treating us as suspects. And I was hoping to get home early today.' Her tone had turned whining and sulky.

'You'll be home soon enough,' Pat soothed. 'And you'll change your mind about giving your notice in. We're a great team, you and me. We have a lot of laughs, don't we? And this is just a once-in-a-lifetime thing.'

'A bit final for Mrs Farrell, though,' Meg observed grimly — a woman who knew how to have the last word.

Two hours later and Swift had set off back to the station having left Laura and Doug Wilson at the crime scene, in the hope that Professor Patel might arrive home and that they would have the chance to speak to him.

'A sharing of information, is how the guv put it,' Doug told Laura as they settled down for an indefinite wait.

'Hmm.' Laura contemplated the grim task of breaking the news of Moira Farrell's death to her husband. 'He probably knows far more about the death than we do,' she commented. 'What are the statistics on men killing their wives?'

'Not exactly cheering,' Doug said. 'In which case he's not very likely to turn up, is he?'

Further calls to the conference venue at which Professor Patel had registered indicated that he had not yet been located in the conference area. It seemed that he must have left quite soon after the lectures started as no one had seen him leave, but no one had noticed his presence either.

'Things are not looking good for Professor

Patel,' Finch commented, swinging into the incident room and watching as Swift began to pin up photographs of the crime scene on the whiteboard. Several other officers assigned to the case were standing around in groups, chatting and occasionally glancing towards the whiteboard.

'No,' Swift agreed. 'And he's got his mobile switched off.'

'Anything interesting on her phone?'

Moira Farrell's mobile phone had been found on a table close to the body. It had been bagged up in preparation for being sent for analysis. But at this moment it was on Swift's desk, and switched on to receive calls.

'Most of the calls were from Patel telling her he was just setting off from work, that he'd be home soon. Very brief, not at all emotional.'

'And outgoing calls?'

'Very few. Patel's mobile number came up of course. And in the last week there were three calls to another line. We're checking on that.'

'She might have made more use of the landline.'

Swift wondered if Finch truly believed he wouldn't have been able to think of that himself. He stared thoughtfully at the whiteboard. 'We're checking on that. And we're bringing in her computer.'

'And we mustn't forget that some people still communicate face to face. Or even by letter,' the superintendent commented, whilst reflecting on his wife and his married daughter whose cell phones spent a good deal of time clamped to their ears.

Swift tapped a pencil against one of the photographs, pointing to the pool of blood which had surrounded the dead woman's body. 'SOCOs thought there was just a chance we could get an image from marks found on the edge of the blood spill.'

Finch squeezed his eyelids together in an attempt to see more detail. 'It looks like a long shot to me, but while we're waiting for forensics it would be worth drawing up a list of regular visitors to the Farrell house and then setting up a shoe search.'

Swift nodded, noting that Finch was showing all the signs of a senior officer who had no qualms about telling grandmothers how to suck eggs.

'Good old police foot slog,' Finch concluded turning on his heel, and Swift had the impression his boss was pleased to have seen the last of the days when he himself would be out on the streets wearing out his shoe leather.

The hours went by and it got to 5.30 in the

afternoon. Swift was once again in Damian Finch's office, giving him a disappointingly unfruitful update, and Doug was phoning his wife telling her that he was probably not going to get home in time for supper.

On Swift's desk Moira Farrell's mobile remained stubbornly silent.

2

Around the time Swift had been talking with Tanya Blake at the crime scene, Rajesh Patel was setting out to walk up Ingleborough, one of the three most well-climbed peaks in West Yorkshire. He parked his car in the village of Ingleton, killed the engine, then shrugged off the jacket of his suit and laid it on the back seat. From the boot he took out the waterproof and wind-proof clothing he always kept stored there, and pulled them on over his work clothes. Having exchanged his black lace-up brogues for sturdy walking boots, he called in at the local mini-market and purchased a cheese and tomato sandwich, a hefty slab of dark fruit cake wrapped in cellophane and a bottle of mineral water. He placed the items in the small canvas rucksack he had used for years when hill walking. Ensuring that his phone was switched off he tossed it into the glove compartment and shut the door with smart click.

The weather forecast indicated that the snow falling some miles to the east was steadily moving westwards. There was a possibility it might turn to rain as the temperature hovered uncertainly around the freezing point.

Rain or snow, it didn't worry Patel. He had done the Ingleborough walk countless times before. He knew all the routes and pitfalls of the climb, just as he knew his own capabilities and stamina.

The steady, rhythmic tramp of walking and the slow, deep breathing required to make the ascent began to calm his earlier agitation. He regretted having left the conference like some truanting adolescent, slipping away without offering any reasons or farewells. There had been no doubt in his mind: he had known as soon as he had endured the first round of reunions with medical colleagues from all over the UK that he hadn't the stamina to face any further social encounters.

Recalling the news Moira had broken the night before had jarred his nerves and sent him off balance. The simple fact of having been forced into an emotional encounter with raised voices and ugly facial grimaces had distressed him. He was a contained man who prided himself on his self-control, who indeed relied on it to get him through the difficulties that even the most ordered life is strewn with.

His palms still prickled with sweat each time he re-ran the dismal scene. He told himself that the best cure was to keep the images as far from the front of his mind as possible. To this end, as he walked, he began to recite passages from Dryden and Milton. When he exhausted those he could move on to Shakespeare. In his youth, at his local grammar school, he had been highly praised for the quality of his voice, his clear enunciation and his exceptional interpretive ability when reading aloud from the great texts of English literature. He had sometimes thought with longing of embarking on a career in the acting profession. But both his parents were successful doctors and, as he had been their only son, there had never been any question as to which profession he would choose.

The sky lowered as he walked on. At the summit he turned his back to the prevailing wind and sat down on a rock, opening his rucksack and taking out the refreshments he had carried with him. A group of hardy sheep regarded him with interest, moving cautiously closer.

'You will have something all in good time,' he told them, knowing that Yorkshire sheep were partial to a slice of rich fruit cake. The thought made him smile. The first time he had done so in many hours.

As he made his descent big soft snowflakes began to fall, sticking to his face and lying on his shoulders and chest. By the time he reached his car a thin blanket of snow had rounded its contours and blunted the pointed tips of the roofs of the houses in Ingleton village.

As the light faded, the now rapidly falling snow drove against the windscreen with dizzying ferocity. Patel slowed his speed to a steady forty-five. He wondered whether to stop and phone Moira once again, warn her that he might be a little later than he had previously thought. He drove on. Moira would appreciate that driving conditions were difficult, would anticipate some delay. She had always been a balanced, practical woman. He gripped the wheel more tightly. Thoughts of his wife prompted him to run through the scenes of the previous evening once again, making him cringe with regret at the way things had run out of control.

His face became fixed and grim as he blanked out memories of Moira and concentrated on steering a steady course through the onslaught of rushing white flakes. As he turned off the main road into the interconnecting avenues of big stone houses which fanned out from the river, under the shelter of Ilkley Moor, he schooled himself to be calm.

It was at that moment when he saw the

white vans parked near his gate, the lights and figures in the driveway, the loops of tape protecting the house and proclaiming that it was now the province of the police.

A tall, gaunt man with auburn hair came forward as he drew the car to a halt. Glancing into the man's solemn face Patel froze into stillness. He pressed the button to depress the window. 'What is the matter?' he asked, surprised to hear his voice emerge quite naturally, as though nothing was amiss, when in his heart he knew that desperate news was rolling towards him like a great unstoppable boulder.

He heard the man introducing himself and then asking if he was Professor Patel the husband of Moira Farrell. And even then he was able to speak quite naturally, confirming his identity, restating his original question.

'I think it would be better if you came into the house and sat down,' the man said.

Patel did not move. In his mind's eye he saw a scene of terrible carnage: rage and violence and blood. Sprays and daubs and rivers of blood. 'Please, just tell me what I need to know.'

'Professor Patel, I'm sorry, but the body of your wife was found this morning in the sitting-room of your house.'

Patel heard the words, allowed them to

penetrate his consciousness, and knew that from this moment he would never experience complete happiness again. He felt a need to cut through his internal confusion, to inject an element of rationality into this incredible situation. 'Might I see your identification?' he asked the solemn-faced man. After a few moments he said, 'I think you are right, Chief Inspector Swift. I should come inside and sit down. But not here. Not yet. I'm happy to speak to you at your station if that would be convenient. Or wherever else you suggest.'

The chief inspector took him to a squad car and got into the back with him, while the uniform officer at the wheel waited impassively for instructions, then fired the engine.

'How did my wife die?' Patel asked the chief inspector.

'We believe she was attacked. She was stabbed in the neck.'

A long pause. 'She was murdered,' Patel exclaimed in soft tones, finding it necessary to say out loud those dreadful words, not to shy away from any of the grief and shock which were attacking his nerves and his viscera, sending stabs of agony through to his brain.

'We believe so.' The chief inspector gave a respectful inclination of his head. 'I'm very sorry for your loss, sir.'

'Where is she now — in the mortuary?'

'Yes.'

'Who will perform the autopsy?'

'Dr Tanya Blake.'

'Ah, yes. I know her work. She's a competent young doctor.' He stared out of the window, realizing that all that had been private between him and Moira would soon be out in the open, in the police files, in the press. In the public domain. 'I'd like to be quiet for a few moments,' he said to the solemn-faced detective. 'But when we get to the station I shall be happy to answer any of the questions you need to ask me.'

A strange calm had settled over him. He closed his eyes and allowed an image of Moira to fill his mind: Moira alive, Moira strong and decisive and capable. He almost wished he could feel more, but his emotional system seemed to have shut down. He guessed the police would think him a cold fish. Many others thought that, and over the years he had become weary of trying to make other people understand him.

★   ★   ★

Grief attacks the body and can shrink people both physically and mentally. When Swift and Laura Ferguson entered the interview-room where Professor Rajesh Patel was waiting, they saw a man with hunched shoulders, staring blankly at the wall, an untouched styrofoam beaker of tea sitting on the table in front of him. As Swift and Laura entered the room he placed his hands on the table as though preparing to stand up. The sleeve of his thick sweater caught the beaker and it toppled it on to its side, sending a wave of tan-coloured liquid rolling over the desk top. Patel reached for the beaker and righted it, looking in dismay at the spilled tea.

Laura offered reassurance. 'Don't worry, Professor Patel,' she said, guessing that Patel was nervous about what was coming. 'Shall we get you another cup of tea?'

Patel stared at her, then shook his head.

Swift sat down opposite the bereaved man, suspecting that Patel was not troubled by nerves about the forthcoming interrogation, rather desperately grappling with the shock of coming up against the sudden death of a loved one. He recalled his own responses to the news of his wife Kate's death in a rail crash. The disbelief, the denial, the panic of wondering how life was to be gone through without her. He knew, too, that time did not necessarily heal, that for a while it simply rubbed at the wound. And that for some people, going on feeling the pain was the only way to keep the person alive in the memory.

Watching the mask of dignity and stoicism of Patel's face, he had the strong impression that the man was deeply and genuinely affected by his wife's death. Which did not, of course, rule out his having killed her.

'Professor Patel,' Swift said gently, 'we believe you're a professor at the Leeds Medical school. Is that correct?'

Patel raised his head a little. 'That is correct. I divide my time between administration, research and some teaching.'

'Were you in your office at the university this morning?'

'No, I went to a conference in Sheffield.' He levelled with Swift's steady gaze. 'But I expect you already know that. I would presume you've been making enquiries about me — and my whereabouts.'

'Yes, we have. We know that you registered at the conference, but it appears that you left quite soon after that. We asked the conference staff to locate you on several occasions, but without any success.'

'No, they wouldn't have,' Patel agreed, showing no signs of discomfiture. 'Did you telephone to tell me . . . about Moira?'

Swift nodded. 'We also rang your mobile, but it was switched off.'

37

'Yes.' Patel spread his fingers and stared down at them.

'Professor Patel,' Swift prompted, 'what time did you leave the conference?'

'Around a quarter to ten.'

'And where did you go?'

'I drove north up the M1, then took the M62 going west.'

'And where then?'

'I drove to the village of Ingleton. I parked my car in the village, and then I went . . . for a walk.'

'You went for a walk,' Laura echoed. 'In this weather?'

Patel turned slowly to meet the constable's gaze. 'The snow hadn't yet reached that part of the county.'

'No. But the weather must still have been pretty unpleasant for a stroll. Where did you go?' Laura asked.

'I walked up Ingleborough.'

No easy walk, Swift thought, having climbed the same peak himself the previous autumn as part of a charity raising venture. He recalled feeling uncomfortably creaky around the joints the next day. He inclined forward a little. 'What time did you leave your house this morning, sir?' he asked.

'About five-thirty,' Patel answered, appearing in no way perturbed by the swerve in the line of questioning. 'Or maybe nearer a quarter to six.'

'Registration at the conference started at nine-fifteen,' Swift pointed out. 'Why did you set off so early?'

'I anticipated the journey might be slowed down by the weather conditions,' Patel said, 'and there's always the danger of traffic queues getting into Sheffield in the rush hour.'

'And how was your wife when you left, sir?' Laura asked gently.

'She was still in bed. She — ' Here he stopped, closing his eyes.

'She what, sir?' Laura injected a touch of pressure into her voice.

'She said she hoped I'd have a good day.'

'And she was fit and well when you left her?'

Patel paused for a moment. 'Yes. Yes, she was.' He dipped his head and fell silent. 'I didn't kill her,' he added, his tone weary rather than challenging. 'And indeed, I'm very willing to offer any help I can give you in proving that. For instance providing a sample of my blood or a DNA swab to help your investigation.'

Laura glanced at her boss, wanting to know if she should dig deeper, but Swift shook his head.

'I've just one more question, sir,' he said, 'and then we'll leave you in peace. Do you know of anyone who would want to harm your wife?'

The delay stretched on. A nerve vibrated at the side of Professor Patel's mouth. 'I can think of no one who would want to kill her,' he said eventually.

'Did she have any enemies?' Swift followed up, his glance intent.

Patel sat back in his chair and sighed, his gaze falling blankly on the wall behind his questioners' heads.

Swift kept a constant watch on the professor's face, wishing he had the means to access the tangle of thoughts which were passing through the bereaved man's mind.

'Everyone has foes, Chief Inspector,' Patel said, rallying from his torpor.

'Does that mean you can think of someone who would have a serious grudge against your wife?' Laura followed up.

'No, it doesn't,' Patel said with a degree of sharpness. 'Not the kind of grudge that would make someone commit a murder.'

Laura glanced once again at her boss. He made a small negative gesture.

'Does Sylvia Farrell know?' Patel asked. 'Do I have to tell her?' The reluctance was patently clear.

'She's already been informed, sir.' Swift was watching the widower closely.

Patel nodded. 'I'll contact Moira's colleagues at the hospital,' he offered, 'although I suppose that will hardly be necessary, given that her body is already there.' A spasm of pain twisted his face.

Swift left a short silence and then said, 'Your house is now a crime scene, Professor Patel. We shall need to have it sealed off for a time whilst the forensics team gather evidence.'

Patel nodded in numb acceptance.

'Is there anywhere else you can stay?'

'Yes,' Patel said after consideration. 'I have the keys to my neighbours' house. They've just gone away for a month's holiday in New Zealand and asked if we — ' He stopped, his face stabbed with pain. 'If I would keep an eye on it for them. I'm sure they won't mind if I stayed there for a short time. It would only be for sleeping; I shall spend most of my time at work. That's the only way I can see of getting through.' His head sank down towards his chest.

Swift clicked his pen closed and got up. 'We'll leave things there, sir,' he said, going on to offer the services of a family liaison officer if Patel so wished, even though he guessed that the doctor would decline. Which was the case. And done with a degree of sadness and dignity which both officers could only admire.

★ ★ ★

'What do you think, sir?' Laura had cajoled beakers of coffee from the machine and brought them into Swift's office. Feeling peckish she took a banana and a Mars bar from the plastic box she had filled at the canteen earlier. She knew she should choose the healthy banana, but it had been a long hard day, and chocolate was what she needed. 'You had the good doctor worried when you pushed him on the enemy scenario,' she said, peeling back the Mars bar's shiny brown wrapping. 'He knows a lot more than he's telling us.'

'Agreed. So what is it he knows that he doesn't want to tell us? That his wife had enemies in the family? Or maybe at work? I'd guess that being a hospital consultant could involve getting on the wrong side of a number of patients for starters, that's before you start considering the rivalries and jealousies within the staff structure.' Swift took a sip of his coffee and made a little grimace of distaste.

'Or that she'd been playing away and Patel had a massive grudge?' Laura offered, her mind suddenly veering away once more to her impulsive exploits with Saul the night before. But at least she wasn't an adulterer; or not knowingly so at least. Her heart gave a rabbit's foot thump as it occurred to her that Saul might be married. The issue had never been broached; he'd always struck her as a man with no ties.

'Fair enough.' Swift picked up his beaker and then laid it down again. 'It was interesting that he didn't try to provide himself an alibi. In fact, he didn't even ask us when she died. And he didn't appear to respond any differently to our questions about what he did after he'd left the conference than he did with the questions about what happened before he left the house.'

'Which is, of course, what we'd most like to know.'

'He must be tough,' Swift said, 'climbing Inglelborough on a day like this.'

'Or indeed, any day at all,' Laura responded with grimace, being a girl who believed in the car rather than the feet as a means of getting from one point to another. 'And I'll bet you don't get many folks who could provide an alibi up there.'

'Any more than you would regarding the time he left the house earlier,' Swift mused.

'It's not overlooked by either of the neighbours' windows. Which doesn't really matter, because our present time frame for the time of death isn't precise enough for us to be able to eliminate him, even if he was seen leaving the house.'

Laura stretched, sensing that their discussion and the long day's work was coming to a close. She wondered what she had in the fridge for supper. And the thought prompted her to remember that when she had left her flat, Saul had still been there. She sent up a fervent prayer that he would be nowhere in sight when she eventually arrived back. Not tonight, not ever again. 'So, what next?' she asked her boss.

'We do the usual,' he said. 'House to house. Talk to the nearest and dearest. Talk to the work colleagues. Find any witnesses. Set up a fingertip search for the murder weapon. Wait for what forensics can tell us. Find out who regularly visited the household, follow them up. The old story: trace, investigate, eliminate.'

Laura popped the final piece of Mars bar into her mouth, and looked doubtfully at the banana. Boring old footwork, she thought. She reminded herself of her Mini out there in the car park and permitted herself an inner smile.

A few miles from the elegance and comfort of Moira Farrell's house in upper-class suburbia, Shaun Busfield, twenty-four years old, pale and lanky with the look and demeanour of an agitated rodent, left the pub and made his way down the main road with jagged, stamping steps. The colours in the sky were lime and slate-grey, the pavements greasy black. Cars dazzled him with their piercing white headlights and rusty red tail lights. Outside the fish shop there was the smell of burning fat and a scattering of congealing chips which made his stomach heave. A sobbing girl broke away from her boyfriend and jumped on a waiting bus. The boyfriend sprang forward and banged on the closing door, 'Ay! Michelle! Come back 'ere you dozy cow!'

Muttering to himself Shaun turned into the estate. It had been built in the fifties on the edge of a wood. There wasn't very much wood left now, just intersecting rows of ugly concrete-rendered semis lining the broad streets. The houses near the main road had neat little gardens and bright windows with ornaments showing through the net curtains: a china dog, a vase with plastic flowers. As he went further into the maze of roads the windows of the houses were dark and stained with oily grime. Bare, feeble light bulbs hung from the ceilings. The low walls were cracked and crumbling and the gardens were full of junk and rubble and wire. What a hell hole.

Shaun felt the bile rise up his gullet. He leaned over a wall and threw up the contents of the last four hours' drinking and the meat pie that he had eaten at teatime. He trudged on, wiping the dribble from his lips. With the vomiting the alcohol seemed to have rushed out of his brain, its anesthetizing properties all deserting him.

The memories came sliding back. He didn't want to remember. And he didn't want to think about his gran dying before he'd been able to tell her he was sorry for all the bad times, all the mean things he'd said and done. 'Oh, Gran. I'm sorry. I'm so sorry,' he sobbed.

He walked up the path to the back door. He'd had a go at knocking the two front windows into one big window. But somehow it hadn't worked. He couldn't get the surround right, and the white PVC frame was still perched inside chipped and crumbling brick, letting the wind sigh through.

He could hear the TV blaring out in the living-room; some trashy late night film. Tina couldn't get enough of them: love stories, thrillers, westerns. She'd watch any old rubbish they put on. 'Ay, get a move on, I'm freezing out here,' he shouted, staring moodily at the thin yellow curtains and trying to make out what was going on behind them. He banged on the glass with clenched knuckles, then pulled back; if he kept on going like this the whole blooming pane might fall out.

The front door opened and Tina poked her head out and peered through the gloom. 'Is that you, Shaun?'

'Who do you bloody think it is?' He stamped inside and followed her into the living-room. She was wearing a short pink dressing-gown and high-heeled navy court shoes with fluffy yellow socks underneath. There had been a time when the sight of all that would have charged him up with longing. But tonight, there was something about those socks that sent a wave of anger through him. He pushed it away; anger was dangerous — terrifying, if you let it loose.

He threw himself on the green velvet settee which stood against the wall, an overflowing ashtray and several stained mugs balanced on one of its arms. 'Make me a cup o' tea,' he told Tina.

She pouted, hesitated, then clopped across to the sideboard and switched on the kettle which was sitting there.

As Shaun stretched out the ashtray slid to the floor scattering stubs and ash. 'Why don't you ever clear up this rat-hole?' he demanded of Tina.

'Why don't *you* ever finish doing up the kitchen?' she snapped back, flinging a tea bag into a mug. 'I hate living like this.'

'Do you think *I* like it?' he demanded, anger lapping inside in fresh red waves. Steady, boy, steady.

'It wasn't me that pulled everything to bits,' she whined, sloshing not quite boiling water over the tea bag.

He raised his hand, jabbing a vicious finger in the air. 'Ay! Just watch it, girl!'

Tina flinched but wouldn't be stared down. 'You ever lay a hand on me again, and I'm out of here,' she said, her eyes flaring with defiance and fear.

'Oh, come on! It was only the once.'

'Once too many.'

'Ah, shut it, Tina. You're doing my head in.'

'Your gran was longing for you to get this place and hers sorted,' Tina said, dumping the hot mug on the arm of the settee. 'But, oh no, you wouldn't be bothered to stir yourself. And now it's too late.'

Shaun felt the turn of a knife and his eyes flooded with tears. His heart felt as if it would burst, he wanted his gran so much. He felt as if he was on his own for eternity: he would just drift forever on a grey endless sea. He jerked upright, then dropped to his knees and curled his body into a ball. 'Oh Gran, if only you hadn't gone and died,' he exclaimed, burying his head in the crook of his arms and weeping like a distressed toddler.

Tina looked on in bewilderment, having never seen him shed a single tear before.

3

The press conference was packed. On the raised platform a technician checked the microphones. TV cameras were in evidence and the press group were testing their tape recorders. Those who still favoured spiral-bound notebooks had their ballpoint pens ready for the off. A reporter from Sky News was talking earnestly with the press and public relations officer. A BBC Radio reporter was waiting her turn. The atmosphere was tense and anticipatory; the cold-blooded murder of a prominent member of the medical profession had attracted national attention.

There was a hush as the Deputy Chief Constable of West Yorkshire led the panel on to the platform and took the central seat behind the long table covered with a blue cloth. Damian Finch took the place on his right, smart in a sombre slate-grey suit, with flashes of pale-blue collar and cuffs. Swift sat on the DCC's left, his face calm and neutral. Going through his mind was the ongoing network of the investigation: Doug gathering information on people who regularly visited the victim's home, Laura talking with Moira Farrell's mother, the uniform foot-soldiers knocking on neighbours' doors in the hope of finding a witness, and searching for the murder weapon, the SOCOs team working to find clues at the death scene, forensics analysing what had been found so far.

It was now more than twenty-four hours since Moira Farrell's death, and the investigation didn't really seem to have kicked off. Outside, winter was proceeding: the sky as brooding and sulky as a disgruntled adolescent, the precipitation coming down from the clouds unable to make up its mind whether it wanted to be rain, sleet or snow.

The deputy chief constable started the proceedings by telling the audience how shocked and distressed everyone present would be at the death of a woman so respected in her valuable work as a doctor and her contribution in the local community. She was a woman who had given her life and considerable abilities to the care of others, a woman who had been brutally cut down in the prime of her life by an evil and pitiless attacker; murdered in her own home whilst she was alone and defenceless. The police would maintain a grim and unflagging determination to catch and bring her killer to justice.

He turned to Swift and introduced him as the senior investigating officer who would be directing the hour-by-hour grind of the murder inquiry.

The first question rang out almost before the deputy chief constable had finished his brief speech.

'How was Mrs Farrell killed?' The questioner was a middle-aged man, thickset and bulldog-like.

Swift leaned forward. 'We can't give you that information until we're in possession of the results of the post-mortem.'

'Is it true that Mrs Farrell was the subject of a sex attack?' Bulldog knew his job. Lob in a question based on simple guesswork and with any luck you could stir up an uproar which might just lead to the dropping of a little gem.

'Any such rumours are purely speculation,' Swift said.

'OK, but this killing is sounding a bit like one we had last year in the area. A middle-aged woman stabbed in the living-room of her home by an intruder. Do you think there's a connection?'

'I can't comment on that at this stage.'

'If there is a similarity, will you be liaising with the team who worked on that death?' Bulldog wasn't for letting go.

Swift would not be drawn. 'If we find any connection, we will, of course, make contact with the team conducting that investigation.'

'That investigation has been a bit of a damp squib, hasn't it? One or two arrested, but no one charged. It doesn't give the local people much confidence.' Bulldog buttoned his lip, his point made.

Swift gave an internal sigh. He knew the Bulldog would be slipping a few broadsides into his article, drawing attention to the disappointing performance of the police in a similar murder investigation to the one recently committed. 'I think we need to concentrate on the death of Moira Farrell,' he said. His glance moved away from Bulldog and swept the audience. 'Can we move on please?'

A woman reporter wearing a bright red jacket put her hand up. 'Any suspects yet, Chief Inspector Swift?'

'Not as yet.'

'Any leads?'

'We're exploring all the relevant avenues.' Swift was aware of sounding like a pre-programmed robot.

'Motive?' Red jacket was beginning to look a little smug.

Swift imagined her tapping out an article subtly castigating his team for not coming up with very much during the precious twenty-four, so-called golden hours, of a murder investigation. 'We don't yet have a specific motive.'

There were further attempts to discover details of the killer's *modus operandi*, the inevitable demands to know how soon a suspect might be named. Unruffled and firm, Swift parried each one.

And then a young woman on the second row jumped up to speak. She was tiny, wearing battered biker's leathers, her short black hair sticking out in all directions. 'Dr Farrell worked in the gynaecology department at the hospital, didn't she? I've heard that there've been some difficulties in that section. Staff at each other's throats, daggers drawn.'

Swift felt a tingle of instinct run down his spine. The listening audience drew in a collective breath of tension. 'And your question is?' He levelled a steady gaze at the woman. She looked no more than a girl, hardly out of her teens.

'No question, Chief Inspector. Just a thought to kick-start your investigation.'

The audience was emitting a bumblebee buzz. All eyes were now on the girl, who sat down, her cat-like features mainly unreadable, although Swift sensed a manipulative gleam of triumph in her eyes.

'Rather than indulging in what is simply speculation,' he responded, 'I'd like to remind all of you present that we shall be appealing to the general public to help us by coming forward to talk to us if they saw anyone outside Dr Farrell's house in the early hours of yesterday morning, between five-thirty and around six o'clock. This was a sudden and vicious attack on a defenceless woman. The killer is dangerous, so if any members of this group, or anyone else hearing this appeal have any information, however insignificant it might seem, we would invite them to contact us. We will, naturally, promise complete confidentiality.'

Judging it time to wind things up he glanced at the deputy chief constable, who instantly took the hint, rising to his feet. 'Gentlemen,' he said. 'Ladies. Thank you all for your time.'

★ ★ ★

Watching Swift advance across the car park, Doug fired the engine of his car and gave it a couple of short revs. He waited for his boss to climb in. 'How did it go, sir?'

Swift shut the door with a firm thud, his face giving nothing away.

Not too brilliant then, Doug decided.

Swift pulled at the seat belt and clicked it in place. 'The usual,' he said evenly. 'Mostly routine damp squibs, but there was a bit of a firecracker at the end.' He gave Doug a brief account of the spiky-haired newshound. 'She's just joined *The Yorkshire Echo*. Her comments could be pure fancy, and I'm guessing she's simply wanting to make a name for herself and get noticed.'

Doug grinned. 'Still, if someone chooses to throw us a juicy bone, we might as well go and have a chew on it.'

'It'll have to wait its turn,' Swift said. 'First on the list is the post mortem.' Regrettably, he added to himself.

★　★　★

Sylvia Farrell, the widow of Moira's father, lived in a square stone house standing on the eastern fringes of the town of Ilkley. The entrance door was painted dark blue, its centrally placed brass lion's head knocker polished to the colour of silver.

In response to Laura's two short raps, the door was opened by a woman in late middle age dressed in a plain black skirt and a pale-blue sweater. She had the thick white hair of people who have turned grey in early

56

middle age, and whose hair has now lost all its pigment. It was rolled into an immaculate French pleat in the style worn by film stars in the 1960s. Around her neck was a single string of pearls, illuminating the woman's face and highlighting her chiselled bone structure. Laura showed her ID. 'Mrs Farrell?'

'Yes, I'm Mrs Farrell. I've been expecting that someone from your department might come today.' She was perfectly polite, yet her voice managed to convey a hint of disapproval. 'Would you come this way please, Constable?'

The Lady of the Manor dispensing largesse to the lowly serfs, Laura thought, pulling a little face at the woman's departing back. And, oh, what a very straight back.

The drawing-room was large and square, painted in a soft sea-green, and furnished in a conventionally elegant style which Laura surmised would have been favoured by comfortably wealthy people around thirty years ago: linen covers on the sofas, gleaming walnut tables, oil paintings showing country landscapes, looped curtains framing the tall windows through which a glimpse of the River Wharfe could be seen beyond the long garden, its shifting waters the colour of a grey pearl. A huge vase filled with deep pink stargazer lilies stood on top of the grand piano in one corner of the room, scenting the air with their pungent sweetness.

A small slender woman in her mid-twenties was sitting at the keyboard, picking out a soft, mournful melody with the fingers of her right hand. She turned as Sylvia Farrell announced Laura's presence. As her head tilted, her long straight black hair fell across her shoulders like a ripple of silk. Her delicate, clean-cut features carried an air of shock and quiet despair. 'Jayne Arnold,' she told Laura, getting up from the piano stool and offering her hand. 'I'm so pleased you've come. All this sitting and waiting is horrible. It makes you feel so helpless.' She released Laura's hand and seated herself on a sofa close to the fireplace.

Mrs Farrell instantly joined her, crossing her legs and neatly folding her skirt before placing a hand lightly on that of the younger woman. 'Jayne is my daughter,' she told Laura.

Laura began the interview by murmuring respectful condolences.

'How can I help you, Constable Ferguson?' Mrs Farrell asked abruptly, barely giving the constable time to finish her short speech.

Looking at the mother and daughter duo, sitting so formal and upright on their grand sofa, Laura felt rather like a hopeful job candidate in front of the selection panel. She reminded herself that her boss Ed Swift would have no truck whatsoever with such concerns. And neither should she.

'Were you were aware of anything troubling Moira in recent weeks, Mrs Farrell?' she asked, getting straight to the point, even though coming face to face with others' grief never ceased to trouble her. And the questions she needed to ask seemed worryingly intrusive.

'I'm afraid I wouldn't know,' Mrs Farrell said. 'Moira and I weren't very close, I'm afraid. Well — not since she married Rajesh.'

She glanced across to her daughter, who gave her a gently sorrowful look in response, suggesting her complete agreement with her mother's implied dissatisfaction with Rajesh Patel.

'It wasn't that her father and I had anything against Rajesh,' Sylvia Farrell went on. 'But after they were married, Anthony and I seemed to see Moira rather less than we did before. And sadly Anthony died three years afterwards.'

'I see,' Laura said, injecting a touch of sympathy into her voice. 'How long had Moira been married, Mrs Farrell?'

59

'Seven years.' As she spoke, Sylvia Farrell's face was set and stern rather than sad. 'They were married around the same time Anthony and I were.'

She raised her head, as though staring into a lost past. Jayne reached out and touched her arm for a brief moment.

'So you are Moira's stepmother?' Laura said, enlightenment dawning. She turned her attention to Jayne.

'I'm Moira's stepsister,' Jayne explained, before Laura had time to ask the question. 'My mother has been widowed twice. Her first husband, my father, died when he was only thirty-eight.'

'How I dislike that term stepmother,' Sylvia commented, her tone suggesting a degree of exasperation at being faced with such irrelevancies at a time of deep crisis.

'I'm sure Moira never thought of you as the kind of stepmother portrayed in fairy-tales,' Jayne said soothingly.

'Moira was dedicated to her work,' Sylvia Farrell said, steering the conversation away from delicate issues. 'Highly committed. Although I believe nowadays it's called being a workaholic.' She looked thoughtful. 'Rajesh is rather the same. In fact, Anthony and I sometimes wondered how much time they could have spent together.'

'And they had no children?' Laura asked gently.

'No,' Mrs Farrell said curtly.

Laura had an uncomfortable feeling that Mrs Farrell was silently adding that it was just as well. So, what was the problem, she wondered? Had Sylvia and her late husband thought a child would get short shrift with workaholic parents?

'Actually the issue of children had caused Moira a great deal of sadness,' Mrs Farrell offered spontaneously. She paused, considering her next words. 'She and Rajesh very much wanted children, and Moira had in fact become pregnant more than once. But each time she had had a miscarriage. It caused a great deal of sadness for them.'

'Poor Moira,' Jayne said. 'It must have been hell losing those babies.'

'Yes,' Sylvia said pointedly, 'I've been through it myself.' Her eyes were suddenly pink with mounting tears.

Jayne squeezed her mother's hand. 'You've got me, darling.'

Sylvia looked gratefully at her daughter. 'Poor, poor Moira!' she exclaimed bowing her head and appearing suddenly overcome with the gloom and sadness of the situation.

'Did Moira have any other sisters or brothers?' Laura asked.

61

'Moira has a brother who practises medicine in the States,' Jayne said, continuing her role of facilitator in this difficult interview. 'My mother has contacted him and told him of Moira's death. He and his wife will be flying over for the funeral. At such time as the body is released to us.'

'I see.' Laura left a small pause of respect.

Jayne reached for her mother's hand. 'We'll get through this, Mummy,' she said gently. 'And you know I'll always be here for you.'

Sylvia lifted her head and permitted herself a tiny, regretful smile. 'Thank you, darling.' She looked across at Laura. 'I'm aware of the things the police want to know when conducting a murder enquiry,' she said, her voice thin and shaky. 'So before you put me through the embarrassment of asking the vital question of where I was when Moira died, I'd like to say that I was at home all that morning. On my own. My housekeeper didn't arrive until eleven-thirty as she got held up because of the snow and ice.'

'Thank you for that,' Laura said, writing down Sylvia Farrell's formal words in her notebook.

'Jayne was in Prague when Moira died,' Sylvia continued, her voice shaky with emotion. 'She came back immediately I called her.'

Laura turned to Jayne, who nodded agreement.

'Now, is that all, Constable?' Sylvia demanded, her self-control restored.

'Almost, Mrs Farrell.' Laura cleared her throat. 'Would you describe Moira's marriage as happy?'

Sylvia and her daughter exchanged glances. 'I have no reason to believe they were unhappy,' Sylvia Farrell said, formally. 'Moira certainly never mentioned it.'

In the ensuing silence the air within the room seemed to gather itself together into a sigh of regret. Sylvia linked her hands together and laid them on her lap. It was a gesture which indicated that the interview was at a close.

Jayne got up and politely escorted Laura to the outer door, having carefully closed the door of the living-room behind them.

'This has been a terrible shock for my mother,' Jayne told Laura, as they stood on the outer steps. 'Especially as I was away at the time. Of course, I came back as soon as she telephoned me with the news. But that's not the same as being here.'

Laura nodded in respectful agreement.

'She's had more than her fair share of sudden death,' Jayne continued. 'Her first husband, my father, died of a stroke in his sleep. And Anthony, my stepfather, died of a heart attack whilst playing billiards at his club. Neither of them had suffered any previous illness, so the shock was terrible. And now, Moira . . . '

Laura left a respectful pause. 'Were you and Moira close?' she asked.

Jayne considered. 'Not really. I mean we got on perfectly well when we met at family functions. But there was quite an age difference between us and we didn't really socialize together. Moira was wrapped up in her work and with Rajesh — and the whole medical scene; she was a dedicated, caring medic.' She paused.

'And you?' Laura prompted.

'Ah, well, I guess I'm a bit of a lightweight. I got a big legacy from my grandparents on my father's side and basically I don't have to work. I entertain myself going to music concerts around Britain and Europe and to teaching the clarinet to a few hand-picked pupils who show genuine promise.'

Laura found herself warming to the other woman's frankness and her air of gentle self mockery. She felt no envy of those rich enough not to work. She would have chosen to join the police even if she'd had millions. Well, she was pretty sure she would.

'I had the impression your mother was

holding back on her opinion of Professor Patel,' Laura suggested.

Jayne inclined her head in agreement. 'Rajesh is not an especially easy person socially; he's very talented, and not very much interested in socializing. And he's very much his own person. He doesn't show his feelings or share them with anyone. He and Moira's father didn't really hit it off at all as Anthony was just the opposite.'

'And your mother? Did he get on with her?'

'No, not really. But she wouldn't ever admit it. My mother's proud, you see — one of the old school. She likes to show a good front. And she believes that our family should share vital information, that we shouldn't keep secrets from each other. And maybe that's not such a bad thing to aim for.' She glanced at Laura to gauge her reaction, then stepped back into the hallway and opened the squashy leather bag sitting on a chair beside the door. She took out a small white business card and handed it to Laura. 'My contact details. Please get in touch if there's anything else you'd like to ask about.' She hesitated for a moment. 'I'd rather you spoke to me than my mother. You understand, don't you?'

'Yes,' Laura said, whilst privately reflecting that at this early stage in this investigation it would be presumptuous to think one understood very much at all.

Feeling that the interview hadn't gone too badly on the whole, Laura slotted herself behind the wheel of her elderly Mini and headed back to the station. On the way she stopped at a corner shop and treated herself to a Snickers bar and a fizzy drink packed with sugar. Sliding behind her desk in the incident room she tossed her notebook on the desktop, logged on to the computer, took a sip of her fizzy drink and then unwrapped her chocolate bar with a sigh of anticipation. Before taking a bite she leaned back in her chair letting her mind re-run through the minutes she had spent with Sylvia Farrell and her daughter.

'So, what's our little Highland lassie been up to?' Doug had stolen up behind her and was whispering into her ear. He came trailing the bleak cold of the January day, frozen rain glistening on the shoulders of his coat. He shrugged it off, shook it and tossed it on the back of a chair.

Laura straightened herself into a more professional position.

'Hey, I'm not anyone's little anyone,' she responded merrily, 'and I'm from Glasgow.' She ran a hand through the back of her hair, her fingers rustling through the mass of pale-brown strands and making them stand out from her scalp in a messy shiny tangle.

'Where the good townsfolk like to commit dental suicide,' Doug teased, eyeing her chocolate bar before picking up the discarded wrapper crumpled on the desk and lobbing it with commendable accuracy into a bin some feet away. 'So how did things go with the victim's parents?'

'OK, I suppose. Both Moira's natural parents are dead.'

'So who was left for you to speak to?'

'A stepmother and a stepsister. Her only brother is in the US.'

'Could be some family intrigue there, then — with the step-contingent.'

'Possibly. The stepmother was obviously shocked, but not grief-stricken as far as I could tell.'

'And the stepsister?'

'The same really. She was in Prague at the time of the murder, but the stepmother was at her own house. And she's readily admitting to being without an alibi.'

'Fair enough,' Doug commented. 'But don't you forget to check the airline records for the sister, that'll be the first thing the boss will try to trip you up with.'

Laura glanced at him.

'Not the DCI,' Doug said, grinning. 'Our

new super. I get the feeling he hasn't got to the high pinnacle he's sitting on by being kind and gentle to his troops.'

'Yeah.' Laura smiled agreement.

'So you just take my advice,' Doug remarked, his smile holding a trace of fatherliness. 'Dot all your is and cross all your ts.'

'Yep.' She gave a smug little smile. 'I've already done my checking.'

'Good for you! Any joy?'

'She was booked on a flight back from Prague, January 19th. She cancelled that and booked for a late afternoon flight on the 16th, the day of Moira's killing.'

'No excitement there then.' Doug picked up a piece of A4 paper lying on the desk, folded it into the shape of a dart and lobbed it at the whiteboard. 'I drove the boss back from the press conference,' he told Laura. 'Apparently one of the up-and-coming young journalists there suggested all was not well with staff relationships in Moira Farrell's team at the hospital.'

'Oh!' Laura's eyes gleamed.

'Yeah. I've just been to the hospital to follow up. Two of Moira Farrell's closest colleagues were in theatre dealing with a caesarean, and the sister-in-charge was nowhere to be found.'

'Probably on the fire escape having a quick fag,' Laura said.

'Waste of a trip. Not to worry, I'll just have to go back in an hour or so.'

'You're disappointing me, Doug. I'd been counting on you to come back from your travels with a brilliant lead.'

Doug eyed her dolefully. 'I've done nothing more than make my poor feet throb with frozen misery trudging around in the slush. We haven't had weather like this in years — aren't we supposed to be in a global warming situation? My poor old bones ache with cold. I think I'm getting past all this legwork.'

'Oh, come on, you're as fit as a flea,' Laura said, smiling.

'Fit to drop,' Doug countered. 'I've been all round the town checking out folks who delivered to the Farrells' household. Professor Patel drew up a list as long as your arm. They've had major work done in the house recently — plasterers, plumbers, joiners, decorators — you name it.'

'So, anything of interest?'

'I did get two pairs of trainers which could have some correspondence to the size of the prints SOCOs found at the scene. I've taken them round to forensics which must be a prime example of a triumph of hope over experience — what murderer is going to go to work in the same footgear he had on when he did the deed? The two guys concerned both said they could provide alibis from girl-friends and neighbours if necessary.'

Laura put on a suitably sympathetic and resigned expression.

Doug smiled, gave a shrug then picked up his wet coat and draped it over a radiator. 'Oh!' he said, remembering. 'We've got a name and address for the number that came up on Moira's mobile. A Dr Serena Fox. Seems like she's some sort of shrink. The boss'll no doubt want her checked out ASAP.'

'Well, well.' Laura slithered a pencil back and forwards through supple moving fingers. 'So — Moira's father was a professor at Sheffield Medical School,' she mused. 'And her husband Patel is a Professor of Orthopaedics at Leeds Medical School. And she was a consultant anaesthetist working in the gynaecological department. And she has a friend who's a shrink. All high-powered medics.'

'And?'

'So, it's interesting,' Laura said. 'Murder and medicine.'

Doug headed off towards the coffee machine, shaking his head in despair.

4

Tanya Blake was peeling off her bloodstained gloves as Swift entered the morgue. 'I'm sorry,' he told her. 'The press conference went on longer than I'd thought.'

She dropped the gloves in a plastic-lined bin. 'I knew you'd get held up, so I went ahead anyway. And the most grisly bits are over.'

'I can't pretend to be sorry about that,' Swift admitted.

Tanya had covered the body with a green cloth, leaving just the victim's head showing. She herself, being tiny and slender, was almost swamped in the standard issue green overalls. He noticed a row of four tiny silver studs glinting in her right earlobe. In the left was a single shining star. Just enough to mark her out as on the edge of unconventional.

She gave him a reassuring smile, sympathetic in the knowledge that attendance at the post-mortem scene was not one of his favourite tasks. 'I thought it would be useful for you to have the main findings right away. It might be a little while before I get the chance to file a written report.'

'Right.' Swift was looking at the dead woman's face. Cleaned up and laid on the slab, she looked strangely at peace, and strikingly beautiful; her thick black hair framing the whiteness of her face.

Blake followed his glance. 'It seems such a waste, doesn't it?' she murmured reflectively.

'The loss of life at a comparatively early age?'

'That certainly.' She laid a hand on the dead woman's cold forehead, gently touched her waxen eyelids. 'But think of the loss of all that vitality: the shutting down of a body which was working perfectly. She was a fit and healthy woman: her physiology and biochemistry were all in excellent working order. And all of that has gone.' Blake looked thoughtful for few moments before snapping back into crisp professional mode, tapping her notes with the tip of her pen.

'OK,' she began. 'Moira Farrell was a healthy woman in her early forties. The cause of death was a single blow to the carotid artery. She would have died almost instantly. There are no defence wounds, suggesting that she was surprised by the attack, didn't see it coming — both in the literal and metaphorical sense.'

'An attacker she knew and trusted, perhaps?' Swift said.

'Possibly.'

'And someone who knew what they were doing. A fellow medic?'

Blake nodded. 'Unless it was a lucky strike as I mentioned before.'

'She was still in her nightclothes, which we've bagged up and will be sending on for forensic examination.' She pointed to a nearby table on which was laid an evidence bag containing bloodstained clothing. 'A cotton nightdress and a chenille dressing-gown. No underwear. Pink leather ballet pumps on her feet.'

Swift glanced obediently at the contents of the bag then moved his gaze back to Blake.

'There were no signs of sexual assault. Nor of any recent sexual activity.' Blake drew a folded sheet from the front of her notebook, and opened it out. 'I sent a blood sample to the lab yesterday evening. This is the report they came up with. It tells us that she had no diseases or abnormal conditions. There was no alcohol in the blood, nor any signs of drugs.'

'A commendably clean bill of health,' Swift commented drily.

'You could say that. And I can also confirm that she was pregnant — around twelve weeks.'

Swift suppressed a sigh.

'With twins. I've asked for a DNA analysis on the foetuses.'

There was a pause.

Twins, Swift thought — a double loss. It then came to him that Professor Patel had made no mention his wife's pregnancy. So why not?

Back at the station he gave the two members of his team present a brief account of what he had learned at the post-mortem, then requested that Laura should accompany him to interview Patel once more.

'It's a sex thing,' Swift told Doug, as Laura sprang up with enthusiasm and wound a scarf around her neck. 'Nothing personal.'

Doug glanced out of the window at the heavy, lowered sky. 'Don't you worry, boss, I'm only too happy to stay in the warmth and put my feet up.' He glanced at his notebook which was crammed with jottings waiting to be keyed in to his computer. 'Metaphorically speaking, of course.'

⋆ ⋆ ⋆

Patel was in a small office at the end of long echoing corridor. He was sitting at his desk, the top of which was almost completely clear apart from a telephone and a plastic funnel containing pens and pencils. Rows of shelves ran around the four walls of the room, each of them filled with medical texts.

It was clear that he was not in a fit state to do any work requiring steady concentration. He had the air of a man who had simply been sitting, absorbed in his own thoughts and misery for the past few hours. Without getting to his feet, he gestured to Swift and Laura to sit down.

'Professor Patel,' Swift said evenly, 'why didn't you tell us that your wife was pregnant?'

Patel's head sank down slowly as though his neck could no longer support it. It was like watching a prisoner in the dock receiving a life sentence. The kind of prisoner who had no fight left in him, who was totally resigned, bowing his head to fate. The two detectives watched him, putting their natural human sympathy to one side and making a professional assessment. Either Patel was a very good actor, or Moira hadn't told him anything.

Whatever the case, clarification was needed. 'Did you know Moira was pregnant?' Laura asked.

Patel rested his forehead on his spread fingers. 'No.' His voice broke up in his throat.

'She must have known, though,' Laura pointed out gently. 'She was a doctor, she of

75

all people must have known.'

'Yes,' Patel agreed.

Laura shot Swift a glance.

'Would you like us to leave, sir?' Swift asked the stricken man. 'We could talk further later.'

'No.' His voice sounded as if it was struggling through the slush lying on the pavements outside. 'Let's do it now. Get it over.'

'What is it you want to tell us?' Swift asked gently, watching Patel carefully and following his own intuition.

'Moira and I had been wanting children for several years. She became pregnant three years ago and we were overjoyed. She miscarried at twelve weeks. The same thing happened six months later. And then a year after that.'

'Did she have treatment?' Laura asked.

'Of course. We went to an ex-colleague of mine in Harley Street.'

'And you kept trying — for a baby?'

'Yes.' Patel removed his head from his fingers and raised it slightly. 'We had sex at the appropriate times.'

Laura felt a raw prickle down her spine. It didn't sound as though the marriage had been too good, certainly not in the bedroom. Her thoughts veered back to the electric excitement of the touch of Saul's lips on hers — a man about whom she knew virtually nothing. She took in a breath and pulled herself back to the present.

'How advanced was the pregnancy?' Patel was asking, speaking slowly and carefully as though afraid his voice might let him down at any moment.

'Twelve weeks.' Laura could see the pain in the man's eyes, the hopeless misery. She was on the point of reassuring him, offering an explanation on the lines of Moira's being hesitant or suspicious about sharing the good the news until she was well past the danger point of a further miscarriage. She reminded herself that she was a detective constable. That what was required was some comment from Patel himself regarding Moira's reason for secrecy. Patel's silence grew.

'She was expecting twins, sir,' Laura said.

Patel closed his eyes for a few seconds.

Glancing at Swift Laura noted that he was still waiting patiently for Patel to speak. When the bereaved man turned his head slightly and sank into gloomy retrospection, Swift got to his feet. Quietly and respectfully, the two officers left Patel to his inner torment.

'Poor guy,' Laura said, as they walked away from the bereaved man's office and its heavily charged atmosphere of tragedy.

Swift nodded agreement. 'And, of course, we'll need to grill him further about this pregnancy,' Swift said, 'and why she kept it from him.'

'Not Patel's baby?' Laura suggested.

'Well, that's the obvious issue to get to grips with.'

'Who might she have confided in?'

'Who would you have confided in?'

Laura considered. 'I'm single. She was married. Patel was the obvious one, or the boyfriend.'

'How about your mother?'

Laura's eyes went wide with horror. 'God, no!'

'Let's go for the boyfriend theory, then. Maybe it was a colleague.'

Laura grimaced. 'Sounds a bit like incest. But yes, a line to follow.' Privately her mind had begun to fill with the whole issue of pregnancy, and the notion that she could be pregnant herself. Dear God! It was now way too late for any thought of the morning after pill. She'd call at a chemist at the first opportunity and get a pregnancy testing kit. How long before the test was valid? A week? Two? She really had no idea. She had never put herself at risk before. Her palms felt clammy with foreboding.

★ ★ ★

Patel sat motionless at his desk, staring blankly at the door through which the police officers had passed. Thoughts flickered in his mind like darting insects. Buzzing, angry insects which scratched at his feelings, grazing and wounding him. Gradually his agitation eased as he reached back into his memory allowing images from the last few brittle, difficult weeks to be temporarily replaced by pictures from a more distant past some years ago: joyful images of Moira before her happiness began to fragment. It was a day in April, the sky was a deep cobalt blue, the blossom from the trees shimmering in the brilliance of a sun which seemed to have been reborn after a long, cold absence. She was in the garden, sipping a long drink, waiting for him to come home. When she saw him, she jumped up and ran across the grass, reaching her arms out in welcome, the miraculous news of her first pregnancy tumbling from her lips, because she simply couldn't hold back the flood of her delight. They had hugged and kissed each other until they were breathless.

He lifted his hands, touching his lips — the lips Moira had kissed. He recalled the soft sweetness of her breath on his cheek, the warmth of her lips. He fought to push away the last memory of her face as it had been when he made the formal identification earlier. A face waxen and still, her beautiful lips tinged with blue, her body covered with the white mortuary sheet.

He closed his eyes tightly shut, bracing himself against the pain of loss, willing himself not to cry out.

Why hadn't she told him about this pregnancy? And, of course, why hadn't he, himself, noticed or formed some intuition about it? The answer lay in the coolness that had been growing between them. Nothing shattering, nothing made ugly with cold silences or insults hurled in anger. Just a slow distancing, a gradual erosion of their need to share thoughts and feelings, both negative and positive. They had been polite strangers. Apart from that early morning back in the autumn when they had come home from the hospital ball and made love, their senses fuelled and blurred with the champagne they had been drinking through the evening. It was then that she must have conceived: the very last time they had had sex.

He told himself she must have been waiting to get well past the dangerous twelve-week stage; that must have been the reason she hadn't confided in him. But he didn't believe his own reassurances. Something had been going on in her life. Something much more menacing than her recent disturbing determination to commit professional suicide.

And now he had lost her, his dearest wife. And the baby he would never know. No! The *two* babies he would never know. He had lost an entire family.

⋆　⋆　⋆

Swift sent his team home for some well-earned rest at seven that evening. He judged that the start of the investigation had not been too promising. So far they had no witnesses, nothing from house to house enquiries, no CCTV footage to help them, no weapon come to light.

After reviewing the information sheets in his desk he decided to call and see Serena Fox, the doctor whose number had kept coming up on Moira Farrell's mobile. Her address brought him to a renovated Victorian semi-detached on the outskirts of the town. As he got out of the car he saw that the house was in darkness apart from a pale white glow shining from behind blinds on the large window flanking the doorway. A brass plate with Dr Fox's name and string of medical qualifications gleamed faintly beside the door as he pressed the bell.

Eventually he heard footsteps. A shadow moved behind the door and the lock made a click.

'Yes!' The woman who opened the door had a strong fearless gaze and a challenging note to her voice; clearly not a person to be dismayed by an unannounced caller on a dark winter evening.

Swift had his ID ready. 'Dr Fox?'

She took a careful look at his identification. 'You'd better come in,' she said.

Following her down the hallway he noted that she was tall and bony, her long frame clad in a flowing African-style garment made up of red and orange cotton.

She gestured him to a chair beside the fireplace where a wood burning stove blazed, then took her place on the chair's matching mate at the other side of the fire. The large mantelpiece was crowded with African face masks and carvings of human heads, the floor stripped and painted black with African rugs scattered over it. The only light came from an anglepoise lamp on the chunky desk placed in the bay window. Dark shadows crowded together in the corners of the room.

Dr Fox sat staring at her visitor, her eyes steady and unflinching.

'I believe you were a friend or counsellor to

Moira Farrell,' Swift said.

Her eyes held his, sharp and wary. She inclined her head. 'Yes, both.'

He drew in a silent breath. 'Doctor Fox, I have some bad news. I'm afraid Dr Farrell was found dead in her house this morning.'

She raised her head; her gaze slipped away from his for a few seconds and then returned. Although her expression and her facial colour remained unchanged, he saw a tightening in the muscles of her throat. 'Moira,' she said to herself softly. She held herself very still. 'You're a chief inspector,' she went on. 'And visiting late on in the day. That means there must be something unusual, something very irregular about her death.' The piercing eyes bored into his as though he himself might have played part in Moira's tragedy. 'She was killed?'

'We believe so.'

'But you're not going to give me any details?'

'Not at present.'

She pressed the fingers of both hands against her cheekbones and took in some deep breaths.

Swift considered her composure remarkable — whether impressive or simply strange he was not able to judge at this point. 'You described Moira as both a friend and as a client.'

'We have been friends since medical school,' Serena Fox said. 'But in recent months she turned to me in my professional capacity.'

Swift waited.

'There was a problem she wanted help with. I was reluctant to act as a doctor or counsellor to her. To act in such a capacity a with a friend is very difficult — and possibly irregular. But she was insistent. So — I eventually agreed. We had a number of sessions together — here, in this room.'

'I see.'

'And maybe it's worth saying that I wouldn't accept a fee. Instead she gave generous donations to a charity I support in West Africa.'

'And the nature of the problem?'

'You know I'm not going to tell you that, Chief Inspector Swift.'

'Medical confidentiality?'

She shrugged. 'I'm quite aware that confidentiality doesn't apply once a patient is dead, but I'm still not going to tell you. Even if you start advising me of my legal obligations and so on.'

Swift ignored the challenge. 'Did you know Moira was pregnant?'

'Yes.'

'And that she was expecting twins?'

'Yes.'

'Did she have any concerns about her pregnancy?' he asked softly.

'No more than every woman experiences,' Serena Fox commented crisply.

'Or about her marriage?'

She jerked her head around and shot him a withering look. 'I don't know — and even if I did, I wouldn't tell you, not at this juncture anyway.'

Swift got up. 'You might be enforced to do so at some point, Dr Fox,' he pointed out quietly.

She rose too. 'When that point comes I shall certainly take legal advice on the matter,' she said. 'But Moira's killing might have nothing to do with the discussions she had with me. So what good do I do her by giving out information that might reach all and sundry? I mean no offence to you personally,' she told Swift, 'but you have responsibilities to your superiors and your press officers and what have you. Anything I say will be all over the media in the blink of an eye.'

Swift did not bother to dispute this. 'When did you last see Moira?' he asked.

'Last Friday. She came here for a consultation at four o'clock.' Her eyes levelled with his. 'And left around half past five.'

'Thank you.' He paused. 'And could you tell me what were you doing, Dr Fox, between five-thirty and six-thirty yesterday morning?'

For the first time there was a small flicker of uncertainty in Serena Fox's ice-blue eyes. 'I'm a poor sleeper,' she said. 'I was here in my study, keying in reports to my laptop.'

'Alone?'

'Yes.' She gave a slight frown of impatience. 'Will that be all?'

He considered. 'For now.'

She led the way to the front door and pulled it open, letting in a rush of freezing night air. As Swift moved through the doorway she called him back.

'I don't mean to appear obstructive,' she said. 'This has been a traumatic shock for me. I need to think things through before I speak.'

He lifted his eyebrows.

'I'm not planning to tell you any lies, Chief Inspector. I simply want to be as truthful to Moira's memory as I can be.'

It was hard for him to keep the scepticism from showing in his face and she seemed to pick up on his doubts and to want to make amends in some way.

'If it's any help,' she told him, 'I can tell you categorically that Moira did not come to talk to me about her marriage.' She took in a breath to speak again and then stopped.

'I'll be back to talk to you again,' Swift said. 'And I'd advise you to think very carefully about withholding any information which could be relevant to this investigation. Or indeed attempting to select what you consider relevant from what isn't: I'll be the judge of that.' Without waiting for a response he turned and walked to his car.

Back in his own apartment he poured himself a glass of red, slipped a fish curry into the microwave, punched in a cooking time of four minutes and telephoned his daughter.

'Dad?' Her voice came on the line, all clarity and crispness, and with a slight question on the upper inflection. It meant she would be in the middle of something absorbing and not really wanting to be disturbed. That was absolutely fine; he just needed to check in with her from time to time and ensure she was safe and as happy as one could expect a 20-year-old student to be.

'Nothing urgent,' he said.

'I'm doing OK,' she said. 'Just putting the finishing touches on an essay due in tomorrow. And you?'

'The same. I won't keep you from your finishing touches,' he said. In his head he saw her pushing strands of dark hair away from her face, her eyes glinting, a witchy grin on her fine-boned face.

'Hey, I hear you were on national TV this morning. Some of my friends caught it.'

'Press conference,' he told her. 'A high profile homicide.'

'Next thing you'll be getting offers from Hollywood.'

'I doubt it.'

'Stay just as you are, Dad,' she said, which was nice even though she said it in tones that gave the clear signal, 'Got to go now'.

He clicked off the connection just as the microwave began to beep. Sliding the carton from the oven, he smiled, reflecting that he could always rely on his daughter not to push up his phone bill too far.

★ ★ ★

Swift slept fitfully. Just before he woke he had a dream in which Naomi somehow aged and metamorphosed into someone else, someone with the face and body of Moira Farrell. He pulled himself from the dream feeling on edge with anxiety — a poor way to greet the day.

He stood under the shower for twice as long as usual, letting the hot water wash over his head and shoulders as he soaped himself, then turned the control to provide a final burst of cold to purge himself of the dream before stepping out.

He made fresh coffee, black and strong, put bread in the toaster, then stripped the bed and stuffed the results into the machine. From the garden flat below there were sounds of joyful dog barking intermingled with strains from Radio 3: Schubert maybe, or Beethoven. He had new neighbours, a smiling, busy couple in their thirties. Self-involved and busy they gave him no worries, a welcome improvement on the former tenant, a widow of a certain age who had developed a brief infatuation for him and provided quite a number of concerns.

Beyond the windows it was another grey, grim day, the sky the colour of ageing slate, ice gleaming and dangerous on the surface of the pavements.

In the car he listened to the local news and was informed that his investigation was into its third day. 'Detectives inquiring into the murder of local doctor Moira Farrell are no further forward in providing any information about possible witnesses or suspects.' He switched over to Radio 4 and listened to an account of British soldiers being ambushed in Basra.

Arriving at the door of his office around 7.30, his general mood was not at a high point. In moments, however, things began to shift.

Tanya Blake was on the line wanting to speak to him. 'Good morning, Chief Inspector!' Her voice was bright with her enthusiasm for her job. 'How's it going?'

'There's room for improvement.'

'Here's something that could be of interest,' she said. 'Moira Farrell's twin foetuses don't share the same DNA.' There was a thread of excitement running through the announcement.

Swift was at a loss for a few seconds. 'So — presumably they're not identical?'

'No, most certainly not. Identical twins are the product of one egg which after fertilization splits and forms two separate embryos which inherit identical characteristics.'

'Right. Of course.' Swift began to think things through.

'But one of Moira's embryos doesn't share Professor Patel's DNA,' she said, as though encouraging Swift to complete the puzzle.

'So, the babies have got' — he paused, trying to get to grips with the information she had given him — 'different fathers,' he finished.

'You got it,' she confirmed cheerily.

He took a few seconds before replying. 'I was thinking of asking if that was possible.

But clearly, from you've just told me it is.'

'Thanks for your vote of confidence. Yes, it is indeed possible. If a woman releases more than one egg during her cycle, then each one has a chance of being fertilized. For most women who have non-identical twins each separate egg has been fertilized by the same man's sperm, usually her husband or partner. However, if a woman ovulates, produces two eggs and has two sexual partners during the time of fertility, then she can produce children who have different paternity.'

Swift glanced towards the window looking out into the raw damp of the morning as he absorbed the information.

'The phenomenon first came to light on the slave plantations in North America,' Tanya continued, helpfully. 'One or two doctors noticed that black women slaves who produced twins sometimes had one baby who seemed to have different characteristics from their own ethnic group — facial bone structure which was more Caucasian than African, a lighter skin, unusual eye colour and so on.'

Tapping his fingers against the desk-top, Swift traced the descent of a teardrop falling from an icicle clinging to the window-frame and sliding down the glass. 'White plantation owners raping African women?'

'That's the general idea.'

Swift clicked off the connection, wondering if there would be anything he would hear that day to top Tanya's twin story. And then there was the issue of breaking the news to Rajesh Patel.

5

Shaun Busfield was drinking his mug of morning tea, muttering to himself and roaming restlessly around the room, unable to settle. Freezing damp was seeping from the walls which Shaun had stripped of their paper and Tina had inadequately tried to patch up with pink emulsion the colour of Elastoplast. And because one of Shaun's recent DIY efforts had been to pull out the old storage heaters used by the previous tenants, the only heat in the room came from a single bar electric fire which had once belonged to Shaun's mother, and was probably a relic from the 1950s.

'Sit down, will you,' Tina nagged him. 'You're making me feel all on edge.' She was standing under the single light-bulb hanging from the ceiling, putting on her mascara, staring into a tiny pocket mirror and concentrating hard. She was dressed for work; a tight white sweater, a tiny black denim skirt and black high heels.

'Why do you make funny shapes with your lips when you're messing about with your eyes?' Shaun demanded.

'I'm not,' she said.

'Yes, you are.'

'Oh, stop trying to stir things.' She glanced at him, anxious yet defiant. 'What's up with you, anyway?'

'Nowt. I'm just thinking.'

'What about?'

'Oh, Jesus! Shut it, woman.' He felt a sense of hopelessness flood over him. Thoughts of his gran hurt so much, of how he'd treated her, taken her for granted, ignored her, made her feel a useless old bitch. How he'd not realized what she'd meant to him until she'd gone. He hated hurting, in fact he didn't think he could stand it another minute.

He turned his thoughts to work the day before, the way the police had come swaggering in, accusing folks right left and centre, nicking their shoes for Christ's sake. Cocky bastards, they thought they could do what they bloody liked. 'A murder investigation,' they'd said, all puffed up with their own importance. Not only could they do what they wanted, they could *take* what they wanted. Bloody thieving jerks, making him peel off his shoes and hand 'em over. He'd had to borrow a pair of ropey trainers from one of his pals. They didn't fit him properly and they smelled like a fusty fox's den. Not that he'd ever been near a fox's den.

Oh, he knew all about the police all right.

The stirrings of anger made him feel better. Anger was better than hurting. In fact, anger could be bloody brilliant, working you up, right up to a bloody climax. Like sex. Not that he got much of that these days. He'd thought Tina'd be a good lay when he first pulled her. But she turned out to be mostly giggle and tickle, more worried about getting her hair messed up and not doing anything 'mucky', as she called it, than giving him his thrills. He glanced at her now, fiddling around with her nails, silly cow. She was tasty though, nice tits and a good bum on her. He wondered about a quickie before he set off for work. Nah, forget it. She'd just duck and dive and bob away from him. No point getting himself worked up all for nothing.

He pulled his thoughts back to the police. The plain clothes bloke with his smug little smile, the uniforms grinning and showing off, pleased as punch with themselves for having the licence to strut about like turkey cocks and lord it over everyone else. He'd keep that picture in his head today and for the days to come, let his hatred of the police mature and grow, until it was fully ripe, until it was truly sweet to taste — like the best cider.

★   ★   ★

'Twins fathered by different blokes!' Doug's mouth was literally dropping open as he listened to Swift's account of his conversation with Tanya Blake. 'I've always said you've got the chance of learning something new every day in this job.'

Laura agreed. 'It's certainly a good tale to tell my mum.'

'So Moira was cheating on Patel,' Doug reflected. 'And we're going to have to find the guy she was doing it with?'

Swift nodded. 'I'd guess it's unlikely the good doctor Farrell was the victim of rape.'

'Do we ask Patel as first go off?' Laura wondered, giving an internal wince at the prospect.

'That's one way,' Swift said. 'Alternatively we could approach Moira's GP to see what he or she might know. And we should also go back to her colleagues in the hospital team and root them out for questioning, no matter what else they're up to.'

'The workplace being a hotbed of adultery,' Laura commented in support of her boss's final suggestion.

Swift's mobile trilled. 'Yes?'

It was Finch with a summons for the DCI to go to his office. Urgency reverberated in the superintendent's voice.

'SOCOs have found a pair of heavily

bloodstained trainers buried in the Farrell's garden,' he told Swift without preamble as he walked through the door. 'I've had the shoes rushed to the lab; the technicians have promised to get the results through ASAP.' There was a quiet air of excitement in Finch's usually leaden demeanour.

As he listened, Swift was considering the various possible issues behind Finch's words. 'Right.'

'Let's hope we've got our man.' Finch turned back to the paperwork on his desk.

'Yes.'

Finch looked up, noticing that his DCI was still in thought. 'That's all, Ed,' he said. 'For the moment. Let me know when the results are through. I've asked the lab to contact you directly.'

'Thank you, sir,' Swift said, opening the door and reflecting that one must be grateful for small mercies.

★　★　★

The call came through within the hour. A young man's voice, not one of the scientists Swift had spoken with previously.

'DCI Swift?' The voice was soft, hesitant even.

'Yes.'

'I'm phoning with information for you.'

'Carry on.' Swift's attention was totally focused.

'Regarding the pairs of trainers Constable Wilson brought in yesterday for examination, we've found no traces of blood on any of the four shoes.'

Well, thanks a lot, Swift thought. 'Right.' He prepared to close the connection.

'But we've got some further information.' There was the sound of paper rustling, making Swift suspect the technician was nervous, anxious not to make a blunder. He reminded himself how vulnerable professionals were when analysing and interpreting information in a murder case, how careful they had to be.

'There was a significant amount of blood on the shoes SOCOs found in Mrs Farrell's garden,' the technician continued. 'And the blood group matches that of the victim.'

'I'm assuming you haven't got a DNA match as yet.'

'Not yet, I'm making it a priority. But it's not a common blood group so it's very likely to be Mrs Farrell's blood.'

'Any DNA available from the trainers?'

'Yes, we've managed to pick up some traces from a hair in one of the shoes.'

'But, again, another wait?'

'Afraid so. But I can tell you that the size and type of trainer we got from SOCOs corresponds very closely with those of one of the pairs of trainers your constable found. And from the way both pairs have worn, it looks very likely they belong to the same person.'

'Is there a match for the prints found at the crime scene?'

'Unfortunately we can't say that there's any more than a partial match. SOCOs weren't able to get clear photo images, mainly because the amount of blood surrounding the body caused the prints to merge together.'

'But information on the traces of the prints SOCOs sent us do show a number of positive reference points?'

'Yes, but not enough to be certain we're looking at the same trainers.'

'And the trainers our constable brought in belong to?' Swift's habitually even tone was now harsh and urgent.

'A man called Shaun Busfield.' There was more rustling of paper. 'He works at a plumbers' merchants on the Bradford Road in Guiseley.'

'Right, thanks for that,' he told the scientist.

'A breakthrough, sir?' Laura enquired as Swift slipped his phone back in the inner pocket of his jacket.

'Let's hope so.' He gave his two listeners the details, already on his feet, poised to raise backup team and then leave.

Following on behind the younger members of the team, Doug smiled to himself, recalling the footwork slog of the day before which seemed now to be bearing fruit. There was nothing like a piece of solid evidence to make everything else seem like idle gossip.

★   ★   ★

Shaun was just draining the last dregs of his tea when there was a sudden, horrible jangling in his ears. The sound of sirens wailing. Squad cars, yellow, cream and blue screeched to a halt outside the house.

Harsh, scalding breath coursed through his airways. 'Jesus! The flaming filth. They're coming. They must be coming for me.'

'*Now* what have you done?' Tina's eyes were wide with foreboding.

Shaun didn't wait to answer her. He was out of the back door, vaulting over the fence at the edge of the stringy grass and winging it into the wasteland that stretched up the hill at the back of the estate. 'Christ Jesus, save me,' he muttered, his heart pounding as he gathered speed. He put on a monumental spurt, willing his legs to work harder, knowing full well Jesus had never bothered getting him out of a spot before.

★ ★ ★

Followed by Laura, Swift picked his way down the entrance passage in Shaun Busfield's house. The cold of the place struck him as though a freezing cloth had been laid on the skin of his face and hands. And the smell of damp was earthy and penetrating.

'God!' Laura muttered behind him, looking down at the bumpy, undulating floor as she squeezed past a large bike propped up against the wall. The surface was actual dirt, a mixture of sand and clay you could probably grow stuff in, but as it was January the frost was coming through. Scraps of cardboard had been laid down as some kind of protection from the raw elements, but they were fighting a losing battle. Looking more closely she could see that there had been floorboards there once upon a time as there were struts protruding from the wall just above the level of the ground. So was Shaun Busfield a disaster at DIY, or simply a madman?

A small, skinny woman was standing at the door of the living-room. Swift and Laura had to take a steep step up from the hall to join

101

her. Laura felt her feet stick on the carpet, which she guessed had once been a dark blue, but was now covered with dirt trodden in the from the hall.

'He's not here,' the woman said defensively. A statement which was hardly necessary, as a team of uniforms could be seen dashing past the window which looked out on to the back of the house, in hot pursuit of their quarry.

Swift showed his identity. 'May we sit down?' he asked.

Looking agitated the woman gathered up the assortment of newspapers, envelopes and crisp packets littering the cushions of a stained blue velvet settee, then stood aside to allow the visitors to sit.

'And you are?' Swift looked into the woman's face, asking the question with kindly interest.

'Tina.' She quickly dumped the rubbish she had gathered on the floor behind the sofa. The envelopes went behind the clock on the mantelpiece. 'Tina Frazer.'

'Is Shaun Busfield your boyfriend?'

She hesitated. 'Yes, well, I suppose you could call it that. We've been living together for going on a year now.'

'You sound as though you're doubtful about whether you're still friends,' Laura remarked, her tone matter-of-fact and kindly.

Tina Frazer stared at her, suspicious and defensive. 'He's not an easy bloke to live with.' She stopped, as though considering that last statement, and possibly regretting it. 'But he's not all bad.' She glanced down at her watch, a chunky affair with a shiny silver bracelet and a huge lilac face which looked enormous on her slender wrist. 'I should be getting off to work,' she said.

'What work do you do, Tina?' Laura asked.

'I'm a beauty therapist.'

'Facials, manicures and so on?' Laura suggested.

Tina nodded. 'What are you after Shaun for?' she demanded.

'In connection with a murder enquiry,' Swift told her.

She flinched as she took in his words. 'Oh, my God! No!' She fidgeted with the hem of her sweater. 'When was it, this murder?'

'Some time around six in the morning last Tuesday,' Swift told her.

'Do you know where Shaun was at that time?' Laura asked.

'Yeah. He was here. Well, he would be, wouldn't he? He's a bit of lazy beggar, doesn't get up until around seven, and even then I have to nearly kick him of bed.'

'So he was here with you at the time the murder was committed?' Laura insisted.

'Yeah, sure. He was here.' She put the nail of her thumb between her teeth and began to tear at it. Realizing the damage she was doing to her manicure she snapped her teeth shut and yanked the nail back out. 'Was it that woman on the news?' she said, her eyes sharpening with conjecture. 'That doctor?'

Swift nodded.

'Oh, God!'

'Did you know Dr Farrell?'

Tina shook her head.

'Did Shaun know Dr Farrell?'

There was a beat of hesitation. 'No.' She looked from one officer to the other, her eyes wide beneath the flutter of lashes thick with mascara. 'You don't really think Shaun did this, do you? He's not a killer. I mean he can be a bit handy with his slaps when he's had a few drinks — '

Swift broke in. 'Are you saying that when he's had a drink he hits you?'

She coloured. 'Well, just the once or twice. And I've told him if he ever does it again, I'm off — and that's the end of it.'

'Right.' In the pause that followed Swift was aware of the tick of a clock which he hadn't noticed before. 'If our boys don't catch up with him, where do you think Shaun's making for, Tina?'

'I don't know.' She pressed her lips

together, mulish and defiant.

'Does he have a car?'

'No. He cycles everywhere. Or walks.' She eyed the two detectives with heavy suspicion. 'He's dead fit,' she said.

'You must have some idea where he's gone,' Laura pointed out evenly. 'A mate's place, maybe. Or his parents? Brothers and sisters?'

'His parents are both dead. And his sister lives somewhere in London. I don't think he's seen her in years.'

'Do you have an address for her?' Swift asked, suspecting the answer would be negative.

Tina shrugged. 'I doubt if he has, never mind me.'

'Mates?' Laura followed up.

'He doesn't really have any. Well, not close, not the sort he'd go and stay with.'

'He sounds to be a bit of a loner,' Swift said.

'Yeah,' Tina agreed, cheering up a little at finding herself able to make some positive kind of statement.

'So you're all he's got, then?' Laura suggested.

Tina's temporary cheeriness evaporated. 'Suppose so.'

Swift got to his feet, Laura following suit.

They picked their way gingerly down the hallway.

'Let us know if he comes back,' Swift said in matter of fact tones. 'Or if you have any new ideas on where he's gone.'

'Are you sure he's the one you need to be after?' Tina asked, pursuing them to the door.

Swift turned. 'We can't comment on that, Miss Frazer. Not yet.'

Tina stood in the doorway watching them go. Then abruptly slammed the door shut as a gust of icy air rushed into the already freezing house.

'She's scared of him all right,' Laura said, shivering as she waited for Swift to unlock the car doors.

'Caught between a rock and a hard place,' he observed. 'If she tips us off as to where Busfield is, she risks bringing the wrath of hell down on her head from him. And if she keeps her lips buttoned she'll have us constantly on her back.'

'She's rather like a doll, don't you think, sir?' Laura wrapped her skirt around her knees as she settled into the passenger seat. 'Doll as in a child's toy, rather than a bloke's plaything.'

Swift didn't disagree.

'A doll with a chunk of the stuffing knocked out of it,' Laura added, wiping a spy hole through the condensation on the window.

'Impressions of Busfield?' Swift asked.

Laura took a few seconds to get things straight. 'From what Tina said our suspect Shaun doesn't strike me as the kind of boy most mums would be best pleased to have their daughter shacked up with.'

He gave a faint smile of agreement.

'Are we going to keep an eye on where she goes?' Laura asked.

'What choice have we?' he said crisply. 'Because if none of his work colleagues or bosses can give us a clue, she's all we've got. Let's just hope she doesn't have a fancy for leading us a merry dance.'

6

Doug waited in the reception area of the Maternity Unit at the local hospital, contentedly wandering up and down glancing at the posters on the walls and the chalked-up scribbles on the message board. Some minutes before he had been told by a pretty and charming administrative assistant that Mr Cavanagh, the senior departmental consultant in Obstetrics and Gynaecology, would be with him in just a moment.

In time firm, hurrying footsteps came down the corridor, a clear vibrant voice accompanying them, the tones resounding in the corridor. 'I'm so sorry, Sergeant, I was busy with an outside call.' The speaker came forward, smiling and confident, offering a welcoming handshake to each police officer. 'Adrian Cavanagh, Clinical Director,' he announced.

Cavanagh was tall and well built, with stylishly cut black hair, and singularly handsome features. From Doug's perspective he looked unreasonably youthful to be in charge of a department in a major hospital, but then Doug was beginning to feel that no one was old enough to be anything any more. He guessed Cavanagh would be around twenty years younger than himself, and when he made a calculation of the guy's likely salary from the NHS with a possible topping up of around 90% in fees for private work, he reckoned it was up in the stratosphere in comparison with his own. He smiled inwardly: envy had no part in Doug's personality; he had enough for his needs and in his book that made him as lucky as any high earner — or millionaire come to that.

Cavanagh took him into a tiny cubicle-like office, and courteously gestured him to a small and very uncomfortable plastic chair. As the doctor seated himself behind the desk, Doug had a fancy that his room at the private hospital down the road would be somewhat more restful and palatial.

'Before I ask how I can help you,' Cavanagh said, giving the confident impression of being fully in charge of proceedings, 'I must, of course, say how dreadfully shocked and sorry we all were to hear of Moira's death. And in such terrible circumstances.'

'How do you know about the circumstances, sir?' Doug asked.

Cavanagh was in no way disconcerted. 'Simply that she was murdered — that is assuming the information available from the press and the media and your own department is reliable.' He levelled his gaze at Doug, who found himself in the headlight beam of brilliant blue eyes.

'Yes, sir, we're treating her death as murder,' Doug confirmed. 'I believe you worked as a colleague with Dr Farrell.'

'Moira worked with me and other of my gynaecologist colleagues as an anaesthetist,' Cavanagh confirmed. 'She was a skilled and committed colleague. She will be very much missed.'

Doug was beginning to find Cavanagh somewhat sanctimonious, pompous, and quite possibly a very smooth liar. 'There have been suggestions that there've been some tensions in the department, sir,' he said, mild but blunt. 'Personal differences.'

Cavanagh smiled. 'Ah, yes. I imagine you're referring to the assertions of the young journalist who wanted to make a name for herself at the media press conference. I don't think any of us need place too much credence on her attempt to claim a few minutes of fame.'

'So there are no tensions in your department, sir?' Doug asked, as though merely wishing to clarify things in his own mind.

'Good heavens, no!'

Doug nodded sagely. 'I'd say that was pretty unusual, sir. Abnormal even. Most, if not all, working groups experience some degree of strain and personal disagreements from time to time.' He gave Cavanagh a kindly, paternal smile. 'Even in our CID department.'

Cavanagh's smile held a touch of frost. 'I wouldn't wish to challenge you on that, Sergeant. But in the case of my department the levels of co-operation are invariably of a very high standard.'

'I'm glad to hear that, sir,' Doug said. 'And I'm a constable. We'll need a list of all the staff here,' Doug told Cavanagh in his habitual easy-going tones.

Cavanagh's smile melted away. There was a moment when it seemed he was considering making a protest. As it was, he decided to go down the route of dissenting with good grace. 'By all means, Constable. I'll get my secretary to run off a copy for you. I should warn you it's a big department, including nursing, midwifery, auxiliary staff, admin, cleaning and so on, beside the team of doctors.' He paused, the smile inching its way back. 'My guess is you're going to be very busy for quite some time.'

He rose to his feet in one graceful gesture. 'Now, I'm sure you'll understand that I'm under some pressure — you know how it is, needing to be in a number of places at the same time.'

'Please sit down, sir,' Doug said mildly, whilst still managing to convey that they, the arm of the law, would brook no arguments. 'As you appreciate, this is a murder inquiry and we need all the help we can get to find Moira Farrell's killer.'

Cavanagh had reached the door. Now he turned.

'There are one or two further questions we need to ask you — in your capacity as head of the department.' Doug offered the last statement as something of a sop to the consultant's ego. And it seemed to work.

Cavanagh returned to sit in his chair and assumed an expression of due gravity.

'Did you know that Moira Farrell was pregnant?' Doug asked.

Cavanagh frowned and his eyes narrowed a little. 'No, I didn't. But, of course, a pregnancy is a very sensitive and private issue for any woman. Moira would perhaps have preferred to keep it to herself, for a time, at least, especially as she has a sad history of miscarriages.'

'Yes, indeed,' Doug agreed. 'Would you say that Moira had a happy marriage?'

For a moment Cavanagh looked startled at the change of tack. He stared at Doug. 'I

112

would say that that was none of my business.'

'Did you used to visit Moira and Rajesh Patel at their home?' Doug continued. 'Drinks or suppers, perhaps?'

Cavanagh cleared his throat. 'No. Well, not recently. Rajesh has always struck me as a rather retiring sort of person, I don't think he enjoys socializing over much.'

'And, Moira? Did she enjoy socializing?' Doug asked.

'She was more sociable than Rajesh,' Cavanagh said carefully.

'So,' Doug said reflectively, 'you used to visit the Patels in the past, but recently you haven't visited. That could suggest that the friendship between you had cooled.'

Cavanagh threw his glance up to the ceiling, then levelled his gaze at Wilson. 'If you haven't got more weighty and relevant things to discuss, I'd like to get on with my work.' He folded his hands together on the desk and his tone was arctic.

Unperturbed, Doug rose to his feet. 'Thank you for your time. There's nothing further, sir,' he said in courteous, formal tones. 'For the present.'

Executing a neat slide around the desk Doug managed to get to the door ahead of Cavanagh and make a slick exit, leaving the clinical director to trail behind.

Damian Finch looked like a man who has just witnessed the stampede of a herd of cattle through his front room.

Swift admitted that it was mainly bad luck that Traffic had decided to make a swoop on one of the car-thieving lads living next to Shaun Busfield only seconds before he and his back-up car arrived to bring Busfield in for questioning.

'The media will love it, of course,' Finch reflected. 'Police incompetence at its most risible: catching a sprat and letting the shark get clean away.' His smile was grim. 'A shark with a very shady history.' He tapped the printout lying on his blotter. 'Busfield's previous: a couple of TWOCs when he was fourteen, causing an affray at seventeen and an ABH during a street fight three years ago. No wonder he didn't want us to catch up with him.'

Finch swept the team with his cold, meticulous gaze. 'DNA results have just come through. The blood found on the trainers buried in the garden is definitely Moira Farrell's. And the traces from the hair found in the trainers are confirmed as belonging to Busfield.' He paused and pursed his lips. 'Whose DNA, because of the aforementioned

114

charges, was already helpfully on the database.' His tone was pure acid.

Doug and Laura found themselves suddenly heavily compelled to inspect the toes of their shoes, such was Finch's ability to inspire feelings of guilt even in the face of blameless innocence.

Finch was now prowling the strip of carpet behind his desk. 'We also know that Busfield had some kind of connection with Moira Farrell in that his firm delivered plumbing materials to the Farrell household.'

'According to his manager, Busfield's team spends most of their time in the warehouse, sir,' Doug ventured gingerly.

'Does he never go out in the vans?' Finch snapped, wheeling around to glare at the constable. 'Do we know that?'

'No, sir.'

'Well find out, Constable Wilson. And look at the signing out schedules for the vans, with especial reference to the dates around Moira Farrell's murder. Because, as far as we know, Busfield has no other transport than a bike, so he might well have needed to use one of the vans to get to Farrell's house which is some way from his own house and his place of work.' He spoke with slow deliberation, as though Wilson were a young lad with learning problems.

'Yes, sir.' Doug squared his shoulders and cleared his throat.

'And if we find Busfield did have a firm's van that would have enabled him to get to Farrell's house in time to kill Moira Farrell and then get himself into work all cleaned up, then we get that van to forensics and have it stripped down to its axles.'

'We'll find Busfield,' Swift told the superintendent, trying to make himself believe it would be soon. 'People can't stay holed up in a house or a lonely wood, or a field for ever. In the end they have to take risks, venture into the outside world.'

'True,' Finch barked. 'But, on the other hand, Busfield only needs one villainous, police-hating friend to provide him with a safe bolthole in order to turn our job into an extremely expensive, fruitless and embarrassing nightmare.'

Swift nodded silent agreement.

From the wall to the left side of Finch's desk, the *Mona Lisa* remained as self-righteously inscrutable as ever.

⋆　⋆　⋆

'So you think this man Busfield is a suspect for Moira's murder.' Rajesh Patel frowned. He had listened to Swift's account of the

116

discovery of the bloodstained trainers and the details of their owner with his eyes half closed, as though trying to blot out the horror he was going through.

They were sitting in a small study at the back of the house belonging to Rajesh and Moira's neighbour.

Patel was, as usual, solemn and courteous, welcoming Swift and inviting him to make himself comfortable on a chair close to the fireplace in which gas-fuelled mock coals burned with a low glow. He then returned to the small sofa opposite, making a place for himself amidst the albums and loose photographs which were spread over the sofa cushions.

Swift recognized this particular response to grief: the desperate need to try to hold on to the loved one by trawling through the collection of their images recorded on film. He had never found this exercise particularly comforting himself, reaching the conclusion that it merely served to emphasize that the loved one had become part of the past. And the more you looked at static, individual images, the more you began to lose the multiple complexities of the essence of the person when they were alive.

'And are you questioning this man, Chief Inspector?'

'Not at present.' Swift steeled himself. 'I'm afraid he anticipated our arrival. The upshot was that he made a speedy getaway and slipped through our fingers.'

'I see.' Patel showed no surprise or anger. He simply continued to look worn out and irredeemably sad.

Swift had the impression the man sitting opposite him was breaking up inside. 'It goes without saying that we're making every effort to trace him. We've circulated his picture to the press and media. He's going to find it difficult to remain in hiding.'

'Ah.' Patel sighed. He looked utterly spent, as though he was almost indifferent to what Swift had to say. 'This man Busfield,' he said, slowly, 'it means nothing to me, and I can't recall that Moira ever mentioned a man of that name. But then, you see, we never discussed such issues. Moira took charge of everything concerning the house — and indeed the garden, employing workpeople when necessary. She was a highly efficient and organized person.' His voice faded to a mere breath. He picked up one of the photographs and held it in his fingers, but his gaze was fixed blankly on the far wall at the far edge of his vision.

Swift steeled himself once again. 'Professor, we have reliable information from our pathologist that one of the two foetuses Moira was carrying did not share your DNA.' He left it to Patel to work things out.

A flicker of nervous energy travelled over Patel's heavy eyelids as he processed the information. He made some noises in his throat, but Swift was not able to gather any meaning from them.

'Had you had any idea that she was seeing someone else?' Swift asked.

Patel gave a small jerk of his head, indicating a negative response. 'She was constantly working with male colleagues,' he said slowly. 'She was an exceedingly attractive woman.'

'But had you any suspicions that she might be having an affair?' Swift pressed quietly.

'No,' said Patel, and his desolation seemed to invade the room like a creeping fog.

'Maybe it wasn't a sustained affair,' Swift said. 'Maybe just a one night stand, something done on the spur of the moment and instantly regretted.'

Patel considered. 'No, not Moira,' he said with a degree of firmness. 'No one night stands,' he said, distaste distorting his stern features.

Swift left a respectful silence.

'When you discover the identity of the father of the twin that wasn't mine,' Patel said, enunciating his words with great deliberation, 'I would ask you to give me the choice of remaining ignorant.'

Swift guessed that Patel would be aware that there was no possibility of his giving such a guarantee.

'Do you think you will ever find the whereabouts of your prime suspect?' Patel asked. 'This Shaun Busfield?'

'Yes.' Swift had not hesitated.

'And do you really think he killed my wife?'

'As I told you previously, Professor, we have evidence to link him with the crime,' Swift said.

'Yes,' Patel agreed slowly, his expression suggesting that he found the notion of Moira's having been killed by a virtual stranger hard to credit.

Swift got to his feet, bringing the interview to a close. 'You could move back to your own house tomorrow,' he said gently. 'We've finished gathering evidence.'

A tremor crossed Patel's face; he closed his eyes briefly. 'Thank you,' he said. 'I'll bear that in mind. My neighbour is not back for another few days. I know she won't mind if I stay on here for a little longer.'

As Swift let himself out, he asked himself, not for the first time, what he would have chosen to do about his living arrangements if

Kate had been killed in their house. On balance he thought he couldn't have borne to set foot in the place ever again once the body had been taken away. But maybe the reality would have been different.

Later on, when Patel was again on his own he let his thoughts linger on Moira's sudden and brutal death. He forced himself to say the words. 'My beloved wife has been cut down and murdered in the prime of her life. At a time when she was expecting my *child*. And that of another man,' he whispered, his voice crumbling with grief. For a brief moment it occurred to him that his own status as a suspect must have gained some weight for DCI Swift following the discovery of Moira's betrayal. He had a motive to kill, one of the oldest grievances in time. It didn't matter. Thoughts of saving his own skin were irrelevant. He needed to savour his grief.

The world, of course, would move on and forget about Moira. He recalled the stages of bereavement which those who had lost a loved one were supposed to go through — shock, denial, guilt, anger, depression, acceptance. Acceptance! And then you 'moved on'. But he felt himself to be empty. He had nowhere left to move on from, and nowhere obvious to go.

For the police and all those people who

took an interest in violent crime, Moira would become a statistic. Like other wretched victims who had been slain either by loved ones or strangers, she would eventually achieve some kind of sainthood, an angel who had given herself as sacrifice to the forces of evil.

Slowly he gathered up all the photographs scattered around him and stashed them in a folder. Having checked that all the outer doors were locked, he returned the study, gave himself a shot of morphine and lay down to sleep on the sofa without bothering to take off his clothes.

7

The early morning clouds which had sent down a coating of grainy sleet had cleared away and the sky above the moors guarding the valley shone with crystal winter blue, its light glinting off the great rocks crowning Ilkley Moor and tinting the slate roofs of the town to a deep sapphire.

It was the fourth day of the investigation and Swift was considering the way forward. The search for Shaun Busfield was urgent and ongoing, involving a great many staff and a sizeable chunk of Damian Finch's budget — as the superintendent would frequently deplore — but for the moment there was no sign of reaping any reward for the outlay and effort expended.

So far Tina Frazer had shown no inclination to lead the police a merry dance. She went to work, she went to the supermarket, she went home. She stayed in at night and watched TV until around one in the morning when she went to bed. As regards phone contact between Shaun and Tina, Doug's careful investigations had revealed that Shaun's house had no landline, and that

Tina had made no calls from her mobile. If she was contacting Shaun it was either from work, from a friend's phone, or from payphones. But the officers tailing her had not seen her use a payphone and her supervisor had told Doug that all calls made from the salon where Tina worked had to be logged and paid for, and that Tina had not requested the use of the business phone. The issue of discovering friends who would allow Tina to use their phones was much more problematic: friends who were prepared to co-operate with Busfield's beleaguered consort were not likely to spill information to the police.

Swift worked a pencil through his fingers, point down on the desk, top down on the desk, over and over, mirroring his frustration. And maybe all the effort was pointless. Maybe Busfield was a blind alley. A pair of bloodstained trainers hardly made a case to present to the CPS.

He laid the pencil down on the table. He knew he should talk to Patel again, press him on the issue of Moira's lover. He closed his eyes briefly: there was something about Patel which hit a raw nerve. He guessed he must see something in Patel's grief which reminded him of his own pain following Kate's death. In which case, he had to come to terms with that, put it on one side and treat Patel just like any other suspect.

He took up the pencil and wrote 'MOIRA'S LOVER' on his pad. Then underlined it. Then sat back.

He reached for his phone and called the reception desk at *The Yorkshire Echo*.

Putting his head through the door of the incident room, he spotted Laura standing in front of the whiteboard, a small frown of concentration stamping a small V between her eyebrows as she reviewed pictures of the dead Moira Farrell and the portrait gallery of witnesses and possible suspects.

'Any new ideas?' he asked, knowing that neither Laura nor Doug was one hundred per cent convinced about Busfield's status as prime suspect. Not as yet.

She shook her head. She had an air of patient frustration about her.

'Let's go out and do a bit of digging,' he said. 'And I'm not talking about the snow.'

★ ★ ★

The offices of the Women's Page and Features department at *The Yorkshire Echo* were as cramped as those of the CID — and even more grubby and slum-like. Mugs of cold half-drunk coffee littered the desk tops, a number of them crowned with drowned, half-smoked cigarette ends. Balls of screwed-up paper from reporters' notebooks were scattered at intervals over the floor, presumably having been lobbed unsuccessfully in the direction of the one and only wastepaper basket.

There were just two personnel present: a fifty-something woman with a helmet of blonde hair, and the young journalist who had spoken up at the press conference. Once again she was wearing her battered bikers' leathers and her black hair stuck up like porcupine spines. She looked up as the two detectives entered and gave a foxy grin.

In a brief appraising glance, Laura noticed that the young journalist's nose was broad and snubbed, her eyes a brownish-black, lit with a cunning glitter. That, together with her wide, scarlet lips and flashing white teeth gave an overall mad and sexy effect. She wondered what Swift made of her, aware that his assessments were usually quieter and more balanced than hers. She wondered also, how far the reporter would go in keeping them dangling for the information they wanted. And how Swift would deal with that. Anticipation built within her.

'Detective Chief Inspector Swift,' the young reporter said, her voice filled with gruff, ironic welcome. 'I wondered when you'd be coming. Sit down!' Her guileful gaze lighted on Laura. 'I see you've brought a pal along.'

'Detective Constable Laura Ferguson.' Laura returned the toothy grin as she introduced herself, then sat down on an office chair which wobbled slightly on a wonky tubular steel leg.

The older reporter had looked up, faintly concerned. 'Do you want me to push off, Georgie?'

'Nah, Barbara, you're cool. Stay right there.'

Swift sat down and leaned forward slightly. 'Georgina Tyson?'

'You've been doing your homework!' The girl leaned back in her seat, entirely at her ease, giving every indication of having an intention to enjoy herself during the next few minutes. 'Call me Georgie,' she said.

'You've got information we need,' Swift commented.

Georgie Tyson nodded. 'I can't really deny that, can I? Seeing as I decided to torment you with it at the press bash.'

Swift smiled, long beyond becoming riled by cocksure youngsters. 'Trouble at the hospital, you said. Difficult staff relationships.'

'That's right.'

'Issues which could have a bearing on Moira Farrell's killing.' There was an edge to his voice, a warning to the young reporter not to mess with him.

Keeping her eyes on Swift's face as though she had him under surveillance, Georgie Tyson reached into a drawer of her desk and pulled out a brown A4 envelope. With the considered timing of a conjurer she slowly slid the contents from their paper sheath, and held them out, keeping them a few inches in front of Swift's reach so that he had to stretch forward to take them.

He considered the four shiny images Georgie Tyson had offered, then passed them to Laura, who stared in fascination at pictures of Moira Farrell shown engaged in some kind of angry altercation with a tall, solidly built man dressed in a dark suit.

'When were these taken?' Swift asked Georgie, taking the photos back from Laura and slipping them back into the envelope.

'Around a month ago. I took them with my mobile phone. They're still stored there with a date on them if you want to check.'

'Who is Dr Farrell talking to?' Laura asked.

Georgie Tyson smiled. 'Mr Adrian Cavanagh. Clinical Director of Gynaecology and Obstetrics at the local hospital.' Her voice had smoothed and lowered, giving a very creditable imitation of a man charmed with his own status and ability. 'A very important job, and doesn't he know it?'

'How come you took these?' Swift asked.

Georgie stared at him, her eyes laced with the triumph of a secret known only to herself. 'I'm interested in him.'

'For a Women's Page features article?' Swift said. Watching her he saw that with this simple question he had made a small hit on her Achilles heel.

'Maybe.' Her irises stilled and glinted like black ice.

'I don't think so,' Swift said. 'My guess is that you've got your sights on writing something for the front page. Hot news. A scandal involving a local doctor would do nicely, wouldn't it? Get you noticed by the national dailies maybe?'

The spiky-haired reporter gave a studied shrug. Her colleague at the adjacent desk was now listening to the interchange with undisguised interest, her eyes hovering over the younger woman with an air of amused calculation.

Swift stood up. 'Miss Tyson,' he said, 'I've no intention of wasting my time trying to squeeze information out of you. And I'm sure you're bright enough to know that I could come down on you pretty hard if I found you were wilfully withholding evidence relevant to our investigation into Moira Farrell's murder.' Without waiting for a response to this deliberately formal speech he was out of the room and striding down the corridor. The envelope with the photographs was in his hand.

Laura shot Georgie Tyson a confirmatory warning glance and followed her boss, having to break into a trot to catch up with him. She guessed the young newshound would be cursing herself for trying to play Swift like a partly hooked fish. And would be more than a little annoyed at having been deprived of the excitement of goading him. Laura smiled to herself, reflecting that there was nothing worse than being cut off in full flow and being ignored.

'What do you think she knows?' she asked Swift as they fell into step together.

'A little more than she's telling us, at the very least,' he said. 'But maybe not much more. I'd say her main preoccupation at the moment is wanting to leave her desk in Features and become a hard-nosed news-hound writing lead articles for the front page. But she's obviously on to something regard-ing Cavanagh, or she wouldn't have been hanging around trailing him with her phone on photo alert.'

'How long before she gets back to us?' Laura said.

Swift lifted his shoulders, his expression focused and purposeful. 'We don't need to wait for Miss Georgina Tyson to favour us with her tips and innuendos.' He looked down at Laura. 'Do we?'

★ ★ ★

'There's something about a detective chief inspector, isn't there?' Georgie said to Barbara once the two detectives were safely out of earshot.

'Do you mean DCIs in general, or that one in particular?' Barbara asked.

'Both probably. It's that mixture of calm authority with an above average knowledge about the wicked ways of the world and the frailties of its inhabitants.'

'Mmm,' said Barbara, smiling. Georgie Tyson had some wicked ways herself and also a few nice turns of phrase at the ready to get herself noticed by a senior editor who could give her a leg up in her career. Barbara judged her young colleague might not go quite as far as she wanted in the newshound business, but wherever she did get to, it certainly wouldn't be for want of trying.

'Yeah, DCI Swift is one fit guy in my book,'

131

Georgie said thoughtfully, putting her feet up on the desk and twiddling with an ear-ring. 'I've always had a fancy for older men.'

'You mean you think he's worth crossing swords with?'

'That's exactly what I mean, Barbara.'

'So what do you know that you haven't been telling the fanciable Detective Chief Inspector Swift?' Barbara queried.

'About Adrian Cavanagh?'

'Yes.'

'Nothing the chief inspector won't soon find out for himself. And, mark my words, he'll soon be on the trail. Rumours about docs who aren't quite up to the job soon spread like wildfire.'

'You controlling little vixen,' Barbara said. 'Just make sure you don't go too far and get the nice Inspector Swift to set the hounds on you.'

'Ooh, that'd be fun.' There was now an air of calculation and mystery swirling in the room like smoke.

'Well, little Miss Ambitious, are you going to keep me in suspense all day?' Barbara demanded. 'What are you plotting?'

'In my book Adrian Cavanagh is a great big red herring,' Georgie said in a tone of dismissal. 'It's Shaun Busfield I'm interested in.'

Barbara had a quick think. 'The guy the police are looking for to 'help them with their enquiries'? The one whose ugly mug is forever popping up on the TV?'

'That's the one. I used to go to primary school with him. We used to live on the same scruffy estate in Bradford.'

'Really! Were you pals?'

'No. He was two years ahead of me. He was a bit of a wild boy, always bunking off school, running around doing a bit of petty shoplifting and slashing car tyres. And who could blame him? His father cut and ran when he was tiny and his mother was a slag.' She took her feet off the desk and picked up a rubber band lying on her desk. 'He was a bit like me,' she said reflectively, 'an only child with parents who weren't really interested in kids.' She wound the band around her hand, pulling it tight across her hollowed palm and twanging it like a guitar string. 'His mum was the feckless type, sleep with any fella sniffing around and never make the bed in case it might come in handy. Whereas my parents were poor and honest do-gooders, more interested in worrying about starving orphans in Africa than their own offspring. So I spent a lot of time on my own as well.'

'Don't tell me you went on little shoplifting sprees with the delinquent Shaun?'

Georgie grimaced. 'Sorry to disappoint you, but, no. Ten-year-old boys aren't famous for asking girls to join in their petty criminal sprees.'

'What did you do with yourself, then? I don't see you as a kittens and puppies, little-princess type.'

'I used to read boys' comics and then I went on to my granddad's Sidney Sheldon and Ian Fleming paperbacks. And after that I got into the tabloids and the Sunday papers. I used to pick up copies left on the buses and on the benches in the park.' She gave the band a final twang and threw it back on to the desk. 'I've always wanted to be a top journalist,' she said. 'As in chief news reporter. For as long as I can remember really wanting anything.'

'And how is plaguing Chief Inspector Swift going to help you?' Barbara asked.

'I'm not quite sure yet,' Georgie said. 'But at least it'll be fun along the way.'

'Just take care,' Barbara warned.

'Not my style,' Georgie said.

'And where does Shaun Busfield come into this?'

'That's an interesting question.' Georgie frowned in thought. 'It can't be long before the police or some gallant member of the public sniffs him out. And then he'll be taken in for questioning.' She picked up the band again and wound it around her knuckles until they became streaked with red lines.

Barbara sat patiently waiting.

'That's when I'll have to get some sort of strategy up and running.' She thought of the current chief reporter, a portly middle-aged man who still suffered from acne, but continued to think of himself as God's gift. On the rare occasions he sat at Georgie's table in the canteen he treated her with tiptoeing politeness, using the sort of voice adults used to speak to kids. Patronizing bastard. True, he filed good copy. He was the best the *Echo* had, but Georgie knew she could do better than that.

★   ★   ★

Jesus wept! Damn and bloody blast!

Shaun stumbled around the bungalow, cursing the cushions and the edges of the carpets and the fancy jars on the kitchen shelves and the place behind the toilet and the washbasin and the hat boxes on top of the wardrobe and the empty pockets of the jackets neatly lined up on the rails beneath.

He'd searched bloody everywhere — the whole length and breadth of the bungalow and hadn't found so much as a pound coin. There was loose change in a fruit dish in the

135

kitchen: a stack of coppers and five and ten pence pieces. The flaming lot only came to one pound and seventy-four bloody pence. He shook the coins on to the kitchen counter and picked up the fruit dish, recalling it from his childhood as a set of six which his gran would bring out proudly when his aunt and uncle came to tea. She'd put sweet tinned strawberries in the glasses then bring a jug of carnation milk to pour over — as much as you wanted. He twirled the glass between his chunky thumb and finger. It was made of thin yellow glass, the bowl perched on a thin little stem like an overgrown glass for Babycham — one of his gran's favourite tipples, as she liked to call it.

Hiding behind closed floral curtains Shaun had combed through the bungalow as though his life depended on it. Which, in a way, it did. Because if he didn't find any money how was he going to live? He couldn't go to work. He couldn't go to the post office to have a stab at getting his hands on his gran's savings account. He couldn't go shopping. He couldn't step outside the door, or even answer it. He couldn't do a damn thing, because some bloody arse-licking member of the public and lover of the piggy police would be bound to spot him and get him hauled in for questioning about that doctor who'd got herself bumped off. Not that they'd got anything on him, he'd been making sure to watch the news and they just kept banging on about how the police were *wanting to question* a Mr Shaun Busfield. *In connection with the murder of Moira Farrell*, they said, all mealy mouthed like the police had told them to be. What they really meant was the bloody police were going to pin it on him whether he'd done it or not. And by now the whole country would be thinking he was as guilty as hell.

He filled the kettle and set it to boil. There was around enough coffee in the jar to last another day or two, and there was another one in the cupboard. And there were tins of meat and beans to last him maybe into the end of next week. Enough chocolate biscuits to last a bit longer than that. But he'd got no milk, no bread, no butter. He'd had to throw everything out of the fridge; it had all gone bad while his gran was in hospital. A whole week she'd been in that good-for-nothing place and the fucking doctors hadn't done a bloody thing to help her. And then they decided to operate, and about bloody time. And then look what happened. They went and let her die on the operating table. As good as killed her. As good as *murdered* her.

And Tina was no fucking good. He hadn't heard a peep from her, not a flaming dicky bird. He knew she wouldn't shop him — well, for a start, she wouldn't bloody dare. But she might at least have phoned to see how he was getting on, let him know what the police had been up to. She could do it from a phone box for Christ's sake. All anonymous, no way to trace him or her. He supposed he could ring her mobile. Dial 141 so they couldn't get his number. But he wasn't sure if the police couldn't somehow get round that. Phones were all digital and computerized now, weren't they? And he'd heard that whatever you put into a computer, somehow someone really smart could always find it.

The old panic from the past pushed inside him, heating his blood, making his heart gallop, tightening a band around his chest so he could hardly breathe.

What if Tina decided to shop him after all? She'd no backbone, that one — she was nothing but gristle and putty. If they took her to the station and frightened her half to death she'd cough. And even if she didn't he had a horrible feeling they'd track him down in the end. They'd come for him early one morning, a whole bloody regiment of them, armed to the teeth, yelling and battering down the door. Christ! And they'd have made sure he was fitted up good and proper.

He looked down at the glass in his hand, then hurled it against the wall and watched it shatter into a spin and sparkle of fragmenting glass.

8

Adrian Cavanagh looked at the photographs Georgie Tyson had taken and made a very creditable attempt to appear unruffled. He also, very wisely, made no attempt to deny that the pictures told a certain story.

Swift and Laura waited patiently for his verbal reaction.

'I'm afraid that in recent weeks there had been some . . . disagreements between Moira and myself,' he said with low-voiced regret. 'Not personal, I hasten to add. Matters of procedure,' he concluded vaguely. 'Medical procedure.' He gave the impression the police wouldn't be at all interested in the details of such procedure, and would most probably not understand them.

He dropped his eyes to his diary which was lying open on the desk in front of him, then with a sharp gesture he clicked it shut and squared his shoulders, making eye contact with each detective showing his readiness to face whatever was coming next.

'Are you talking about clinical procedures in treating patients?' Laura asked. One of her previous boyfriends had been a junior hospital doctor and it had been impossible not to pick up a few trade secrets connected to the practice of medicine.

Cavanagh's initial expression showed that he was slightly taken aback by the question. The lines of his face settled into new heedfulness.

'No,' he said crisply.

'Surgical procedures?' Laura continued. 'As an anaesthetist I presume Dr Farrell would have a great deal of experience in that area.'

'Moira was a specialist in anaesthetics,' Cavanagh said with one of his smooth smiles. 'She was not in the habit of commenting on the surgical procedures of myself and my team. Or any other team she worked with.'

'Mr Cavanagh,' Swift said, 'would you clarify for us what the dispute with Moira Farrell was about. The photographs clearly suggest that both of you were angry.'

Cavanagh considered for a few moment. 'We had a disagreement about a matter relating to the management. There's a reorganization exercise going on in the hospital, including our department. I'm very keen to divert a sizeable slice of our budget to a new specialist baby unit. Moira had strong feelings that the money should be spent on other projects.'

'I see.' Swift took a moment to process this information.

Outside in the corridor there was the sound of raised voices. Cavanagh turned his head towards the door and glanced covertly at his watch. Swift and Laura's gazes connected, signalling an awareness that the consultant's attention had been diverted from the difficulties ongoing in the little office and were now engaged with potentially greater difficulties beyond.

There was a tap on the door. A young woman with dark curls, and bright scarlet lipstick, popped her head around the door, apology and deference written all over her pretty features. 'I'm so sorry to disturb you, Mr Cavanagh, but your eleven-thirty appointment has arrived.'

Further agitated protests were coming from the corridor close to the nurses' station: a man's voice making demands, a young woman's voice remonstrating with seemingly little effect.

'I really think you need to come.' The curly haired woman's eyes were wide with alarm. 'Shall I call Security?' The anxiety in her demeanour suggested that Cavanagh really needed to deal with the situation right away.

Cavanagh jumped up. 'You must excuse me,' he told the watchful detectives, heading out into the corridor with a purposeful stride.

Swift got up, walked round the desk Cavanagh had just vacated, flipped open the diary and scanned through the current day's appointments. The shouts had temporarily stopped. 'Let's get a ringside seat,' he murmured to Laura, closing the diary and moving towards the nurses' station.

The sounds of angry protests had resumed but were now muted. Cavanagh and the man who had been kicking up a fuss were moving down the corridor, about to disappear into another small office. He noticed that Cavanagh had a guiding hand around the man's shoulders, gently but firmly propelling him away from the exposing publicity of the corridor.

'Dissatisfied patient?' Laura suggested. 'Or rather the relative of one. Men don't have much use for the services of a gynaecologist, do they?'

Swift smiled, nodding agreement.

He got out his ID and went up to the nurses' station. The young woman sitting behind it had her head down, busily making notes as though nothing untoward had happened.

'We're police officers,' he said, placing his ID on the shelf bordering the station. 'Did you know Moira Farrell?' he asked the young woman, who was still desperately trying to pretend she was unable to pull herself from her administrative work, despite the looming presence of the two police officers.

The simple, direct question forced her to look up, a round-cheeked young woman with brown hair cuffed back from her face with a ring of black velvet. Her eyes peered anxiously at him through black-rimmed glasses. 'Yes.' A hot pink blush started up in her pale cheeks.

'As a friend?'

The blush had now spread into her throat and her ears. 'No. I'm just a probationer,' she said.

'Probationers don't become friends with consultants?' Swift suggested.

A glimmer of relief flashed in her eyes. 'You could say that.'

Swift nodded in understanding. 'Did you know her as a colleague?'

'Yes.'

He smiled at her as though she was being really helpful. Then waited.

'She was a nice person.' There was a wistful sadness in the young woman's eyes. 'A really nice person. Like she had no side to her.'

'Nurse Hay,' he said, having taken note of her identification badge, 'would you describe Dr Farrell as generally well liked in the department?'

Nurse Hay opened her mouth to make an instant response and then closed it again. 'Yes,' she said, sounding guarded. 'Oh, yes,' she added with emphasis. She glanced nervously down the corridor, her eyes following the route Cavanagh and the irate visitor had taken.

'Do you think Mr Cavanagh will be free soon?' Laura asked in friendly tones. 'To speak to us again?'

'I don't know.' Nurse Hay's face had lost its flush now, but the guarded air still persisted. She looked down once more at the notes she had been making.

'Thank you, Nurse Hay,' Swift murmured, glancing at Laura and giving a jerk of his head towards the exit door of the department.

'So, where are we at now, sir?' Laura asked her boss, her mind running back through the last two interviews.

'Travelling down a number of seemingly blind alleys,' he commented.

She didn't disagree. 'And squeezing all the sponges dry with remarkable speed.'

'Maybe Cavanagh isn't as safe and dry as he thinks,' Swift said. 'According to his diary his appointment was with someone called Tricklebank.'

'Do you think Tricklebank was Mr

Exceedingly Angry? The shouter in the corridor?'

'Quite likely. So as we haven't many more blind alleys to head down urgently, why don't we wait around and see if we can catch Mr Tricklebank and have a word when he emerges from his clash with Cavanagh?'

Laura saw the point. 'And if he manages to slip out without our seeing, he shouldn't be too difficult to find. There can't be many Tricklebanks in this part of the world, can there? Or, indeed, many parts at all.'

★ ★ ★

Doug had worked his way through Shaun's workmates, trying to get a handle on the man's daily routines. Nothing of immediate significance had turned up. Shaun had emerged sounding like a guy who kept his private life to himself. His workmates knew that Shaun lived with a girlfriend, but none of them referred to her by name, or seemed to know anything about her or the relationship. The only thing of any possible importance was that one of his mates mentioned that Shaun's grandmother had died recently and that Shaun had seemed pretty cut up about it. Doug had followed this up with a gleam of hope, but neither the informant nor any of

146

the other colleagues knew the grandmother's name or where she had lived.

The manager at Busfield's works knew even less, except that Busfield was a reliable worker who turned up on time and turned in the work. He'd been employed at the firm for two years. And as regards what he did in his spare time, well, the manager considered that was none of the firm's business. And no, he couldn't put his hand on the references Busfield had come with when he got the job.

Doug doubted there'd ever been any question of formal references. Probably no more than word of mouth of the last employer who more than likely wanted to get shot of Busfield. And predictably this present manager had stated that he couldn't imagine Busfield being the sort of bloke who would run amok and kill a woman in her own house in cold blood. Whereas we old cynics in the police know that there's no such thing as the sort of bloke who wouldn't commit murder, he told himself. Everyone's the sort of bloke when you get down to the nitty-gritty.

'Do you have a signing out policy for using the vans?' Doug asked, having noticed two cream vehicles painted with the firm's logo standing out in the yard behind the warehouse.

The manager eyed the constable with a

world-weary stare. 'In theory, yes.'

'Do you keep a book?'

'Yeah. Don't run away with the idea we're a slack outfit here. Drivers have to sign in to get issued a key.'

'But there can be occasional slip-ups,' Doug commented, his tone non-committal.

The manager shrugged. He guessed the constable understood the situation only too well.

'I'd like to see the book,' Doug said.

The manager rummaged amongst the piles of papers on his desk. 'Here — help yourself!'

Doug leafed through the pages for January, but found no entry in Shaun Busfield's name. However going back a few months provided evidence of three weekends during the autumn when Busfield had signed for one of the vans. Pointing this out to the manager he intimated that the police would need to take the vehicle in for examination.

The manager threw his eyes to the ceiling. 'Is this really necessary?'

'Yes.' Doug disliked outright lies, but found this one not too difficult when he considered the issue of covering his back as far as reprisals from Superintendent Finch were concerned.

Leaving the manager sighing in weary disbelief at the demands of the law, he went on to Tina's place of work and dragged her from the task in hand which was painting a bored-looking client's fingernails with bubble-gum pink varnish.

Tina was not at all pleased, and decidedly on edge. Which was exactly what Doug had aimed to achieve.

'I don't like you coming to my work,' she said, tight-lipped, as she spoke to him on the little platform forming the stepping down place from the fire escape at the back of the building. In the cruel rawness of the grey, darkening afternoon she was soon shivering in her thin pink gingham work overalls and she wrapped her arms tightly around her chest in a gesture of protection and protest.

Calm but insistent, Doug kept up a steady bombardment of questions as to Shaun's whereabouts. But despite her agitation, Tina was firm and steadfast in asserting that she had not seen or heard from Shaun since his disappearance at the time the police came looking for him.

'He's not stupid,' she told them. 'He'll keep his head down.'

'And why would that be?' Doug asked.

'Because he'll know he'll be in bother if you find him.' She rolled her eyes in exasperation at the banality of the questions.

'When we find him, love,' Doug corrected gently.

'Huh!'

'And why should he think he'll be in bother?' he continued.

'Who wouldn't think that if they knew the police were after them for murder?'

'But he didn't know that when we came for him, Miss Frazer,' Doug pointed out.

'But he certainly will now! Don't you CID guys ever watch TV?' She put on a prim expression and enunciated her next words with care. 'Police are still hunting Shaun Busfield, whom they want to speak to in regard to the murder of Mrs Moira Farrell, a local doctor.'

Doug considered this mimicking of one of the *Look North* news-readers to be pretty commendable. 'Well, you've got the spiel off pat,' he remarked ironically. 'I'd say you've been keeping a close eye on what's going on in this murder investigation.'

Tina gave a dry laugh. 'Yeah. And it seems to me there hasn't been a lot. Going on, I mean.' She was smirking like a cheeky adolescent.

During the questioning it had occurred to Doug that Shaun Busfield's girl was quite a hot little piece. 'Aren't you worried about him?' he asked, his mind moving not so much around the issue of loneliness but on the

150

distressing lack of regular and readily available sex when a partner was absent.

Tina gave a foxy smile. 'He can take care of himself.'

'So you're not telling us anything,' Doug commented.

'I've nothing to tell,' she said. 'And if you don't let me get back to work I'll have no job and nothing to live on either.'

Doug nodded assent. They went back into the warmth of the building. Tina turned down the corridor leading to the room where her client was waiting.

'I'll be back,' Doug called after her. He climbed into the car and fired the engine. That one could be a whole lot tougher than she looks, he decided as he waited to turn into the traffic. Although she's hardly Myra Hindley in thrall to Ian Brady. He turned on Radio 2 and tapped out a rhythm on the wheel.

But he'd be surprised if she didn't know something his team would find interesting. And even more surprised if she let on where he was hiding out.

★　★　★

Reinstalled in Beauty Therapy Room 3 with her now gratifyingly curious client, Tina reloaded her brush with a fresh coating of Sizzling Pink and painted a large framing U around the client's thumb nail. All in all she felt the interview with the police had gone well. Let Shaun sweat. Let the police sweat. It felt good having a share of the power for a change.

★ ★ ★

Swift stepped forward as the man he assumed to be Tricklebank walked through the automatically opening exit doors of the hospital. 'Mr Tricklebank?'

The man turned, a stocky figure in his thirties with light brown hair. His eyes were hollow with weariness as though he hadn't had a proper night's sleep for some time. He was wearing a crumpled grey suit, a badly ironed white shirt and a blue tie. His clothes suggested that he was bound for some kind of middle manager job, but the dark stubble of his unshaved chin didn't quite fit that assumption. He brushed a hand over his forehead and Swift could tell by the tremor that he was drinking too much on a regular basis.

'Who wants to know?' His voice was filled with the same exhaustion as his face, and it was hard to believe he was the man who had made such violent protests in the hospital corridor.

Swift showed his ID. 'We wondered if we could have a word with you, sir. It's in connection with the murder of Dr Moira Farrell.'

Tricklebank stared at him in bewilderment. His face crumpled as though being approached in this way was just the last straw.

'It's just for information, sir,' Swift said gently.

'Don't tell me I'm a suspect,' the man said with grim resignation. 'I've enough on my plate without that.'

'We're simply making enquiries at the hospital, gaining background information from people who worked with Dr Farrell and who knew her as a colleague, or as a patient.'

Tricklebank was paying full attention, looking from Swift to Laura as though assessing their trustworthiness. 'I didn't know Dr Farrell, but I can give you chapter and verse on that slimy bastard Cavanagh. If anyone needed putting behind bars, it's him.' He spoke with soft venom.

Swift began to walk away from the busy entrance, leading the three of them to a less crowded place at the edge of the ambulance parking area. 'Go on,' he said.

Tricklebank looked undecided, as though

the impulsive urge to unload had vanished as swiftly as it had arrived. He pulled a packet of cigarettes from his pocket, turning it around in his fingers as he pondered.

'This is a murder investigation, sir,' Swift said, reflecting on the countless number of times he must have said those words. 'Anything connected with Dr Farrell's life and her work could be relevant to our enquiry.'

Tricklebank lit a match and cupped his hand around the tip of his cigarette, shielding it from the raw wind which was gusting around the edges of the building. 'That man, Cavanagh, has ruined our lives,' he said. 'Because of him, my wife lost her baby.' He took a long pull at his cigarette, inhaling into his lungs. 'And I've more or less lost her.'

Both Swift and Laura began formulating follow up questions to that last statement, and both simultaneously decided that silence was the only possible way forward.

Tricklebank exhaled and then said, 'She's in a wheelchair, she can't speak properly; she wets herself; she shits herself: she wishes she was dead.'

Prickles ran up the back of Laura's neck at the sounds of this man's raw grief. She glanced at Swift, recalling that he had suffered the sudden brutal loss of his own wife and guessing that he was sharing the emotion. 'When did you lose the baby?' she asked Tricklebank.

By now their informant had no need at all for prompting. The grief-stricken man couldn't wait to tell his story to a sympathetic audience.

'Thirty-two days ago. They've been the longest days of my life.' Again he drew hard on his cigarette. 'It was our first baby — we'd had no trouble getting started with one and she was fine in her pregnancy, so we didn't expect any difficulties. I brought her in when the pains started coming regularly, and everything was going to plan until the second stage. The baby seemed to get stuck in the birth canal. The midwife started getting a bit twitchy and talking about foetal distress. That's when Cavanagh came on the scene. The big boss, the top man.' Tricklebank's face twisted with scorn. 'He tried to get the baby out with forceps but that didn't work. So they whisked my wife off to theatre to do a Caesarean. About half an hour went by and Cavanagh came out to tell me they'd lost the baby. He was very kind and sympathetic. He told me there'd been a risk that both the baby and my wife would die. She'd started haemorrhaging badly. He'd wanted to avoid doing a hysterectomy because he knew we'd want to try for another baby. But in the end he had to do one.' Tricklebank snuffed out his cigarette and stared moodily into some far, unseen distance.

'He made it sound as though he'd been a bit of a hero to save my wife, and I went along with it and thanked him like the gullible, grateful fool I was at the time. It wasn't until later I realized something really bad had happened during the operation. When she came round, it was as if she'd had a stroke; her speech was all slurred, her hands and fingers lifeless, her legs so weak she had to have a wheelchair issued.' He looked at the cold, dead cigarette butt in his fingers and carefully placed it in his pocket.

'I took her home and we soldiered on for a time and it was hell. I got to thinking that some awful cock-up had taken place. I went to see Cavanagh again, but he just insisted he'd done all he could. And then a friend at work told me his neighbour had had surgery from the smarmy bastard too and she was in a right mess as well. She was thinking of suing.' He stopped and breathed in deeply, a breath of exhaustion and total frustration.

'But you can't get to grips with these guys. Cavanagh just smiles and keeps on saying he did all he could. And the management lot at the hospital won't give an inch. I've been asking to see my wife's medical notes over and over again. They kept saying they'd get them for me. Then they said they couldn't seem to find them, and after that it seemed they'd gone missing — for eternity. They made a real show of being oh so sorry about it! And do you know what? I can't do a damn thing about it.' He eased his weight from the stone pillar he'd been leaning against, stoic resignation on his features. 'So there's a story to brighten your day,' he told his two grave-faced listeners.

Swift nodded in respect of the man's suffering. 'Are you're sure you didn't meet Dr Farrell?' he asked gently. 'She worked as an anaesthetist in the gynaecology department.'

'Sorry, no. The only doctor I got to see was Cavanagh. The nurse on duty was very kind and the midwife was great too. But what could they do?'

'Do you have their names?' Laura asked.

Tricklebank shook his head. 'I'd know them if I saw them again,' he said, kicking out at a small stone lying on the ground. 'But what I want now is simply for Cavanagh to admit he made a mistake. To admit he's ruined our lives.' He glanced at his watch. 'Got to go. I couldn't get anyone to watch the wife and she gets in a bit of a state if she's left alone too long.'

Swift and Laura watched him walk away.

'Any thoughts?' Swift said.

'Still digesting.' She wrinkled her forehead as she reflected on what they had just heard, and as usual a small inverted triangle appeared between her eyebrows. 'It might be interesting to talk to the neighbour of Tricklebank's friend — the one who's considering suing Cavanagh.'

'It would certainly be interesting.' Observing her eager expression, he smiled. 'But maybe not relevant to the case.'

As they walked to the car park he reflected yet again on the current pulse of frustration running through this case, their failure to flush Shaun Busfield out from whatever sanctuary he had found for himself. He conjured up an image of the information on the whiteboard in the incident room. The pictures of the slain Moira Farrell, the names of possible suspects and leads, and at the centre of the display the blown-up photo of the bloodstained sole of Busfield's trainers standing out like a reproach. Hard evidence which was of no use whatsoever until Busfield was flushed out.

He caught Laura's quizzical gaze. 'You go track down the neighbour if you think it might be productive,' he told her. 'Why not?'

* ★ ★

Damian Finch summoned Swift and his team into his office. As usual coffee was percolating in his machine sending out tantalizing wafts of burnt vanilla through the air. Finch was prowling up and down behind his desk clutching a mug of coffee. On this occasion he did not invite the team to join him in taking some refreshment.

'So,' he said, speaking in low icy tones as though musing solely to himself, 'it seems that we are well and truly stuck in the unfortunate situation of having identified a prime suspect, and having allowed him to elude us and lead us a merry and protracted little dance.' Finch sighed, his glance flashing over the team, flaying each one of them with the severity of his glare. Whilst he had been in post only a few weeks his subordinates were now well aware that his dark moods could infect the whole station, ensuring that it was in everyone's interest to keep him happy. 'And from the look on all your faces,' he continued, 'I am assuming that little has happened so far to encourage us to have hope of finding our suspect with due haste.'

'As you know, sir,' Swift said, unruffled by the superintendent's ice-man tactics, 'we've got our press officer to set up an appeal through all the relevant TV, radio and press outlets to alert the public to Busfield's disappearance and our need to find him.'

Finch blinked and frowned as Swift spoke. 'What about the girlfriend?' he barked, cutting his DCI short before he could continue his account. 'I don't suppose she's showing any signs of changing her mind and favouring us with some clues as to Busfield's whereabouts? No, don't bother answering that, you'd have told me already, wouldn't you?'

'Of course, sir,' Swift said quietly. 'We're continuing our house to house questioning with Busfield's neighbours, and any other contacts who might be able to help us.'

'But from the look of it having little success,' Finch suggested, grim-faced. He took a sip from his mug and waited for some kind of response from someone. 'And sadly we've got next to nothing from the search of the van Busfield used during last October and November. Forensics have been over every square inch with a magnifying glass. They've removed all the seats and taken them apart — a painstaking piece of research which revealed nothing but a few dust balls, some dead cigarette ends and a ten-pence coin. The floor mat revealed some traces of earth which have been sent to the lab for testing. But I can't pretend that I hold out much hope of their setting fire to our damp squib of an enquiry.' He paused. 'I've asked the lab to do further testing on the trainers SOCO found, letting them know that even the most miniscule shred of further evidence would be like a gift from heaven.'

Laura marvelled at the superintendent's chilling eloquence: it was rather like an ice cube slipped into the collar of your shirt on a warm day.

Doug shifted on his chair, feeling little beads of sweat breaking out on his forehead.

Swift reflected on his experience in the past of working with superiors who considered themselves lower in rank only to God and his angels. It made a difficult job somewhat harder.

'We shall press on,' he told Finch. 'And we shall find Busfield.'

'I hope so,' Finch said with pointed scepticism. He took a sip of his coffee. 'Thank you for your time,' he told the team. 'I suggest you go away and get on with what has to be done without delay.'

Laura and Doug rose smartly to their feet and made for the door. Swift remained behind, sensing that Finch had something more to say to him, something which needed to be said in private.

'I've read the reports of your various visits to the hospital,' Finch said abruptly. 'And I agree that some interesting points have emerged. But as regards Adrian Cavanagh, we have nothing to place him at the scene, we have no forensics, we have no clearly demonstrable motive.'

Swift nodded acknowledgement.

'And there's something further I need to say,' Finch continued ominously. 'A part of me considers that I shouldn't speak out on this matter, but I'm going to anyway.'

Swift waited. Yes you would, he thought, guessing what was coming.

'I've familiarized myself with your recent work, Ed — as indeed I have familiarized myself with the work of all the professional staff working in this station.' He placed his coffee mug down on the desk with slow deliberation. 'And I've noticed that you have a history of being something of a doubting Thomas.' He stopped, the expression on his face indicating that it was almost too painful for him to continue. But that did not stop him doing so. 'There seem to have been a number of occasions when you appear to have doubted — or even disregarded — the evidence against prime suspects and gone off on a trail of your own devising.'

'That is true,' Swift broke in steadily, before Finch could go any further. 'And on more occasions than not, I've been proved correct in doing so.' As he spoke the words they sounded more pompous than he would have liked, but so be it, some sort of stand needed to be made.

'Quite so,' Finch said. 'You might not agree, but I'm a reasonable man, Ed. I wouldn't disagree with what you say, or presume to criticize your methods of working.'

Swift waited silently through the ensuing pause. He waited for the *but*.

'Nevertheless,' Finch continued, 'in this particular case, I think it would be most unfortunate to undermine the team's keenness to flush out Shaun Busfield, by actively pursuing other lines of enquiry. We have strong forensic evidence — fresh blood matching that of Moira Farrell on Busfield's shoes, and also a hair carrying his DNA. We know that it's possible Busfield might have had the opportunity of visiting the house previously in order to deliver materials. We also know that he has a history of violence. *And*, he's worried enough to have gone missing.'

'Strong indications,' Swift agreed. 'But, of course, as yet we have no motive. And his girlfriend has given him an alibi.'

Finch gave a dismissive snort at the latter remark. He frowned and a long, deep furrow appeared between his eyebrows. 'We have facts, Ed. Facts. Those are what interest me. Hard evidence. Backed up by the forensic team. That's what we've got with Busfield. And when we find him he's going to have difficulty getting round that. As to motive — well, yes, that's something to think about. But at present we're a long way from needing to do that. I sometimes feel that theorizing could be seen as mere icing on the cake.'

'Yes, sir,' Swift said.

'You speak with the calm assurance of a confirmed sceptic,' Finch observed. 'And you have a right to do so if you wish, Ed. But I'd like to ask you to keep your scepticism to yourself in this case, and indeed generally. Going against the flow isn't necessarily good for team morale. I want our team to be like a pack of hounds scenting out the prey, not sniffing around randomly like lapdogs being taken for a walk in the park.'

Swift found himself mildly entertained by the canine imagery. He got to his feet and moved to the door. 'I appreciate the points you've made, Damian,' he said. 'And you can rely on me and my team to continue driving every possible effort into finding Shaun Busfield.'

Walking away down the corridor Swift examined his current thoughts on the new superintendent. He judged there could have been a time, when he was a young rookie just starting off in the force, that he might have had to struggle in order not to be intimidated by Finch's covert bullying. Things were different now — he had the confidence of experience and success. But over and above that he had the strength and changed perspective on life which had come following the tragedy of losing Kate. Beside that loss, Damian Finch and his machinations were a mere pinprick. He smiled at the choice of words his mind had thrown up for him. Pinprick, indeed.

In the CID room Laura and Doug were waiting anxiously for the emergence of their boss from the den of Superintendent Finch.

'Finch,' Laura was musing. 'What sort of a name is that?'

'A bird's,' Doug said.

'Well, I suppose it's better than Tit.' Laura grinned, before snapping to attention as Swift appeared in the office.

His mobile trilled before he could speak to his colleagues. On answering he listened for a moment then turned away.

Both Laura and Doug bristled with alertness. Some breakthrough in finding

Busfield? Things moving at last?

Swift's call was brief, mainly listening, little talking. 'I'll call you back,' he said. 'Give me just a few minutes.' A stillness came over him, some inner focus which instantly communicated itself to Laura and Doug. They watched him get slowly to his feet.

'I'm sorry,' he told them. 'There's something urgent I have to deal with. You carry on.'

He disappeared through the door and into the corridor beyond, leaving Laura and Doug exchanging glances of conjecture and concern.

9

The voice on the phone had not been recognizable for few moments, but the message it was carrying was enough to throw Swift temporarily off balance.

The voice belonged to Cat Fallon, a DI Ed had worked with some years ago before he joined West Yorkshire. She was now with the vice squad in Durham, a tough, sharp-nosed detective with a strong, striking face and a heart of 22 carat gold buried deep so that not all her contacts and colleagues were aware of just how genuine and shiny it was.

After introducing herself and reminding him who she was, she came straight to the point. 'Ed, I'm afraid I've got some difficult news to give you — '

'It's Naomi, isn't it?' A pit of hollowness opened in his stomach.

'Yes. It's not the worst, Ed. She's alive and well.' There was a pause. 'She's been arrested.'

Swift closed his eyes, bracing himself against the edge of his desk with his spare hand. 'Go on.'

'For possession of drugs.'

'What kind of drugs?'

'Coke.'

'God!' The word was no more than a whispered rasp of shock. 'Are you sure?' He quickly corrected himself. 'Sorry, Cat, forget that. How much coke?'

'About three grams.'

He drew in breath through clenched teeth. 'So are you charging her with intent to supply?'

'No. At least, not at this point. It's . . . complicated.'

'Is someone else involved?' he came in quickly.

'Yes. I can't really give more details over the phone. My senior officer wouldn't be too pleased if he knew I'd contacted you on the quiet. I got the chance to talk to Naomi on her own a little while ago. She asked me to phone. Said she couldn't bring herself to do it.' There was a short pause. 'I think she feels she's let you down, can't bear to disappoint you.'

'Yes, yes, I appreciate what you're saying, and thanks for making the opportunity to talk to her.'

'My SIO's a touch bullish,' she said, and there was meaningful caution in her tone. A warning. 'I can give you his extension number if you like. His name's Len Craven.'

'No, I'll drive up right away.' He judged the timing of the journey up the A1, given that he would hit the evening rush hour as he approached Durham. 'I should arrive in a couple of hours at the latest. Perhaps you'd let Naomi know I'm on my way. And that I'm not disappointed in her, however things turn out.'

'OK, Ed. And take care when you're driving.' She said it as though she meant it.

Swift found his palms were sweating as he broke the connection. He had a sudden huge longing for Kate; someone to share this blow with, talk through the ins and outs of how to handle things, the conclusions to be drawn, the way forward. Because even if Naomi had had the coke planted on her and was completely innocent, which he hoped against hope she would be, things could still be difficult.

Especially with a bullish SIO in charge at the Drugs Squad.

He rang through to Damian Finch's office. Mercifully he was not on another line. His voice rang out, grim and confident. 'Ed?'

'Damian,' he said, instinctively going for the personal touch, 'I'm going to have to go up to Durham for a day or so.' He took a breath and gave Finch the bare, simple details as Cat had explained them to him.

Finch was instantly understanding. 'Get off right away, Ed. Just drop everything. I'll act as SIO on the Farrell case while you're gone.' He was all decisiveness and pragmatism.

Swift was appreciative and impressed. 'Right. Thanks for that.'

'Your team will have my full support,' Finch said. 'And I'll be sure to make time to supervise the case, whatever the pressures of the rest of my workload.'

'They'll value that,' Swift said, unable to stop himself giving a tight smile of irony.

★ ★ ★

The journey up the A1 was surprisingly free of hold-ups, despite the weather which had taken a turn for the violent. As the night gathered, a black velvet stain raced across the sky sending down a burst of sleety rain so heavy and abrupt that the motorway was temporarily awash with flood water. Black streams poured down the windscreen as the wipers struggled to gain control.

He took the turn off which approached the city through Bowburn village and the stern countryside to the east of the town, dropping down a slight hill as he drove through the suburbs, then turning left towards the centre and passing the turning to Naomi's college before he reached the station where she was being held.

There was a fracas going on outside the entrance where a pink-faced male uniform was trying to calm two drunken men who were engaged in some heavy physical action. One of them was trying to squeeze the throat of the other man, whilst his opponent reached back, flailing about in the attempt to find a target to thump. It struck Swift that they were way too old for a fight, their podgy bodies and rheumatic legs cramping their style. Swift left the PC to it and went inside the main entrance which was empty apart from a single pathetic-looking small man in his fifties who was sitting on a chair with a wad of tissue stuffed against the end of his nose trying to staunch the bleeding.

Swift made himself known to the officer at the front desk, a young beefy constable, with blond hair and a cheery pink face. 'I've been told you're holding my daughter, Naomi.'

The young man's eyes sharpened. 'Oh, aye. Just one moment, sir.' He disappeared through a door into the main body of the station.

Moments passed. Swift shifted from one foot to the other, his glance roaming around the reception area. The man with the bleeding nose caught his eye and gave him a

171

sympathetic smile. 'Your little lass in trouble, is she, man? That's bad luck.'

Swift nodded agreement. Blood was still gushing from the man's nose. 'Shouldn't you get that seen to at the hospital?' he asked.

'No way. My missus has gone mental. There's no way I'm leaving here until she's calmed down. Safest place to be.'

There was that, Swift thought.

The beefy constable was back at the desk. He leaned forward to speak to Swift. 'If you'd like to come this way, sir. Inspector Fallon would like to speak to you.'

Swift guessed it would be five years since he'd seen Catherine Fallon. She'd aged during that time, but if anything had become even more striking than he remembered. Her strong, even features were framed with dark-brown hair silvering at the temples and cut in a short bob. She was wearing a black suit with an open-necked pink shirt. She got to her feet, smiling and offering her hand, her brown eyes warm with welcome. 'Ed! Long time.' Her grip was also warm, holding his hand firmly for a few seconds longer than a stranger would have done.

Swift appreciated her greeting which he felt to be unstudied and genuine. 'Cat! It's good to see you. And thanks for the help so far.' He sat down, his face sobering as the issue of

Naomi's situation hit him afresh.

'I'm really sorry about what's happened.' She stopped, considering how to elaborate.

'I'm guessing you're skating on thin ice with this one,' Swift said.

'Sticking my neck out,' she agreed. 'It's something I'm no stranger to. But I have to be a bit careful here. As I said, Len Craven, my senior officer, has a reputation for not taking a softly-softly approach when it comes to apprehending drug offenders. And dealers are definitely not his favourites.'

'Which I wouldn't expect them to be as far as the head of the Drugs Squad is concerned,' Swift pointed out. 'But I can't believe Naomi's been dealing. I can't really believe she's been using. But then I'm her father.'

'Let me tell you what information I've gathered so far.' Cat opened her hands in a gesture which indicated there was going to be some plain speaking. 'She was travelling as a passenger in a car going along the A167 road in the town, heading south. The car was stopped because there'd been a road rage incident just moments previously. A car had mounted the pavement and one of the pedestrians was taking a pretty serious view of what had happened. He'd pulled a knife on the driver.'

Swift grunted in dismay.

'It was just routine,' Cat said. 'They were stopping everyone passing the place where the incident occurred.'

'So why detain Naomi? What did she do?'

'It wasn't her, Ed; it was the guy she was with.'

'Who was?'

'Jasper Guest. He's a tutor at Naomi's college.'

'Ah.' He looked at Cat, nothing the question in her eyes. 'I don't think I've even heard her mention him. She's got a long-standing boyfriend from a few years back.' Come to think of it, he hadn't heard Naomi mention him either for a few weeks.

'He's an interesting guy,' Cat said. 'He's got the looks and charm of a TV soap star and quite a lot of attitude to go with it. He got a First at Oxford. And he's also got previous.'

Swift groaned.

'Nothing too dreadful. Suspicion of selling dope when he was a student. Possession of cannabis.' She stopped.

'Tell me the worst.'

'And there was a charge for an affray around the time he graduated, some demo on the campus. He got a few months' probation.'

Swift blew out a long breath. 'I suppose it could be worse.'

'He's the sort of guy who wouldn't be able to simply keep quiet if he was stopped while driving and required to get out of the vehicle. Articulate some would call it. The two constables pulling him in to the kerb didn't take it quite that way.'

Swift had to smile. The picture Cat was building of Guest was not especially pretty in his eyes, but he could imagine Naomi being intrigued by a guy like that. An older man with style and clout.

'And when they brought him in,' Cat continued, 'he rubbed my boss up the wrong way, big time. And not for the first time. Len's had Guest in before and he made a pretty good sparring partner — which Len kind of loves and loathes at the same time.

'Len's currently under some pressure to squeeze the local dealers. And according to him he's got the whisper from the ether that Guest might be moving up into a different league from cannabis.'

Swift heard extra meaning behind her words. Her eyes met his and he knew that he was right, but that she felt she couldn't say anything further. Fair enough, as long as Naomi was released and totally exonerated pronto.

'So Craven's holding them both, with

Guest as the main suspect and Naomi an accessory?'

'Well, the stuff was discovered in the glove compartment in which her purse was also placed. Len's suggesting she knew about it.'

'Not the hardest of evidence,' Swift said.

'No, but not good for her either.'

Swift sighed. 'What has Naomi said about all this?'

'She said she knew nothing about the drugs in the locker. And following that she hasn't made any further comment.'

'Is Craven holding her in the hope she'll shop Guest?'

'I'd guess so.' She paused. 'Yes.'

'But she's not been charged?' His voice was hard now.

'No.' She looked away and bit down on her lip. 'He's a risk-taker, Ed. He wants results whatever it takes.' Her eyes held his once again. *Don't make me say more.* 'How's the new Homicide and Major Enquiry team in Bradford?' she asked.

'Generally working well, I'd say.' His tone was non-committal.

'And the Moira Farrell case?'

'You've been doing your homework,' he said. 'We're stuck. The prime suspect's gone to ground.'

'Every SIO's nightmare,' she said.

'We'll find him — at least that's the official line.'

Cat smiled. 'I've applied for a DCI job with the Bradford Central Major Enquiry team,' she told him.

'Really.' He heard the pleasure in his exclamation and was faintly surprised to register how pleased he felt. 'Good luck. When are the interviews?'

'A couple of weeks. I'll let you know.' She smiled.

'What made you think of a change?'

'Oh, chance of promotion. A change of scene.' She meant a change from Craven, but was too loyal to come out with it. 'The kind of thing that brought me up to this part of the world three years ago, mainly prompted by a split up with my husband.' Noting his expression of regret, she smiled. 'It's OK,' she said, 'water long under the bridge.' She glanced into his face. 'What about you?'

'Life without Kate,' he reflected, allowing a rare admission of sadness into his voice. 'Well — it goes on.'

Cat refrained from probing further.

'Is Craven still on duty?' he asked her.

'No, he's gone home on time for once. Leaving Guest and your daughter to sweat it out in the cells.' She scribbled on her notepad, tore the sheet out and handed it to

Swift. 'His home address,' she said. 'Do you want me to come with you? I'm game.'

'That's great of you, Cat, but no, I won't drag you in.'

'I'm so sorry,' she said again. 'This must be a nightmare for you. I haven't any kids but I've got an imagination.'

As he left the room she put her hand briefly on his shoulder.

★ ★ ★

He found Naomi sitting cross-legged on the bunk in her cell, her gaze directed at her fingers which she was bending then flexing into a steeple. He noticed that there were thick stripes of blonde in her dark hair and that her body looked thinner than he recalled. Her head jerked up as she heard the key in the lock of the cell.

'Dad!' She uncurled herself and stepped up close to him, letting him enclose her in his arms. 'Sorry,' she muttered. 'I'm really sorry.'

He held her in an easy but reassuring grip. 'For what?'

'Causing all this trouble. Dragging you up here.'

'Is that all?'

She sniffed as though to ward off tears and nodded vigorously.

'I've no idea where the coke came from. And I'm not a user. I don't need the stuff.'

'So what's your version of events?'

'I think someone planted it.'

'That's a convenient get-out which is something of a cliché,' he observed.

'God!' she exclaimed. 'To be accused of peddling clichés on top of everything else. But that's what I truly believe. I can't think of any other explanation.'

He let his arms drop away from her and the two of them sat on her bunk.

Swift gave her a few moments. 'What about Jasper Guest?'

A small stain of colour crept up her neck. 'I should have told you about Jasper when I was home at Christmas. I've been seeing him since last November.'

'Seeing — as in . . . ?' He raised his eyebrows in query.

'As in being an item.' There was a pause. 'And sleeping with him.'

Quizzing her on why she hadn't told him before seemed inappropriate at this point. He decided to leave that for another time. 'Is Jasper a user?'

'Cannabis occasionally. But not since I've been with him. I told him I didn't like it. And as for being a dealer. Absolutely not.'

'I've heard from Cat Fallon that Jasper's

179

had one or two run ins with the police. That he's not exactly Mr Popular.'

'He's pretty well endowed with the grey matter,' she commented. 'He's got an Oxford First and he's not one to hide his light under a bushel.'

'Clever, cocky, arrogant?' Swift suggested.

She smiled. 'Probably all of those. I don't think the average plod is quite on his wavelength.'

'How's he going to react to me?'

'You're not the average plod. And you're my dad.'

'Cat Fallon thinks maybe Jasper's got on the wrong side of the head of the Drug Squad,' he told her. He guessed Cat also thought Craven might be involved in collusion with known dealers. There was no need to burden Naomi with that.

'That could well be the case. But Jasper hasn't mentioned it to me.'

Swift straightened up. 'OK. So you're telling me you're entirely innocent. You're not using, you're not dealing. And you didn't know anything about the drugs found in Jasper's car next to your purse?'

She nodded.

'How come you didn't see the stuff when you put your purse in the glove compartment?'

'I just stuffed it in without really looking.'

She frowned. 'I know that sounds feeble, but it's true.'

Swift thought things through. 'Fair enough. I believe you.' He guessed Naomi's attention had all been for Jasper the quick-witted charmer.

'And where were you going, when you got stopped?'

'To a party in Tudhoe village.'

'Jasper's friends?'

'His sister, actually.'

'Ah — meeting the family.'

'Dad!'

He gave an absent smile. His mind was working on the way forward for the immediate future.

'Interrogation over?' Naomi asked.

'Yep.'

'So, what happens now?' A thread of raw anxiety ran beneath the words.

'I'll have a word with Craven. Aim to get you out of here as soon as possible.'

'That'd be nice,' she said, aiming for her usual brittle, ironic tone, but turning away as her voice began to break up and tears were almost impossible to hold back.

He got to his feet and paused, looking down at her.

'There's a lot of time for reflection in here,' she said.

'Maybe that's no bad thing.'

They sat in silence for a few moments. The custody sergeant came to the door and called time. Swift dropped a kiss on the top of her head. 'I'll be back.' He walked through the door, hearing the dull clang as the door closed, internally wincing as the sergeant turned the key in the lock.

Using the number Cat had jotted down for him Swift made a call to Craven. Fifteen minutes later he was standing outside a crumbling Georgian house, one of a terrace of four standing on a ridge at the end of a small cobbled road. The house was divided into three flats, Craven's occupying the ground floor. A black 1980s BMW 3 series convertible stood on the cobbles opposite his door, immaculately waxed and gleaming like polished granite under the nearby streetlamp.

Craven appeared in the doorway as Swift got out of his car, a muscular man in his mid-forties. His hair was dark and close cropped, his face gaunt and tough-looking. He was dressed in black jeans, and a dark grey V-neck sweater. His mobile phone was clutched in his hand like a gun at the ready. 'Ed Swift?' he asked, cold and terse.

He led the way through a dark hallway painted in brown to an equally dark living-room with two long windows and a high ceiling. The room was almost empty: a sofa, a sleek hi-fi system in one corner, a revolving CD stack full of discs, and a modestly-sized plasma TV. Swift had the impression if he called out his voice would probably echo. Craven gestured him to sit down in a corner of the impressively large brown leather sofa. He himself sat in the other corner.

'I've been trying to get some sleep,' Craven said pointedly. 'Had four late nights at work, one after the other. Knackered. You know the scenario.'

Swift nodded. 'Thanks for making time to see me.' He asked Craven how things were going in the Drug Squad.

For a few uneasy minutes they swapped tales of life in the police force in the twenty-first century. Craven was openly bitter. Work conditions, pay, image, public indifference. You name it, they had to deal with it. And as for the punters! 'Every toe-rag dealer out there on the streets is carrying a neat little firearm in the pocket of their designer jeans,' he grumbled, 'or stashed under the seat of their spanking new Mercs. And all I've got is a finger to point at them if I catch them with some crack. I've had two officers take a bullet in the leg in the past year, but if our lot so much as put a foot wrong our elders and betters at headquarters are down on us like a ton of bloody hot bricks.'

Swift put on a neutral expression and said nothing.

'Your little lass,' Craven said. 'She's got herself into a bit of a scrape, hasn't she? Big mistake to get involved with Jasper Guest. And to get herself in the situation of looking as though she was carrying for him.'

Swift schooled himself to stay calm. 'Were you hoping she'd give some information on Guest?'

Craven gave a dry laugh. 'What else? But it doesn't look as though it's going to turn out like that. She's a toughie, isn't she? And not one to squeal.'

'I'd say that was about right. What can you tell me about Jasper Guest?'

'A smart arse. Of the first order. Fancy degree from Oxford. Nice cushy job as a lecturer in one of the poncey colleges here in Durham. Lecturer! More like a licence to pull any juicy 18-year-old he fancies. Lecher's more to the point.'

Swift had to restrain himself from rounding on Craven and shaking him by the neck. 'You're not the Vice Squad,' he said, forcing a smile. 'Why the interest in Guest?'

'Oh, his name started cropping up in the

nightclubs. A bit of dealing here and there.'

'Hard drugs?' Swift asked sharply. 'What have you found?'

Craven shrugged. 'Nothing more than a bit of weed until this little haul. We've had him in a couple of times. He gets on my tits. Clever bastard who can't get enough of the sound of his own voice. He thinks he's God's gift, can do whatever he fucking likes, fuck any brainy posh little tart he takes a fancy to.'

Swift felt the rage rising in him, a flooding red wave. He pushed it down.

'Listen, Ed. Don't get on your parental high horse and upset the applecart for us. We think we're close to hooking a really big fish. And Guest makes good bait.' He tilted his head. 'Get my drift?'

Swift nodded agreement. 'And what happens to Naomi?' he asked softly.

'She's free to go. I'll make a call right now. You can go get her as soon as you like.'

Swift let out a silent sigh, relief drowning out the anger. 'Thanks for that, Len.'

Craven shrugged. 'What about your wife? What does she think of all this? Not so good for a mother when the daughter slips off the rails.'

'My wife was killed in a train crash. When Naomi was fifteen.'

The muscles around Craven's mouth

twitched. 'Sorry,' he said, before spoiling it by adding, 'mine walked out on me.'

Swift stood up. 'What about Jasper Guest?'

Craven grinned and shook his head in pity for a man who could show such concern for a jumped-up little turd like Jasper Guest. 'We'll keep him in one piece in case your lass wants him back when we release him.'

He led Swift back into the hallway and opened the door. 'Did Cat Fallon give you my number?' he asked.

Swift hesitated. 'Yes, she did.'

'Yeah.' He drew the word out. 'She's a good officer, our Cat. And very tasty with it. Pity she's leaving us. She'll get the Bradford job. With the reference I've given her they ought to make her bloody chief constable.' His eyes glittered with a malicious know-what-I-mean glance.

Swift couldn't remember ever wanting to wipe the smile off a man's face quite so much.

★ ★ ★

At the custody-sergeant's desk Naomi was reunited with her watch, her purse, her phone, the belt of her jeans and the small pearl ear studs that had once belonged to Kate. She signed the itemized receipt the grim-faced sergeant handed her.

As she and Swift passed the front desk at the entrance, the young beefy constable leaned his impressively muscled elbows on the counter. 'You just take care, pet,' he said to Naomi, stern but kind.

'You bet,' she told him.

She and Swift walked out into the car park. It was late now. The night was clear, the sky black and scattered with stars like spilled milk.

'Hungry?' Swift asked.

'I could murder a steak and chips.'

'Do you know somewhere good to get them at this time?'

'Yep.' She gave directions. 'Dad?'

He waited, expecting something about Jasper Guest. 'Cat Fallon's been a real star in all this. Do you think she'd like to join us?'

'Sure.' He wondered if Naomi was shying away from a heart to heart with him over the steak. Or maybe she really liked Cat Fallon, wanted to say thanks. 'Give her a call.'

Cat was free. She was up for a steak. She'd meet them in ten minutes. Swift wasn't sure whether to be glad or sorry.

At the café bar Naomi had recommended he ordered a bottle of red and a litre of mineral water. Naomi poured herself a glass of water and drank it in one go. She was unusually quiet. He could almost track the thoughts in her head, the conflicts, doubts. And very probably, knowing her, a strong loyalty towards Jasper Guest.

Cat swung in through the doors, still in her black suit, but with the addition of long swinging silver ear-rings and improbably high-heeled strappy shoes totally unsuitable for the bitter cold of the evening.

Naomi got up and went forward to greet her. Swift was surprised to see his undemonstrative daughter give Cat a quick hug.

Cat's presence somehow eased the thread of tension which had been running between Swift and Naomi. They ordered steak, fries and a salad. Cat helped Swift along with the bottle of red. They made light, general conversation about the weather and Naomi's course and a couple of the new films showing at the multi-screen.

Cat shot brief glances at Swift and then Naomi, curious as to what had gone on since she spoke to Swift earlier. 'So Craven wasn't as gung-ho as I'd feared,' she said, breaking the ice and bringing the topic they were all privately preoccupied with out into the open.

'He was fine,' Swift said in non-committal tones.

'He didn't see you as the villain after all,' Cat said to Naomi.

'No, thank God.'

Cat kept watching her.

'And I wasn't,' Naomi said quietly. 'I don't know where that coke came from. And I don't believe Jasper did either.' Her voice was soft but there was a vein of steel in her words.

'I'm satisfied to go along with that,' Swift said, the policeman now rather than the father.

'Well DCI Craven has his good and bad points,' Cat said with a grin. 'You can count yourself lucky when you're on the receiving end of the former.' She turned the grin directly on Naomi. A jest and a warning.

Watching his daughter, Swift knew that somewhere along the line, for whatever reason, a wrong turning had been made. He had the impression she was trying desperately to get herself back to that fork in the road.

'Are you going back to Yorkshire tonight, Dad?' Naomi asked.

'No. I've booked in at The Crown.' He didn't mention that during the past few hours his nerves had sometimes seemed as thin as frayed cotton. He was OK now. But the last thing he needed was a long drive in the dark with the threat of another heavy snowfall.

'Nice,' said Cat. 'They'll give you a super breakfast.'

At the end of the evening Swift drove

Naomi back to her college. Cat refused a lift and phoned for a taxi. She kissed both father and daughter with cheerful warmth as they parted.

'She's great,' Naomi said, as they fastened their seat belts. Her glance swivelled towards her father, a glitter of conjecture there.

'Do I hear an attempt to match-make?' he asked.

'You know me,' she quipped. 'Would I do that?'

Swift wondered how well he did know her. His little girl, who was now a woman and had been driving around with a suspected drug dealer, along with a considerable amount of cocaine.

★ ★ ★

Contrary to his expectations Swift slept like a rock. The call from reception woke him and he got up instantly, showered and shaved in the warm, gleaming bathroom, its bright mirror lights showing up the pallor and strain in his face from the events of the day before.

The dining-room was also bright and warm, smelling of toast and coffee and bacon. He ordered a full English and made himself eat it all. He thought of calling Doug or Laura and getting an update on the Farrell case. Instead he left a message with the front desk sergeant to say he'd be back mid to late-morning.

The sun was shining, low and golden, sending down slanting daggers of brilliance. He got into his car, squinting against the sun's dazzle through the windscreen, and drove around to Jasper Guest's flat, the address of which he had found listed in the phone book. He guessed Craven would have released Guest after letting him stew in the cells for the night. Whatever Craven had been up to as regards Guest, either using him as a pawn in some projected big swoop, or simply planting stuff on him in a fit of vengefulness, had backfired, and the devious DCI would have lost interest. For the moment, at least.

The house in which Guest had a basement flat was eerily similar to Craven's: Georgian with tall windows and walls as thick as those guarding a castle moat. Swift went down the steep steps and rang the bell. When it wasn't instantly answered he rang again, twice.

The door was pulled open to reveal a sleepy-looking man with a thatch of foppishly cut hair the colour of conkers. Swift could see where the attraction would be for women, especially young ones. Guest's face had breathtakingly regular features, cheekbones with razor sharp definition and blue eyes framed with luxuriant lashes perfectly matching the hair on his head. 'I'm Naomi Swift's father,' he said, stepping forward into the entrance hall and forcing Guest to step back.

'OK, OK!' Guest put up his hands in surrender. 'I can see you'll be none too happy with what's been going on.'

'You could say that. But I'm not here to do the heavy father bit. Naomi's an adult — at least in the eyes of the law. But I think you need to do some talking.'

As Guest nodded his forelock fell over his eyes. He pushed it back. 'Fair enough. Come through and sit down.'

Swift sat down on a black leather sofa and looked around. Guest had a stereo system and CD stack, almost identical to Craven's. But there the resemblance ended. Guest's room was stylish, warm and instantly welcoming. A place you felt you'd be happy to spend time in. One entire wall was lined with books, neatly stacked on pine shelves. There was an assortment of casual chairs; 1930s Lloyd Loom and big squashy armchairs covered in faded brocade as though they had just been pulled out of someone's great-grandmother's parlour. A goldfish bowl filled with daffodils stood on a round walnut table.

Swift pictured Naomi curled in one of the

chairs, reading. Maybe listening to music or just dreaming. Or naked, making love with Jasper Guest.

'Is she here?' he asked Guest.

'No.' There was a moment of indecision in his eyes. 'She's coming over later in the morning.'

'Just think of me as an arm of the police,' Swift told him. 'Reviewing your previous form.'

Guest sank down in one of the armchairs. 'Fair enough. I'd want to know the same if it was my kid. I got into trading a bit of dope when I was at Oxford. I might look as if I was born with a silver spoon lodged in my gullet, but my father made his living from being a vicar and we were pretty poor. Trading gave me a bit of spare cash to keep up with the Eton set.'

'And you got caught?'

'I pinched someone's girl. He shopped me. Again, fair enough.' Guest's rueful smile would have charmed birds from the trees.

'Charged?'

'For possession of a small amount of cannabis resin. It wouldn't count for much now, would it? No one in the drugs squad would be getting excited. Even back then I only got a suspended sentence.'

'OK. And then there was some trouble

before you left Oxford?'

'God! That. There was a demonstration just before graduation. Some fascist anti-abortion Jesus followers making their point in a college debate. I wasn't the only one who got a few thumps and gave some back.'

'But you got yourself apprehended?'

'Yep. A telling off and two months' probation. My poor pa wasn't best pleased.'

'You don't have a lot of success in keeping a low profile, do you?' Swift commented evenly.

''Fraid not.'

Swift could see Guest was a martyr to his spectacular charm and looks. There was something about the man he liked. But maybe not as a charmer with Naomi on the receiving end of his allure.

'And the three grams of cocaine in your car? Was that simply for personal use? I can't bring myself to believe that.'

'It wasn't mine.'

'And it wasn't Naomi's,' Swift said firmly, a statement not a question.

'Good God, no!'

'So, how come it was in your car?'

'It was planted.'

'By yet another of your enemies?'

'As a matter of fact, yes, I suspect it was.'

There was a long pause. Swift ran through a likely scenario. Guest running up against

Craven and his colleagues. Getting himself well on the wrong side of them. Getting them well on his trail. Goading Craven who didn't seem a man much troubled by moral integrity.

'Have you any evidence for this possible plant?' he asked.

'As a matter of fact, I do. One of the locks on my car was tampered with the night before last while Naomi and I were out eating with friends. I drive a 1989 Alfetta. Its security is somewhat primitive, no alarm, no immobilizer. It's an easy target.'

'Would Naomi be able to confirm this?'

'Yep. Just ask her.' Another rueful smile. Another toss of the conker-coloured forelock. The man oozed sex appeal. Swift could see why Naomi was hooked. From experience of his own and observation of many others, Swift knew that sexual infatuation was like influenza, it got you in its grip and you just had to wait until the fever died down and your immune system worked the bugs out of your bloodstream. And maybe it would never happen. Whatever, he couldn't do much about it.

He got up.

Guest shot to his feet. 'I'm really sorry that Naomi's been pulled into the this mess of mine.'

'Fair enough,' Swift said, feeling this was a phrase Guest could connect with. 'Just make sure she doesn't get into this sort of mess through you again.' He moved out into the hallway. Guest went ahead and opened the door. 'I'm no hawk,' Swift told him, 'but if there's any hint of trouble I'll be back up here in a flash. And you won't like it.'

Guest nodded acceptance. He extended his hand. Swift took it. Then got into his car and set off on the drive back to Yorkshire. It struck him that, on balance, he had probably not succeeded in avoiding the playing the heavy father role.

Fair enough.

10

On the north side of Bradford that same morning the weather was becoming grey and cloudy once again, the sky filling up with further snow which had driven in from the west. Straight from the Arctic as far as Shaun Busfield was concerned. The heating in his gran's house had gone on the blink and the place was like a morgue. Damned under-floor heating which he couldn't get at to see what was what. He'd fiddled with the fuse box, but being no electrician had merely succeeded in fusing the whole blasted shebang. So now he had no heat, no light, and no way to heat up any of the endless cans of beans in the cupboard.

Stomping through to the main bedroom he rifled through his gran's wardrobe and found an ancient fur coat, swaddled in plastic and reeking of mothballs. The sleeves only came down to just below his elbows but the rest of the old girl's coat did the trick as far as getting a bit of warmth back into his frozen body was concerned.

Returning to the living-room he aimed the remote at the TV, forgetting for a moment that that too wasn't going to work. Frustration rolled through him. He swore and kicked out at the dainty little table on which his gran had kept her knick-knacks. A china shepherdess fell on to the hearth and shattered into fragments. Tear of rage and helplessness stood in his eyes. He went through into the tiny garage annexed on to the kitchen. His gran had never had a car so the space had been used to store garden furniture used in the summer and bits and pieces of old furniture and scraps of carpet that might come in handy. He remembered there was a cupboard where she kept a torch and light bulbs. Maybe there'd be some spare fuses he could use to get things started up again.

Looking in the cupboard he found nothing of much help. He closed the cupboard door and laid his head against it. His heart began to speed up as he considered the desperate nature of his situation. How long could he go on hiding like this? It was a question which he had kept trying to bury over the past few days, but this morning it wouldn't go away.

Straightening up, he noticed a box pushed against the wall beneath the cupboard. It had a Christmassy label on it saying it was from Jim and Pat with love. He vaguely remembered some well-to-do cousin who'd gone on sending his gran stuff at Christmas. Opening the box he found twelve bottles of wine inside. Six white, six red. Posh expensive stuff as far as he could judge by the labels. He grinned. Jim and Pat had wasted their cash, his gran never touched wine, just the odd glass of sweet sherry or Babycham on special occasions. Well, at least he could have a drink to cheer himself up.

He pulled the bottles out of their cardboard housings and lined them up on the garage floor. As he bent to grasp the final two bottles he noticed that that the box itself was stacked on a long parcel wrapped in brown paper. He shifted the box and looked more closely. Then tore off the wrapping paper. Inside was the money he'd always been sure his gran would have stored up like a busy anxious squirrel. Sweat prickled under his armpits as he began to count the ten pound notes. Minutes passed. He paused to unscrew a bottle of white and take a long swig. And then he went on counting. And on. A smile spread over his increasingly flushed face and fixed itself there. He'd found himself a bloody little fortune.

Going back through to the living-room, he pranced about for a time, singing and swigging. The room became darker and darker as the snow began to fall. He risked parting the curtains a fraction. The snow was driving down as though the clouds had detonated it. Euphoria seized him. He was rich. Rich people could do anything they liked, couldn't they? Although, even so, he couldn't quite think what he might do to get himself out of the mess he was in, how to free himself from the prison of his gran's prissy bungalow. His head was beginning to swim. He'd think things out when he was sober. For now he'd just enjoy getting totally plastered.

★ ★ ★

'Did things go OK, boss?' Laura asked with concern as Swift walked into the incident room. 'With your daughter?'

'As good as could be expected.' He didn't want to talk about it. 'What about here? Anything new?' It felt as though he had been away for weeks.

'Not really. Busfield's still safe in whatever bolthole he's hiding in. The super's not looking one bit happy, and Doug's talking to Tina, yet again.'

'Someone must know where Busfield is. Even if they're not aware they know,' Swift said. 'Get out all the transcripts we've got concerning him and we'll go through them again.'

Over freshly brewed coffee they went through the transcripts ringing round names of every contact they'd spoken to with regard to Busfield.

'Problem is,' Laura said, 'they all gave the impression he wasn't one to chat much about friends and family.'

'There's the grandmother,' Swift said slowly, noting the comment made by one of Busfield's friends. 'She died recently and he was upset.'

'So did she live alone?' Laura mused. 'Did she own her own house? And if so, is it somewhere Busfield could use as a safe place?'

Swift frowned in self-reproach. Why hadn't they thought of that before?' Why hadn't *he* thought of it? He was the one who had the overview. 'I suppose we were pretty sure we'd get a bite when we put out a general alert for him,' Swift said evenly, not one to cry over spilt milk. 'And in these cases we usually do fairly soon.'

'We don't have a name. But Tina'll know,' Laura said, keen to put her shoulder firmly to this particular wheel.

'Yes. But if the grandmother is the key to where Busfield is, will she tell us?' Swift said. 'From what we currently know of Tina she's showing a lot of determination to keep what she knows to herself.'

'She either loves him to bits,' Laura reflected, 'and wants to shield him at any cost, or she's scared out of her wits he'll somehow get his revenge if she rats on him.'

'Agreed,' Swift said. 'But Doug can be very persuasive.'

Laura smiled. 'He's a dark horse, our Doug. Hidden depths.'

'Did you follow up with the neighbour Tricklebank mentioned, as regards Cavanagh?' Swift asked.

Laura's eyes widened in mock horror. 'We've been working directly to the super's directions. Nose firmly to the grindstone on finding Busfield.'

'Why not have a short break?' Swift suggested.

After she had left, he sat in thought. And then reached for his phone and dialled Cat's number.

★   ★   ★

Laura parked her cherished old Mini in the driveway of a neat detached house with a blue slate roof and rows of windows in a cross-hatch of small rectangles. She guessed the window cleaner must sigh each time he embarked on them with his soap and leather.

The front door was immaculately painted in blue and the thickness of the paint had an oily gleam to it. She entertained herself with a little fantasy of a maid opening the door, the frilly-cap-and-apron sort of maid who appeared in period TV dramas. She supposed in the twenty-first century any servant available would be from Estonia or the Philippines. In fact the lady of the house answered in person. She was dressed in pale-blue jeans and a thick granite-coloured wool sweater.

'Mrs Juliet Cox? I'm Detective Constable Laura Ferguson. I'm involved in the investigation into the murder of Moira Farrell.'

Juliet Cox nodded. 'Yes, I've been following it on the news.'

'I believe Mr Tricklebank might have told you I'd be calling. He gave me your address.'

Juliet Cox gestured Laura to come inside and led the way through a thickly carpeted hallway into a long living-room at the rear of the house. 'Sit down,' she said, 'I'll get the coffee. It's all ready.' She went away leaving Laura to look around and observe the gleaming, polished French windows which led into a hexagonal-shaped conservatory whose roof was rapidly becoming a collecting point for the snow which was still driving down hard. The living-room was faultlessly tidy, carpeted in the same thick pile as the hallway, with Chinese rugs scattered about as a luxurious extra. The fireplace was filled with an artistic arrangement of winter greenery. Portraits of teenage children stood on an oval glass table at the side of the room. The whole place was warm as toast with heat pulsing from somewhere Laura couldn't manage to identify.

'Do you like black or white?' Juliet Cox said returning with a tray.

Laura asked for white, and accepted one of the chocolate biscuits Juliet Cox offered. 'Mrs Cox, we gather that you were recently treated by one Mr Cavanagh at the District Hospital — '

'He actually did my surgery at the Willsdale Clinic,' Juliet Cox interrupted. 'My husband's firm provides a private health package for us all. Not that it makes any difference, he's just as useless wherever he's operating: private or national health.' She looked hard at Laura. 'Is he a suspect? For Dr Farrell's murder?'

'We're simply gathering any relevant information,' Laura said carefully.

'Well,' Juliet Cox commented tartly, 'whether he killed that poor woman or not, he's certainly a butcher, and I'm only too pleased to talk about my experiences at the hands of Adrian Cavanagh. The sooner he gets a stop put on his antics the better.' She took a sip of coffee and put her cup down. 'Fourteen months ago I had a routine prolapse repair.'

Laura felt slightly uneasy. Middle-aged gynaecological problems always sounded messy, worrying and ultimately depressing when you considered where, as a young woman, you were heading.

Juliet Cox gave the faintest of smiles. 'You only get a vaginal wall prolapse if you have a baby and you're not too posh to push. The choice is yours.'

'All pain and no gain,' said Laura, aiming for a light tone, although internally she was wincing, reflecting on her own situation — the constant nagging fear that she could be pregnant, and what she would do if it turned out to be so. She'd bought a testing kit, but it was too early yet for it to give reliable results.

Juliet Cox offered Laura a second biscuit which she declined. 'The first operation seemed to go all right. Until the second day. I started having quite a lot of bleeding. The sister who was in charge of my case rang Cavanagh, but he said not to worry, to make sure I had bed rest and he'd be in to see me the next day.' She toyed with a chocolate biscuit then put it back on the plate. 'I did just wonder if it had anything to do with the fact that it was a Sunday and he had jolly social things planned with his family. However, being at that point still quite a nice reasonable woman, I put up with the bleeding and the pain and waited until Monday. He came along said he didn't want to give me a proper examination as it could disturb the stitches. He said some bleeding and discomfort was quite normal at this stage and he prescribed painkillers to make me more comfortable, as he put it. In the night they had to get him in to see me again, as I'd passed out through loss of blood. The nursing staff set up a transfusion and the next day I went back to theatre to have some further repair work done.'

Laura put down her chocolate biscuit and began to scribble furiously in her notebook.

'Subsequent to that I had two further ops before I could go home. And, somehow, although he talked to me very sweetly he never really told me what the problem was. And whatever it was it was certainly not his fault. Sometimes I even got the impression it was somehow my fault, which I suppose it was partly, because by this time I'd become quite emotional and demanding. I was desperate to get better, desperate to find out what was going on. I asked him if I had cancer, but he said no. But I felt dreadful and

I was still in pain and losing quite a lot of blood. Every time my husband came to visit I burst into tears, and generally I was in a mess, both literally and personally. It got to the point where the insurance company wouldn't pay for any more treatment and I was presented with a huge bill from the clinic for the cost of the stay. And all the time Cavanagh was as nice as pie and constantly protesting that everything was going fine.'

She put down her cup. Suddenly her eyes filled with tears and she was unable to continue. 'Sorry,' she whispered. 'Just give me a minute. I want you to know the whole story.'

Laura waited patiently. She looked at the chocolate biscuits left on the plate and found they were no longer tempting.

Juliet Cox swallowed, blew her nose and mopped the skin beneath her eyes. 'In a nutshell,' she said, her voice husky from crying, 'I eventually went to see another consultant gynaecologist in Leeds and had two further operations in an attempt to put my insides in order.'

'Did he tell you what the problem had been?'

'It was a her. And she didn't tell me anything directly. Medics don't grass on each other, I've learned that. They stick together like glue. But from what she said about the number of stitches she had to put in my insides it was obvious Cavanagh had made a complete bungle of the surgery he performed.' Her eyes rested on Laura then slid away to the floor.

'I was in a real state by then. I had to have psychotherapy and take anti-depressants. I couldn't do my job. I've worked for twenty years as a manager in the children and family section at social services, but you have to be right up to the mark and feeling fit and well both physically and psychologically for that kind of work. I had six months off and then, in the end, I applied for early retirement on health grounds. And I'm still on anti-depressants. If I didn't take them I don't think I'd get through the day.' She was fidgeting with the ends of the silk scarf around her neck, her composure steadily breaking down. 'And I'm bitter and paranoid and hell to live with. My husband's soldiering on, but only with the help of a little affair on the side with one of his work colleagues.'

'Why did you want to spend time telling me this?' Laura asked, fascinated by Juliet's story, but beginning to feel uneasy about the time she was spending gaining information on a personal disaster which seemed unlikely to be related to Moira Farrell's murder.

'I want Cavanagh stopped. I want to make sure he doesn't work again as a surgeon. Not out of revenge, just out of consideration of all those women he could damage in the future. He's dealing with pregnant women, with the deliveries of little babies, for God's sake. It's not as if he's a novice just starting out: everybody makes mistakes — but he doesn't learn from them. And that means he's a fuckwit — and yet he keeps his job!' After this outburst Juliet Cox's face was flushed with angry resentment and frustration.

'Jack Tricklebank told me he's thinking of going down the road of getting a solicitor involved and getting legal aid and so on,' she continued. 'But he won't get anywhere — I've been down that road. It's cost me thousands and I've got nowhere. No one will say that Cavanagh did anything wrong. Not even the press will. It's like he's living in a one-way toughened glass bubble where he can reach out to all his wretched patients but no one can get at him.'

Laura sat in respectful silence as Juliet Cox began to sob openly, wrapping her arms around her chest. Eventually she reached forward, touched the other woman gently on the shoulder and stood up in preparation of leaving.

Juliet Cox blew her nose again. 'I'll see you out,' she said.

They walked together across the sea of royal blue carpet. 'When I said that medics stick together, I maybe wasn't being totally fair,' she said reflectively. 'There's a young registrar called Anderson in Cavanagh's department at the hospital whom I saw when I went for a follow up after the insurance company pulled the plug on my going back to the Willsdale. I gave the poor man an earful about what I thought of Cavanagh, and although he didn't say anything directly I got the impression he was concerned about what was going on, and that another member of the team was also worried. It sounded as though he and this other doctor were going to try to do something about Cavanagh. But I guess it must be pretty difficult for them, grassing up a colleague.' She paused and sighed. 'And the bottom line is, Cavanagh's a consultant and it seems they just don't get touched.'

They had reached the door now. Laura reflected how often it happened that some shining nugget of information popped up after an interview had officially closed. 'Do you think Moira Farrell might have been the colleague the registrar was referring to?'

'It's possible, isn't it?' There was a sharp light of speculation in Juliet's red-rimmed eyes. 'Who better than a doctor to know that dangerous doctors should be stopped?'

Laura's thoughts careered ahead. What if Moira Farrell had been going to blow the whistle on Cavanagh? What if Cavanagh knew and had decided to save his career by taking matters into his own hands?

Laura glanced at Juliet Cox and wondered if she had mishandled this interview, allowing the other woman to manipulate her.

Juliet opened the door. 'I hope your enquiries reach a speedy conclusion,' she said. 'And thanks for listening to all my moaning. It really helps to tell the story over again to someone who shows a bit of sympathy.' She gave one of her half smiles. 'How pathetic is that?' She offered her hand and Laura took it. The hand was warm and sticky with feeling, but the grip was firm.

Outside the snow was falling like freshly thrown confetti, speckling Laura's hair with a thousand shiny white dots as she ran to her car.

* * *

By the time it was dropping dark, Shaun was in a state of drunkenness where reckless

211

optimism and an urgent need for entertainment outweighed caution and realistic thinking. Putting a small wad of his gran's recently unearthed treasure in the pocket of his jeans he ventured out into the wide world once more, bound for the pub at the end of the road around a mile away.

Kicking up the snow which was now hardening as the temperature dropped, he had a sense of euphoria at the thought of the freedom his gran's hidden stash had offered him. And she'd always said she'd leave him the bungalow, so very soon he'd be pretty well set up and bloody stinking rich. He pulled down the woolly hat he had found in his gran's wardrobe. It was one she'd knitted herself. Dark blue wool and big enough to pull down to the tip of his nose. She'd always been like that gran, so worried about knitting things too small she made them flaming huge. She'd been a funny old stick, but he'd really loved her. He just wished it hadn't taken her to die before he realized just how much. He felt the tears welling up again, but he pushed them back. He was going to go to that fucking pub and he was going to have a beer and get clean away with it. And no one would recognize him. He just knew they wouldn't. He'd be fine. He thought of his gran up there in heaven looking down on him, and he knew that no one, no one at all could touch him.

* * *

Swift checked with the Registrar of Deaths. There was no one of the name of Busfield who had been registered in the past few weeks, indeed not in the past five years. But, of course, if the grandmother concerned was a maternal grandmother she would have a different name. He asked Doug to go back to Busfield's place of work and talk again with the colleague who had mentioned the death of Busfield's grandmother. 'What we want is some idea of the date of death and the hospital in which she died.'

Doug went off happily enough. He'd had no joy with Tina. But then Tina had a close connection with their suspect and would be filled with all the usual human complexities and inconsistencies attaching to the dilemma she found herself in. Talking again to a casual workmate of Busfield's was the kind of clearly defined routine policework which provided a little welcome relief.

* * *

Shaun took his pint to a table in the corner of the pub, relishing the warmth of the place, feeling the numbness of cold in his toes begin to tingle with life. He hadn't been here in years, not since he used to pop in as an underage drinker after he'd been visiting his gran. It was all changed, tarted up with rugs on the stone-flagged floor and bowls on the window sills full of poncey wine corks.

He sipped his beer. He was coming down now from the happy feelings the wine had given him. He took long swigs of his beer, wanting a new hit like a man hooked on coke. There were four business types on the table next to him, dark suits and shirts with blue stripes, full of themselves, drinking their red wine and talking in loud voices about the cars they were driving and the holidays they were going on. Resentment rose in him, thinking of all the luck they'd have had which he'd missed. He imagined them with happy childhoods and nice parents who didn't fight each other and having hot dinners made for them, and pocket money. The list went on piling in his head, fuelling his bitterness. His dad had left before he even knew him. And there'd been 'uncle' after 'uncle', none of them any good. Some of them had fun hitting him and some of them jeered and called him a little pissyarse when he wet the bed. His gran had done her best to help but his mum didn't want her putting her nose in.

The thoughts eddied and shifted in his head. He glanced at the business-types from time to time, his rancour intensifying. One of them caught his eye. 'What are you staring at, pal?' he jested, amused and full of himself, eyeing Shaun with the condescension of the landed gentry from centuries past running across some poor wretched peasant.

Shaun scowled and thrust his glance into his beer. He drank some more, but somehow it didn't seem to be doing the trick. There was a tightness in his chest, a sudden stab of panic. He shouldn't have come. He should have stayed safe in his gran's house, scoffing the wine.

The men were huddled together now, conspiratorial and chuckling. Shaun thought he heard the words, 'Catching a bit of a whiff from the local oiks, eh?' Glancing up, he saw the one who had spoken up before look towards him again, his eyes twinkling with amused disdain.

'Fuck off!' he muttered, dipping his nose back into his glass.

The men went quiet for a few seconds then resumed their jolly braying.

Shaun took deep breaths, steadying himself, knowing he had to get out of the pub and get back to the bungalow as soon as possible. With slow deliberation he drained his glass, got up and made for the door. Outside the cold cut like a knife. But the darkness was a security blanket. He set off walking at a brisk pace, trying to keep his staggering steps in as straight a line as possible.

He became aware of footsteps following him, accelerating, catching up. And then they were on him. Shaun knew how to fight, he knew how to take care of himself. He threw a punch and knocked one of the bastards clean out. But there were still three of them. The air was full of flying fists. As he lashed out he thought he'd got another one down. The yells of fury rang in his ears. Lights began to flash in his head. And then the fuzz were there, black uniforms and helmets weighing in.

Oh, Jesus, God! God! God!

Fuelled by a desperate fear for his freedom Shaun managed to squirm free of the tangle of bodies. And then he began to run.

★   ★   ★

Doug sat in his car and phoned in to the station.

Swift took the call. He was in his usual place at the end of the working day, sitting in contemplation of the whiteboard and its

216

charting of the story so far in the Moira Farrell case. Laura was not yet back from her interview.

'I think we might have made some progress, boss. According to Shaun's mate, the grandmother died around four weeks ago. In one of the local hospitals, he wasn't sure which. She was seventy-one. He said that Shaun had mentioned the age more than once, saying she was too young to die.'

'Right, that sounds promising.'

'Do you want me to get straight round to the nearest hospital and get names of female deaths in that age range for the likely dates?'

Swift considered. 'If you do find any leads it would be too late to follow up with house to house calls. We don't want to frighten the general public.'

'Heaven forbid!'

'But if you can get a list of names and addresses we could start following them up first thing tomorrow morning.'

'Right you are, guv. Will do.' Doug delved into the supply of sweets he kept in his car, unwrapped a mint and telephoned his wife. 'Sorry, love, you'll have to put my supper in the oven. Don't even think of putting it in the dog.' He listened to the retort with a grin, popped the mint into his mouth and set off again into the night.

★ ★ ★

Back at her flat, whilst Laura waited for a frozen steak and kidney pudding to warm up in the oven, she mentally reviewed the interviews with Adrian Cavanagh, Joe Tricklebank and Juliet Cox. Was there was a significant and possibly menacing link between Moira Farrell and Cavangah. As she reflected it began to seem more and more likely that Moira had been the doctor who was intending to blow the whistle on Cavanagh's incompetence as a surgeon. It then struck her that the mode of the killing — a direct hit on the carotid artery — was consistent with a degree of medical knowledge.

She'd ask Swift in the morning if she could follow up at the hospital with the registrar Juliet Cox had mentioned. There didn't seem much else to do whilst they went on waiting for Shaun Busfield to emerge into the spotlight.

Her land line trilled. 'DC Ferguson,' she said automatically, ever on duty.

'Remember me?' the voice said, velvet with seduction.

'Saul,' she said crisply, attempting to strip her voice of any detectable emotional response, despite the alarms zinging through her nerves.

'Long time, no see,' he said, his chat-up line cringingly predictable.

'No worries,' she told him. 'I've been very busy.'

'Ah, yes. The Farrell case.'

She made no comment. There was a small silence.

'Am I getting the big freeze?' he asked.

She grimaced. How could she have missed out on the banality of the guy? 'What are you after?' She made her voice pleasantly polite.

'You.'

She made a small noise in her throat.

'OK, OK, I'm getting the message. Couldn't we at least meet for a drink?' he wheedled. 'Mates, huh?'

'Mates,' she commented. 'Sure, let's just leave it like that, shall we?'

He needed a few seconds to consider. 'Just a drink, huh?'

'Saul,' she said, 'we had a lovely fling.' She winced, reflecting on how banality brought out the hackneyed in you. 'Let's leave it at that.'

He was still protesting as she dropped the phone back on its base and returned to the oven.

★ ★ ★

At the mortuary Doug persuaded one of the pathologists who was working late to open up the filing drawer which carried names of bodies who had been passed on from the hospital. He came away with ten names. Tomorrow promised to be a day of interesting foot-soldiering.

11

Shaun woke with a hangover that made him vow never to drink again. White-faced and shaking, he stumbled to the bathroom, threw up in the basin and instantly felt better. The cold in the bungalow was becoming like a physical assault, stiffening his joints and numbing the ends of his fingers and toes. He pulled on jeans and a sweater and wrapped himself in his gran's old-fashioned candle-wick dressing gown, then went back to bed. At least he'd got himself home after the fiasco last night. First those bleeding business-type bastards and then the fucking police. But he'd got the better of the lot of them. He was safe again. When he felt a bit brighter he'd have a really big think about what to do next.

★   ★   ★

Doug and Laura were heading up the house to house calls in search of Shaun Busfield. An escort of two beat cars with a total complement of six uniforms built like tanks was following them, covertly covering back and front exits from the houses targeted before Laura and Doug embarked on their soft-pedal enquiries.

They had to use sensitivity in dealing with relatives who were, in the main, still grieving for lost relatives, and were puzzled and none too pleased to be visited by the police asking questions about their dead wives, mums, sisters, grandmas and aunties.

'I don't think I can take much more of this,' Laura exclaimed after an interview with a tearful, lonely widower in his eighties who was very reluctant to let the officers leave.

Doug nodded agreement. 'High time we got a break and cut to the chase.'

* * *

Shaun gave a start as the door bell rang. Then rang again. Was followed by persistent knocking on the door. He got out of bed and peeped cautiously through a crack in the curtains. Jesus Christ! There was a uniform creeping round to the back door. The knocking went on. He rubbed his chin. So they were at the front as well.

He sat down heavily on the bed. It was all over. He was a fox and the hounds were closing in. A wave of hopelessness and exhaustion swept through him. Slowly, still in his gran's dressing-gown, his feet clad in the socks he'd worn ever since the flight from his own house, he went down the hallway to the front door and opened it. 'If you want a fight,' he told the two officers standing there, gravity, eagerness and tension etched on their faces, 'you're going to be fucking disappointed.'

★   ★   ★

Shaun Busfield was an old hand at being arrested. He knew his rights. He used the one call he was allowed to make in order to contact a firm of solicitors. Within the hour a young man called Tristan Brown had arrived at the station, clutching a notepad and looking concerned and apprehensive.

Swift made both Shaun and his solicitor wait until the results of the initial house search at Shaun's grandmother's bungalow were completed. Nothing of interest was found. He told the officer in charge to keep looking.

As Shaun was ushered into the interview-room, Laura prepared to record the exact time on the tape as the interview commenced. Swift sat alongside her, with Tristan Brown on Shaun's side of the table, his chair pushed a little way back, his pad and pencil at the ready. In the observation room Doug found himself partnered with Damian Finch, not an entirely comfortable prospect in his view.

Shaun had taken advantages of the facilities of the custody suite and had taken a shower and shaved. But he was still in the jeans, sweater and underclothes he had been wearing for days and a faintly sour smell emanated from him.

Swift made the introductions and started the questioning. 'Do you know why you're here?' he asked the glowering Busfield.

'Haven't a fucking clue.'

Swift gave him a long hard look. 'There's a TV at your grandmother's bungalow — haven't you been watching it?'

Busfield thought about it. 'Better things to do.'

'We're investigating a murder,' Swift said.

'Well, I ain't done it. And that's the bloody truth.' Busfield turned to stare at the tape turning in the machine and scowled at it. 'I've never murdered anyone.'

'We're investigating the murder of Dr Moira Farrell.'

Shaun stiffened. 'So? What's that got to do with me?'

'She lives in Ambleside Drive.'

Shaun gave a slow, insolent shrug — a

gesture he had honed to a fine art in his youth. But the irises of his eyes shifted and flickered with unease.

'Do you know Ambleside Drive?' Swift persisted.

Busfield glanced at his solicitor but it was like a swimmer in difficulties appealing to a drowning man. 'I might. Not sure.'

Swift glanced at Laura, who opened one of the files in front of her. 'Do you work at the plumbing suppliers in Denverdale Road?' she asked.

'Yeah.'

'Do you ever drive one of the firm's delivery vans?'

Beads of perspiration glittered on Busfield's forehead. He blew out a breath as though overcome with the heat of the room and pushed up the sleeves of his sweater. His arms were thin and muscular, covered in light-brown hairs. He laid them on the table as though they were prize exhibits. 'Sometimes.'

'Your firm recently supplied a number of items to Dr Farrell's house in Ambleside Drive,' Laura said. 'Your foreman says that some of them were delivered in one of the vans. He said that you sometimes drive the vans when the other drivers are busy or off sick.'

Shaun bit on his lip. 'So, what if I do?'

'Can you tell me where you were on the morning of Tuesday January 16th this year?' Swift came in.

'At work, of course.'

'Between the hours of five-thirty and six-thirty a.m.'

Shaun lifted his sinewy arms from the table and folded them across his chest. Suddenly he felt on much safer ground. 'Tucked up in bed with me girlfriend. I never get up 'til seven, and even then it's a bloody effort.' His eyes sharpened. 'You ask Tina, she'll tell you I was there with her.'

Swift nodded. He reached down, picked up an evidence bag containing a pair of trainers and placed it on the desk. 'Are these your shoes?'

Shaun peered at them. 'How can I tell? They're all mucky, covered in mud. Could be anyone's.'

Swift sat back and treated Shaun Busfield to a long hard stare.

Shaun busied himself peering closely at the trainers in the evidence bag. 'They're certainly not the ones your lot took off me at work. Cheeky bastards, leaving me with nothing on me feet.'

Swift left a long pause. 'The trainers in the bag have Moira Farrell's blood on them. Our forensic experts believe that it's blood which was lost from her body around the time she was killed. They also note that the size of the trainers and the way in which they've worn through use is very similar to that of the trainers you let us take for analysis.' He tapped the bag, making the plastic crackle. 'Take a closer look, Shaun. Tell me you're sure these trainers don't belong to you.'

Colour rushed into Shaun's pale face and he felt the sweat breaking out on his skin under his T-shirt. His eyes shifted from side to side like trapped animals. Beside him Tristan Brown looked almost as panic stricken.

'You can bang on about these flaming trainers as long as you like. I've told you, I was in bed asleep when that woman was killed. Why can't you get that into your thick heads?'

'Forensics found a hair in one of those trainers,' Swift said. 'It matches your DNA profile.'

Shaun swallowed hard. 'How d'you know? You haven't done one of those swab tests, have you?'

'We've already got a record of your DNA on the database, Shaun,' Laura came in softly. 'Have you forgotten that? It was taken on the last occasion you were arrested. For ABH.'

Shaun frowned and he bit down on his lip. 'Aye, well, that hair could have got into the shoe any old how. It don't prove 'owt. You're just trying to pin this woman's murder on me because I've got previous.'

Tristan Brown leaned forward to his client but Shaun put out a hand, batting the anxious young man off. 'Anyone could have put that hair there. You're setting me up, you bastards, planting evidence so you can get a result. Don't think I don't know how you lot go on.'

'You've had plenty of previous experience finding out, haven't you, Shaun?' Swift commented.

'That's all in the past,' Shaun protested, his eyes blazing. 'I've been straight for well on a couple of years now.'

Swift leaned forward and placed his hand once again on the evidence bag. 'I asked the lab to try to get a further sample from these training shoes, Shaun. They found traces of sweat in the grime on the inside of the soles. Traces which have been analysed, and as a result we've got a further match on your DNA. Evidence which proves you have worn those trainers.'

Shaun's Adam's apple did a bungee jump. He was silent for a few moments, feeling the net closing in on him. He thrust his face forward towards the two waiting detectives. 'Listen, I didn't kill that woman. And if you pigs haven't set me up, someone else has. *I didn't do it!*'

He swivelled to confront his solicitor, nodding towards Swift and Laura. 'Can't you do something about this? This lot are the criminals, they're trying to stitch me up.'

'This is evidence which has been collected and analysed according to the laid-down procedures and in good faith,' Swift said formally.

'Hah!' Shaun flung himself back in his chair. 'I'm not saying no more.'

'Shaun — if you're as innocent as you'd like us to believe,' Swift said calmly, 'why did you take off like a bat out of hell when our officers called to speak to you at your house?'

Shaun threw up his hands. 'Jesus Christ, man! Why d'you think?'

'You tell us,' Laura invited.

'It's obvious! You'd decided I'd be a good 'un to pin this one on. You lot'd stop at nothing. I was shitting myself thinking of what you'd do to me.'

'Your alibi's a bit shaky, isn't it?' Laura suggested. 'Your girlfriend covering for you. A touch convenient, don't you think?'

'Piss off,' Shaun growled.

Tristan Brown leaned forward, cleared his

throat and spoke up. 'Do you have any witnesses who saw Mr Busfield at the victim's house or at the murder scene?'

'Not so far,' Swift said.

'Or any evidence of his presence at the house and the crime scene?'

There was a silence.

Shaun straightened in his seat and turned to his lawyer. 'Ay! Good for you, lad.'

★ ★ ★

Whilst Shaun sweated in his cell attended by his solicitor, and Swift conferred with Doug and Finch, Laura slipped out and drove to the hospital and asked to speak to Cavanagh's registrar, whose name was listed on the information the consultant had asked his secretary to provide.

James Anderson was tall and slim with thick blond hair and pale skin. He had wide-set blue eyes and a long thin nose. In her mind Laura noted him down as singularly good-looking, the kind of guy women would fall for. Older women would mother him and young ones sleep with him. She reined in her fantasies and instructed herself to concentrate on the matter in hand as regards the current investigation, namely had there been any connection between Moira Farrell and James

Anderson beyond that of being doctors working in the same department, and if so what was it?

Anderson took her into a tiny office which she guessed had been formed by partitioning a former larger room into two small ones. This office was the one which had retained the original 1930s style central-heating radiator which was full on, making the room stiflingly warm.

Laura took off her coat and unwound her scarf. Anderson watched her then crossed to the radiator and fiddled with its controls. 'Sorry,' he said, 'it's stuck in full steam ahead mode.'

'Not to worry.'

'How can I help you? You've come about Moira, haven't you?' Anderson looked at her steadily, his eyes holding hers.

Laura dropped her gaze to her pad and pen, refusing to engage with his covert seductiveness. She reminded herself that she was here on a nod from Swift, that Finch would be furious if he knew what was going on and that it was up to her to tread very carefully in this interview. 'We're wanting to build up a picture of Moira: her life, her background, what sort of person she was. We'd be glad for anything you can tell us.'

Anderson thought for a few moments. 'She was a damn good gasman,' he said.

'Sorry?' Laura looked up, pen poised over her pad.

'Gasman — it's medical slang for anaesthetist,' he explained.

'Right. So you obviously had a respect for her work?'

'Very much so. She was a good doctor to have on our firm.'

Laura glanced up again.

'That's medical slang for team.'

'Right. And did Dr Farrell get on well with the rest of the team — your firm?'

'Oh, yes. And with the patients. She'd take time to talk to them and reassure them about having a GA.'

'General anaesthetic?'

He smiled. 'Correct. A lot of people get quite uptight about the thought of putting themselves in someone else's hands and being knocked unconscious.'

Laura nodded. She, herself, had never ever been in hospital but she could imagine the anxiety.

'Moira would explain to patients just what was going to happen and how they were likely to feel. Quite a few other anaesthetists don't bother so much. She was just really good at talking with patients,' he added. 'God! It's awful to think she's gone, and the way it happened.'

Laura watched the muscles of his face move, observed the sadness in his eyes. If he was playing a part he was a commendably good actor. 'We've heard that there are some tensions within your department,' she said.

Anderson looked at her unblinking. 'I'd imagine it's rare for there to be no tensions amongst a bunch of professionals when they're in the business of dealing with birth, life and death.'

'Yes, indeed. So there are tensions?' Laura came back at him.

He glanced away. 'Yes.'

'Was Moira involved?'

There was a beat of tell-tale hesitation. 'She wasn't the kind of person to quarrel with colleagues.'

Laura recalled the photograph of Moira and Cavanagh in some kind of confrontation. 'Not even with Mr Cavanagh?'

Anderson glanced down at his hands and pursed his lips. 'Look,' he said, 'it's true that there are some disagreements between some of the staff and Mr Cavanagh at present. It's about medical procedures, nothing to do with your investigation. I really can't say more than that.'

Laura wrote it all down in her idiosyncratic

shorthand. 'Did you know that Moira was pregnant?' she asked.

Anderson flinched. There was an electric silence. 'No.' His voice was a husky whisper and he was unable to conceal a sense of utter astonishment and dismay.

'Were you having an affair with Moira?' Laura asked quietly, having no doubt about the answer. Whether or not Anderson would offer the truth was another matter.

He sighed. 'I only wish I could say that I wasn't.'

'So you and Moira were having an affair.'

He took some time to consider. 'Yes. But I didn't know she was pregnant.' He levelled a glance at Laura. 'How far on was she?'

'Twelve weeks.'

'Could the baby be yours?'

He turned away whilst he considered. 'Yes.' His expression hardened. 'Did you suspect Moira was pregnant with my baby when you started on all these questions? Has someone found out and ratted on us?'

'No,' Laura said. 'I simply had information from the autopsy report that Moira was pregnant.' She saw little point in enlightening Anderson further regarding the question of there being two dead babies, and two different fathers.

'Jesus!' Anderson muttered. 'Patel will kill

me if he finds out.'

He put a knuckle in his mouth and chewed on it. Laura noticed that he had a patch of raw red eczema on the base of his finger. Was it stress-related, she wondered?

'Does this have to come out?' he asked Laura. 'My wife . . . '

'It's hard to say,' she said truthfully.

'Has the pathologist done any testing to discover parentage?' he demanded.

'I'm not able to give you that information at this stage.'

'If this gets out, there'll be hell to pay,' Anderson said. 'I mean I could look like a suspect for killing Moira, for God's sake.' He was really rattled now.

'Yes,' Laura agreed. 'Technically everyone connected with a murder victim is a suspect,' she pointed out.

'I didn't kill her,' he said. 'I loved her.' He stared helplessly at the wall above Laura's head. 'But I expect they all say that, don't they? Cold-blooded murderers.'

Laura sat still and quiet.

'So what happens now?' Anderson asked.

'It would be helpful if you'd tell me what you know about any difficulties between Moira and anyone else in your firm.'

'God! Talk about being between a rock and a hard place!' He bowed his head for a few moments. 'I'll have to get in touch with someone from the BMA before I can say any more. I'm not being obstructive. It's just that if I start telling tales on colleagues, I could run into real trouble with the hospital management. I could get suspended. My job here could be on the line. It's happened to other doctors, so it could well happen to me.'

Laura heard the depth of anxiety in his voice. She asked him to describe his whereabouts around the date and time of Moira's murder.

He leaned his head on his hand and closed his eyes briefly. 'I was here, in my room at the hospital, I was on call.'

'So you weren't on the wards or doing surgery?'

'No.'

'You were in bed?'

'Yes.'

'Any witnesses?'

He sighed. 'Sister Avalon.'

'She works on your team?'

'She's one of the gynaecological ward sisters.' His face had suffused with dark, hot colour, caught out in lying, evasion and serial adultery.

'Right.' Laura stood up, put on her coat and scarf and tucked her notebook in her bag, disappointed to note that Anderson had slipped a peg or two in her estimation. 'You get in touch with the BMA,' she told him evenly, 'and we'll be back.'

* * *

'We haven't got enough,' Swift told the superintendent. 'The CPS aren't going to be happy about this.'

Damian Finch had the transcript of Busfield's first interview on his desk and he wasn't looking all that happy either. But the usual fresh coffee was on offer and on this occasion his DCI was invited to share in it.

'I've already had a preliminary talk with one of their lawyers,' Swift said. 'Their view is that the footprint evidence is circumstantial, certainly not strong enough to build a case on. Moreover Busfield's explanation of his going to ground when we first went for him seems reasonable enough. And if you listen to the tape and imagine how Busfield might perform in court, I think we'd all agree he could well convince a jury.' He paused. 'And, of course, we've still no strong connection to demonstrate a link between Busfield and the victim.'

Finch chose not to argue. 'How are your team holding up? Frustration running high, I would guess?'

'They're a level-headed bunch,' Swift said. 'But yes, there's a degree of frustration around.'

'Any interesting theories, either about Busfield or anyone else?'

'Laura's following up angles that have come out through the hospital team Moira Farrell worked with.'

'Ah, yes, I wondered about that when I read the accounts. Do you think there's any mileage there?'

'Possibly. But it's hard to get information, they're all silent as the grave when it comes to talking about each other.'

'Sounds like us,' Finch said.

'And the alibis we've checked so far on the medics are pretty watertight.'

'What about the husband?'

'I've made a note to see him again later today.'

'Busfield's trainers in the garden with Moira Farrell's blood on,' Finch said, frowning into his coffee. 'Were they just too conveniently available for us to find? Did someone deliberately plant them?'

'Possibly. And maybe wore them to cover their own tracks.'

'So who has access to Busfield's shoes?'

'His girlfriend, Tina. His workmates.' Swift shrugged. 'Maybe a number of others we don't know about.'

'We've checked them out a few times,' Finch commented.

'We could do it again,' Swift pointed out. 'Fine-tooth-comb job.'

Finch chewed on his lip. 'Listen, Ed, I know I've a reputation for being a stubborn, cold-hearted sod, but I'm not a man who's unable to take the wider view. I'm not so keen to nail a prime suspect that I'm blind to other lines of enquiry which might be fruitful.'

Swift nodded, containing his surprise.

'I'm glad you didn't rush to assure me that you never thought that,' Finch said. 'Because I know you did.' He pursed his lips and wrinkled his nose. 'What do you advise at this stage?'

'Just the usual,' Swift said. 'Namely going right back to the beginning. We've got a murder on the victim's own territory, with no apparent forced entry. No one saw anything or heard any noise. We need to be looking again at the family. Any other close contacts.'

Finch's lips were still pursed. 'Go ahead, do whatever you think, I'll back it.' He drained his mug and pushed it away to the side of the desk. 'How is your daughter, Ed?' he asked with a degree of respectful caution.

'She's keeping in touch. She seems her usual self. I'm inclined to believe her story that the drugs found in her boyfriend's car had been planted.' He smiled. 'But then I'm her father, I would, wouldn't I?'

Finch remained as grim as ever. 'That doesn't mean it's not the truth.'

12

With huge courage and steely determination Rajesh Patel had moved back into his own house. He locked the door of the room in which his wife had been killed and moved his clothes from their shared bedroom into a small guest room at the back of the house. In the following days he had been laid low with helplessness and grief. Occasional shots of morphine had got him through the nights, and sheer dogged will power through the days. Patel was not a drug user in the commonly understood meaning of the term. He didn't shell out money to dealers, nor did he self-prescribe. Instead, he had an understanding doctor in Harley Street whom he trusted implicitly, both in terms of medical expertise and in watertight confidentiality. Over the years his doctor had helped him through his recurrent episodes of depression, advising on a carefully thought out drug regime, and on suitable analysts and therapists when Patel had so requested.

But in these days following Moira's death the old demons were returning in force, reminding him of the torments he had suffered as a young man before the psychotropic drugs on offer had become as sophisticated as they were today. There had been days when his mood had been a kind of sludge brown, swilling around his brain and darkening all the pictures there into a hazy fog. He had sometimes felt he was trying to exist on another planet where there was no vegetation, no people, no other kind of life at all, just emptiness.

The only way to get through was to be strict about taking the right kind of drugs, and then to draw up all his strength and struggle back into life, seizing each moment by its throat.

To date Patel hadn't missed a day's work, even though, when in his office, he had spent hours slumped at his desk, sinking into his own world of despair. But now he was going to challenge himself with a mission. And his first stop would be a visit to the hospital's gynaecology ward.

★ ★ ★

Shaun Busfield felt better than he might have expected after a night in the cells. He had not slept at all badly, had appreciated the washing facilities and the central heating at the station. And he'd had a quite decent breakfast, brought to him by a cheery custody constable. Room service!

Swift and Laura had teamed up together to provide continuity from the first interview. Tristan Brown was sitting beside his client, pen poised.

Swift set the tape running and made the usual introductions. 'Let's just go back over some of the things we talked about yesterday.'

'You've the right to refuse to do that, it could be said to be wasting time,' Brown intervened, with a firmness which suggested he had been using the hours since the first interview boning up on criminal defence law.

Busfield nodded agreement, then heaved a dramatic sigh. 'Aye. True. But I don't want to get on the wrong side of the fuzz, do I? Go on, then,' he said to Swift.

'You told us that at the time of Moira Farrell's death you were in bed with your girlfriend, Tina.'

'Yeah.'

'We've spoken to Tina since she told us that,' Swift said.

Busfield affected indifference but Swift could see the jolt of apprehension that flickered across the young man's eyes.

'She confirms what you said,' Swift continued.

'Well, she would,' Busfield said with

satisfaction. 'Because it's the truth. So why don't you stop wasting my time and just let me go?'

'Tina could have made a mistake,' Laura pointed out. 'Sometimes people's memories play tricks. Or sometimes they bend the truth to protect people they love.'

Busfield scowled. 'Very poetic. Why don't you just get over yourself, love,' he snarled.

Swift sat forward slightly. 'Is it true your grandmother died recently?'

Busfield shifted in his seat. 'What's that to do with you?'

'Just answer the question, Shaun,' Swift said.

'Yeah. She did.'

'Was she your mother's mother?'

'Aye.'

'Would you say the two of you were close?'

'Me and me gran?'

'Yes.'

There was a softening in Busfield's normally harsh, defensive expression. For the first time he seemed to want to talk and co-operate. 'She looked after me quite a bit when I was little. When me mum had to work.'

'And did you see her regularly during her last few years?'

'Not as much as I should've,' Busfield said.

'Have you been feeling bad about that?' Swift asked, recalling that one of Busfield's workmates had mentioned how upset he had been at his grandmother's death.

'Yeah. And now it's too bloody late to put things right.'

'Is this relevant?' Tristan Brown chimed in.

Ignoring the young solicitor, Swift gave Busfield a sympathetic nod. 'Did you have a key to your gran's house?'

'Aye. She wanted me to have one in case there was any emergencies.'

'She must have trusted you, then?'

'Aye, I think she did. She used to say I could go live in the bungalow when she was gone. But I thought it would be ages before that happened. She was a tough old bird, didn't ail nothing.' A thought struck him. 'I'll wager you lot've searched her place since you nicked me.'

Swift confirmed this with a slight nod.

'Well, the stash of cash you'll have found in the garage was hers. And now it's mine. So you'd better make sure I get it back. I'll kick up such a stink if there's any dodgy goings-on. Have you lot up for felony. Isn't that right?' he demanded of his hapless solicitor.

'Er, I'll need to have more detail on that.' Brown's pen fluttered and slipped from his hand as he was speaking. He blushed and bent down to pick it up. 'Anything found and taken from the house should be logged,' he added stiffly, as he straightened himself.

'What was she in hospital for?' Laura asked.

Busfield frowned. 'I don't really know. She was on the women's ward, so it must have been women's troubles. Some sort of cyst one of the doctors told me. She had an operation, but she didn't pull through.'

Swift laid a photograph of Moira Farrell on the table, a recent picture Rajesh Patel had allowed him to copy from his own collection of photographs. 'Do you recognize this woman?'

Busfield looked at the photograph. A pulse began to tick in the corner of his left eye. 'No.'

'I think you do,' Swift said.

'No!' Busfield shouted. Beads of sweat on his forehead were clearly visible now, and his upper body was rolling a little from side to side.

'I think you knew her quite well.'

'No.'

'Did you meet this woman at the hospital, at the time your grandmother was ill?'

Shaun shut his eyes tightly and pushed the picture away. 'Jesus bloody Christ!' he whispered. He leaned his head on the table and enclosed it with his arms and hands.

Tristan Brown looked concerned. 'My client clearly needs a break.'

Don't we all, Swift thought privately.

Busfield suddenly moved into a new state of alertness. 'Shit, this is serious,' he said, raising his head again. 'We need to fucking get this sorted out. Now.'

'What do we need to get sorted out, Shaun?' Swift asked.

Shaun jabbed his finger on the photograph of Moira Farrell. 'This!' He licked around his lips, feeling his throat dry. He was at a complete loss.

Laura leaned towards the distressed suspect, but Swift stopped her with a warning raising of his hand. 'Tell us what's bothering you, Shaun,' he said quietly.

'I have seen her. I've met her, but ... ' Shaun's head was swimming with panic.

'But?' Swift's voice was patient. Shaun Busfield wasn't going anywhere for another thirty hours. They had all the time in the world.

'But, I don't *know* her. And that's the truth.'

'OK, let's get this straight: you admit to having seen the woman in this photograph.'

'Yeah.'

'And we can confirm,' Swift went on

calmly, 'that the woman in the picture is Moira Farrell. The doctor who was murdered. The victim in our current enquiry.'

'Yes, right.' Shaun wiped the sweat trickling down his forehead with the back of his hand. He tried to think of a way forward. A way of getting out of this mess.

'So where did you see her, Shaun?' Swift's voice was gentle and reassuring, attempting to allay Busfield's obvious state of agitation.

'At the hospital.'

'And when was this?'

'Just after me gran died.' He pointed to the photograph again. 'She was the one who came to tell me.' He looked to Swift, his eyes full of bewilderment. 'She was lovely, really kind.'

'What did she say to you?'

'She told me she'd got some sad news. She said that me gran's heart had given out. The operation had been going well, and then her ticker just stopped. They'd done all they could to bring her round, but it didn't work.' Tears stood in his eyes at the recollection.

He's telling the truth, Swift thought. But not the whole truth and nothing but the truth. Just those small items of truth he thinks won't get him into deeper trouble.

★ ★ ★

Georgie Tyson and her mate Barbara were in the canteen drinking coffee and eating chocolate muffins.

'God! These are awful,' Georgie complained, picking at the stodgy mess in the middle of her muffin. 'Where do they get them from? The back arse of some dodgy bakery in Eastern Europe?'

'You've such an imagination, love!' Barbara said, ploughing on with her fork through the sugary stodge.

'Imagination! Hmm, wish I could make as much cash from it as John Lennon did.' Georgie took a long drink of coffee. 'Shaun Busfield's been in custody for thirty hours now,' she said. 'And the police haven't given so much as a peep about what evidence they've got. And by tomorrow morning they'll have to charge him, get an extension for holding him, or release him.'

'And?'

Georgie frowned, chewing on her lip.

Barbara swallowed the sticky chocolate crumbs in her mouth as gracefully as possible. 'I'd more or less got around to that. So what are you cooking up?'

'I've been thinking about Tina Frazer, Shaun's girl. What she has to say for herself. And him.'

'You're planning on going to see her?'

'Yeah.'

Barbara thought about it. 'Cash for a good story?'

'Something like that.'

'Our editor won't cough up.'

'No, but I've got some cash of my own. And Tina's not that rich. She'll be mighty tempted at the idea of half a grand to spend just as she wants.'

Barbara watched her young colleague through narrowed eyes. 'Be careful, Georgie. You've been doing OK here.'

'I'm stuck here!' Georgie hissed, kicking the table leg. 'What have I got to lose?'

* * *

Sitting on his own at the nurses' station at the entrance to the gynaecology ward, James Anderson registered the buzz of the entry phone and reached out a hand to press the button to release the door. Still occupied with writing up patient notes he took no notice of the footsteps approaching the desk. It was not until a soundless shadow fell over the desk and remained there that Anderson looked up.

'Professor Patel!' He felt his throat dry.

Patel was in no mood for preamble. 'You were sleeping with my wife, weren't you?'

The grief-stricken man's eyes were as cold

and unanimated as those of a robot, and Anderson felt rising panic. 'Let's go and talk in one of the offices,' he said, rising to his feet and looking across the corridor praying that Sister Avalon's room was free.

'No, we'll talk here. I've nothing to lose, because I've already lost everything.' Patel spoke in flat even tones which sent chills racing down Anderson's spine. For a moment he wondered if the senior medic was armed — a knife, maybe even a gun. He felt sure that Patel would be able to see the throb of his jugular if he bothered to look, he was so alarmed.

'Don't lie to me,' Patel said, 'because I'll find out if you do. And I'll track you down, and I'll kill you. Just tell me the truth.'

Anderson looked around wildly, praying to see some help at hand. But it was a quiet time of the evening; the visitors had all gone and the night staff were occupied with their first rounds, going through the ward. 'Yes, I was sleeping with Moira.' He fell silent, judging it best not to elaborate.

'And were you the person who was urging her to blow the whistle on Cavanagh?'

Cold fear seized Anderson's joints. 'We talked about it, yes. I was just as keen as she was to do something about . . . the situation. I mean patients — ' He stopped, feeling himself trapped in a nightmarish web of lies and doubts and cowardice all of them overlaid with a genuine sense of concern for the welfare of the hapless women who came under Cavanagh's so called care. 'I wasn't urging her on,' he said lamely.

'Patients are at risk,' Patel said. 'And Moria was a very highly principled woman. But her career would have been ruined if she'd turned whistle-blower.'

Anderson sat in frozen silence.

'Did you know she was pregnant?' Patel asked. 'No, don't bother trying to work out what to tell me on that score. It doesn't really matter.' He leaned over slightly, his eyes full of intent, as though he might strike the other man. 'You probably don't know that she was carrying twins.'

Anderson felt waves of shock ripple through him. 'No.'

'One of them carried my DNA,' Patel told him, 'the other didn't. I expect you can imagine what I felt when I discovered that.'

Anderson's mouth fell open. Trying to work out what Patel's intentions were and what the future held for both of them felt like wading through hot sand. He said nothing.

'Did she talk about me?' Patel asked. 'When you were together?'

Patel's eyes seemed to drive into Anderson's soul, and the younger man felt himself pitched back into his childhood, when lying to his father had seemed like the wickedest crime in the universe. 'She worried about you,' he said. 'About your health.' He looked up and saw that one of the ward nurses was coming away from the ward, a little spring in her step. Suddenly Anderson was sick of being intimidated.

'She said it was difficult,' he told Patel, his voice cold and cruel. 'Living with someone who is a depressive and dependent on drugs.'

Patel stood back a little and took in a long breath. 'Yes,' he said. 'Yes, I can see that.' There was a long, stagnant pause and then the older man turned and walked slowly to the exit door. Anderson watched, sensing Patel's dark mood of hopelessness and despair.

'Everything OK?' the nurse asked, swinging herself behind the counter and easing off one of her shoes.

Anderson looked at her unsmiling. 'It's been a hard day,' he said.

13

Georgie treated herself to a smoking session in the car, it was getting to be one of the few places you could have a puff without being reminded of what a filthy and deadly habit it was. Driving through the Bradford suburbs at night-time was hardly a cheering pastime, though it had its interests for a budding journalist. She noticed newspaper hoardings outside shops, tattered and smudged after the day's sleet and icy rain: *Local man in custody for Moira's murder*, they proclaimed. Tipsy folks spilled from the pubs, stopping at late night shops for fattening snacks. The women didn't have half enough clothes on for the weather. They were just girls really, tottering on high heels, their tits popping out of their tight tops, their skirts halfway up their arses. When I have a kid, she thought, if it's a girl, I'm not going to let her out until she's twenty-five. She can wear any gear she likes, but she's staying at home with me.

She turned into the council estate where Shaun lived. The road surfaces on the maze of streets were horrific, all broken up and full of holes. She had to steer like crazy, veering back and forth over the road to miss axle-busting canyons.

She stopped outside Shaun's house, finished her cigarette, squirted Gold Spot into her mouth and then sprayed herself with Miss Dior, because she fancied you couldn't get any classier smell around yourself than that.

Tina was prompt in answering the door. Georgie had her sized up in a split second: tiny, sexy, street-wise rather than clever, and probably as hard and brittle as a walnut shell. And very wary.

Concealing her amazement at the state of the entrance to the house, Georgie picked her way cautiously across the stony damp floor of the hallway, inhaling the scents of earth, drains and stale cooking. Poor Shaunie ending up in this hell hole she thought, keeping an eye on Tina who was leading the way into the living-room, her small bottom wiggling seductively in tight black jeans.

'Sit down,' Tina told her visitor.

'Thanks. Call me Georgie.' She gave an encouraging smile.

'So what do you want then?' Tina's neat little face was tight with misgiving. She had remained standing up.

'Don't look so worried, Tina. I'm on your side. Yours and Shaun's.'

'Do the police know you're here?'

Georgie grinned and snorted. 'No way. You see what I'm after is getting justice for Shaun. Because both you and I know that he didn't kill Moira Farrell.' She spoke with slow steady conviction, at the same time digging into her handbag and taking out a half bottle of Pinot Grigio. 'I guessed you'd be a white wine girl,' she told Tina. 'Could you get us a couple of glasses?'

Still looking doubtful, Tina disappeared into the kitchen. Street-wise, but does what she's told, Georgie thought, looking around the chaotic living-room, and thanking God she didn't have to live here. She got out her mobile phone and pressed the settings so it would record.

Tina returned with two cloudy-looking glasses. 'Sorry about the mess,' she told Georgie. 'Shaun's going to get things fixed up, and it'll be really nice then. But.'

'But he's had other things on his mind.' Georgie unscrewed the cap on the wine bottle and poured herself and Tina a glass. 'Cheers!'

'Yeah,' Tina said doubtfully, perching on the opposite end of the sofa to Georgie and taking a large sip of wine. 'How can you get justice for Shaun?' she asked.

'I used to go to school with him when I was a kid,' Georgie said, not ready to answer

Tina's question yet. 'Ravenscar First school.'

Tina's eyes sharpened. 'Is that really true?'

'Yeah. Mind you, Shaun wasn't there a lot of the time. Bunking off.'

Tina gave a faint smile. 'Yeah. That's Shaun.'

'In those days the teachers used to bawl kids out when they came back into school. So, guess what, they went bunking off again. It was like smacking a runaway puppy when it decides to come back to you.'

Tina took another swig of wine. Georgie could see that she was beginning to relax.

'He had a bad time when he was a kid,' Tina said. 'His mum was a slapper; she went through men like a hot knife through butter. But his gran was nice.'

'There's always a silver lining,' Georgie observed, wetting her lips with the wine. She wanted to stay sober and she certainly didn't want getting caught drink driving.

'It was her house where the police got him,' Tina said looking thoughtful. 'It wasn't me who shopped him, you know. I never told the police, though I was pretty sure where he was. The police found out somehow.'

'Well, sometimes they get things right,' Georgie said with a wry grin.

'I hope he doesn't think I was the one that gave the police the nod.'

'I'll bet he doesn't.' Georgie said. 'He used to be a loyal type, Shaunie. A bit of a delinquent but not nasty, not cruel.'

'No, that's right,' Tina said. Her features registered sadness. She drained her wine. Georgie poured her another glass.

'Have you been to see him?'

Alarm came into Tina's eyes. 'No.'

'Do you miss him?'

'Yeah,' said Tina. 'Yeah, I do.' She stared down into her wine. 'He's been having a bad time.'

'You can say that again,' Georgie agreed.

'Not just all this with the police. His gran died a few weeks back. He was gutted. He cried, he really cried.'

'That's sad,' Georgie's mind began ticking fast. 'You don't believe he killed Moira Farrell do you?' she said, soft and slow.

'No.'

'You gave him an alibi.'

'Yeah. But the police don't care a jot about that. They think I'm a waste of space. A scrote's tart. They think I'd say anything to get him off and keep a quiet life for myself.'

'Do you think Shaun's a 'scrote'?' Georgie asked.

Tina looked up. Her pale cheeks were becoming pink from drinking the wine. 'No,' she said. 'I don't.'

'And was he here with you when Moria Farrell was killed?'

There was no hesitation. 'Yes, he was.'

'Would you stand up and say that in court?'

A tiny pause. 'Yes!'

'So why aren't you speaking up for him, Tina?' Georgie asked.

'What?'

'Why aren't you jumping up and down and making a fuss about his being held for questioning?'

Tina gaped at her questioner and placed the tip of her thumbnail between her front teeth. 'They wouldn't take any notice of me.'

'Why not?'

'I told you, they don't rate me.'

'I don't think that's true, Tina. In fact I think they'd start taking a lot of notice of you if you did a bit of jumping up and down and standing by your man.'

Tina looked baffled, but definitely interested.

'I'll help you,' Georgie said.

'How?'

'First off, I'll write an article about you and him. About how you're determined to stand by him. How you know he didn't do it, and how the police have sidelined you and chosen to ignore your vital evidence. Because, you see, Tina, what you say is proof that Shaun isn't the man the police need to charge as he was here with you at the time Moira Farrell was murdered. End of story.'

'Is it as simple as that?' Tina asked in wonder.

'Yes,' Georgie said, happy to lie when necessity demanded.

'I'll be in the newspaper?' Tina said, like a child being offered an unexpected present.

'Yep, and I'll get one of our photographers to come round to your work first thing tomorrow morning and take a picture. So get your best kit on.' Pleased with Tina's reaction, Georgie pressed on, 'And when the article's published we'll go to the police station together and talk to the big boss in charge.'

'But what if they won't let him go?' Tina asked, wondering through the fuzz of the wine what she'd be feeling like if they did let him go.

'They will,' said Georgie. 'And after that I've got something rather good up my sleeve to make sure the police won't be bothering him again.'

Tina allowed herself to be convinced.

Georgie gathered her gear together and prepared to make a move. Her calculating mind threw up one final idea to leave Tina with. 'So Shaun's gran had her own house, did she?'

'Yeah.'

'Well then, if she remembered him in her will, your Shaunie might be coming into a bit of money, mightn't he?' She winced slightly as she stepped down into the squelch of the hallway.

'I suppose so,' Tina said, as though the idea hadn't occurred to her.

'You could get this place all done up,' Georgie ventured cheerily, being careful where she placed her feet.

'Yeah.' Tina was looking decidedly wistful now, quite the devoted girlfriend and soul mate. 'Yeah, that would be cool.'

Georgie sat in her car for a few moments, and allowed herself a little gloating. She reckoned she had the makings of a good article — *Agony of girlfriend as local man faces murder charge*. Front page stuff. She imagined standing up to the editor, persuading, arguing, wheedling. He'd say he couldn't promise the front page. Other stories might break. Already her article would have knocked a fatal car crash and the rape of a local teacher to the inside, etc, etc. But Georgie knew she could do a fantastic piece. And Tina was just the sort of downtrodden low self-esteem girl who would love the exposure and then playing the noble heroine standing by her man. And she'd photograph well. Moreover there was plenty more up Georgie's sleeve to be toying with if Shaun got out.

And all for the price of half a bottle of Pinot Grigio.

⋆ ⋆ ⋆

Swift drove along the early morning streets, on his way to see Rajesh Patel at his house. It was snowing once again, but not settling: the roads gleamed black against the greying snow heaped at the edge of the pavements. During the time Swift had been planning a slot when he could see Patel once more, the professor had telephoned him with a request of his own for a talk. Swift did not know what agenda Patel had in mind but he knew by now that unless Patel, or someone else, produced some vital new evidence it was more or less certain they would have to release Shaun Busfield within the next couple of hours. Which, on the whole, he judged was probably justified, being privately inclined to believe that Busfield had not killed Moira, despite the evidence supplied by the bloodstained trainers in the garden.

As he drove, thoughts of Naomi rose to the forefront of his mind temporarily pushing the Farrell case on to the back burner. In the past two days he had had more than one phone call from Cat, both indicating that Naomi was doing fine, and, from what he could tell, indicating that Cat and Naomi had formed some kind of relationship. He was interested in how much the idea of it pleased him. His feelings towards Cat involved both warmth and trust, and the notion that she might be offering Naomi a degree of friendship and protection was nothing but welcome.

He recalled that before Naomi was born his and Kate's friends had kept teasing them about sleepless nights and loss of freedom and how their lives were never going to the same. What they hadn't mentioned was how knocked out they would be by how much they'd love her right from the word go. How precious she would be. And after that there was always the fear of things going wrong for her — just ordinary things, falling off a slide, contracting some awful illness, being bullied, getting in the way of a car when crossing the road. All the usual. And then Kate got killed and the worry was how he would ever manage to make the loss up to her. Which, of course, he could never do.

And now, totally unexpectedly, someone was sharing that concern, easing the load.

As he parked his car at the bottom of Rajesh Patel's drive, the professor opened the door and stood waiting for him. He extended his hand as though Swift were a welcome visitor, then invited him to sit in the warmth of the kitchen. 'Can I offer you some refreshment, Chief Inspector?'

Swift shook his head.

Patel sat down. 'I went to see James Anderson yesterday. I don't know if you're aware.'

'No.'

'I challenged him about having an affair with Moira. And he admitted it. And I told him about the two babies, that only one of them carried my DNA.'

He spoke with steady clarity and a reasonableness quite remarkable for a man who had suffered such emotional pain during the last few days. Swift reckoned Anderson would have been seriously rattled if Patel had treated him to all this self-composure, which must surely be underlain by some grave, deep antipathy and menace.

'Did he admit he could be the father of the other baby?'

'Yes. And I happen to know that he's currently having an affair with one of the sisters on the gynaecology ward. I have one or two students who are happy to act as moles.'

'I see.' Swift looked into the other man's

face. 'Professor Patel, what else do you know?'

Patel sighed. 'Nothing that's going to help you find Moira's killer. That's if this man you're holding turns out to be a red herring.'

'Did you really not know about Moira's pregnancy?' Swift asked.

'I'm afraid I didn't, and that has been causing me a good deal of distress, that I should have been so lacking in perception.'

'Was there something else? Some other worry regarding Moira which distracted you?'

Patel offered a fleeting regretful smile. 'I was worried that she was going to destroy her career by making a complaint to the hospital management about Adrian Cavanagh. A complaint of professional incompetence. She'd witnessed it first hand on several occasions. She'd seen patients suffer, she'd seen one or two die. And she was determined to do something about it.'

'But you didn't want her to complain?'

'I knew it would be fruitless and I feared it might even destroy her career. Management don't like to go public regarding incompetence in their consultants, it reflects so badly on hospital performance targets. And whistleblowers are simply not to be tolerated; they get ostracized; they even get suspended. And after that they don't get new jobs.'

'So the bodies are swept under the carpet?'
'That more or less describes it.'
'Did you and Moira argue about this?'
'Oh yes. On more than one occasion. And notably on the evening before she died. It upset us both greatly. I warned her she was going to commit professional suicide by speaking out.' He stared fixedly at Swift and for a moment it seemed that a confession was forthcoming. Swift skimmed through the possibilities: Patel had been driven to a point of utter frustration, had snapped, had dealt his wife one fatal stab. Had somehow managed to frame Shaun Busfield.

'The memory of that argument is unbelievably raw,' Patel said. 'And through the next day my feelings veered between anger and regret. Moira and I hardly ever rowed. We were contained, private, civilized people.' There was a long pause. 'And when I got home it was too late to tell her I was sorry.'

Swift sat motionless and silent.

'I didn't kill her,' Patel said softly. 'That is one act I don't have to agonize about.'

Swift took in and released a long breath. 'Professor Patel, is there anything, anything at all concerning Moira's death that you haven't mentioned before.'

'No. I've come to the sad conclusion that Moira and I were leading very separate lives.

That I knew so little about what she was thinking and feeling. That I've just been wrapped up in myself and my work and all the various preoccupations we humans burden ourselves with.'

'It looks as though we shall have to release Shaun Busfield,' Swift said gently. 'The evidence we have is not strong enough to make a case that will stand up in court. I'm sorry.'

Patel shook his head. 'Better to release a man if there is doubt. Better to do that than incarcerate someone who is innocent. I'm not one who takes the view that catching a murderer brings some kind of relief or satisfaction to the ones left behind. The deed is done. The loved one is lost. That is the life sentence all of us who grieve share. For me nothing can soften the brutality of that sentence.'

Swift rose to his feet. 'If anything comes to mind, Professor Patel,' he said.

Patel got up. 'Yes, of course.' He led Swift to the door. 'I'm thinking of taking a break from work,' he said. 'Maybe a few days in the Lake District. You have my mobile number.'

He stood in the doorway waiting whilst Swift got in his car. A very civilized man felled with grief.

Georgie Tyson's article hit the streets around 2.30 in the afternoon. It had made the front page, and the picture of Tina staring at the camera with her carefully made-up eyes wistful and vulnerable made Georgie hug herself with glee. Even better there had been several requests from the nationals to run the story. The editor had gone so far as to offer congratulations.

Georgie collected Tina from her work and drove her to the station.

Tina was bemused with the attention the young journalist was giving her; half elated, half scared stiff. And whilst she was worried about all kind of things to do with Shaun, she was even more worried about pissing off her boss by asking to nip out of work without due reason or warning.

'Hey! Lighten up,' Georgie told her as they waited for Detective Chief Inspector Swift to collect them from the front desk.

'I'm a worrier,' Tina said, sticking a nail in her mouth, then stoically resisting gnawing at it. She laid her hands out flat on her knees.

'Great nails,' Georgie told, her eyeing the bright pink ovals with a strip of silver down the middle of each one. Did you do them yourself?'

'Yeah.'

'Look, stop fretting. Everything's going to work out fine. Just remember you're on the front page of the local rag. You're a celeb already. And we're going to get Shaunie out of here.'

Tina swallowed hard as Swift appeared at the door of his office. She was well practised at defending herself, but found it hard to know how to behave when she was with someone who obviously thought they were on the attack. There was something worryingly compelling about Georgie Tyson — Tina was slightly in fear of her and on the other hand anxious not to let her down.

Seated in Swift's office Tina noticed that he was taller and thinner than she remembered, and in the light from the window behind his desk she could see that he was a natural redhead, his hair a full rich auburn you couldn't get out of a bottle even in these days of advanced colour technology.

He sat quietly behind his desk, his expression neutral, neither friendly nor intimidating.

'Have you seen today's *Echo*?' Georgie asked him.

He nodded.

'Tina wants to know why you've had Shaun banged up when she's given him an alibi for the time of Moira Farrell's murder.'

'We have to investigate all of the evidence we find,' Swift told her calmly.

'What evidence?' Georgie asked with a degree of challenge. She waited, holding her breath, desperate to know what evidence they had. What juicy nuggets of information there might be which she could work into a new article.'

'Miss Tyson,' Swift said evenly, 'you know very well I'm not going to tell you. When the time is right we shall give out information through our press officer.'

Georgie looked at Tina, wanting to pass on the baton of questioning, but the other woman sat in frozen silence.

'Why won't you believe Tina's alibi for Shaun?' Georgie demanded.

'I didn't say we didn't believe it.'

'Well it's obvious you don't otherwise you wouldn't have locked him up. Tina told the truth and she's prepared to stand up in court and say so.'

Swift nodded his acknowledgement of this intention.

'Tina's come to demand that you release Shaun as soon as possible,' Georgie said, having an uneasy feeling the interview wasn't going as she had hoped.

Ignoring Georgie, Swift turned to Tina. 'Is

there anything you'd like to say?' he asked in even tones.

'I did tell the truth,' Tina said.

'Just remind me what you told us that morning we came to arrest Shaun,' he said gently.

'The morning you let him slip through your fingers!' Georgie said, unstoppable.

'Tina?' Swift said.

'Shaun was in bed with me when that poor woman was killed,' Tina said.

'And you're sure about that?'

'Yeah. I've thought about it a lot,' Tina said. 'That morning, how things were. And I'll swear on the Bible that Shaun was snoring his head off beside me around six that morning, because he woke me up and I couldn't get back to sleep. He's been in the pub drinking most nights after his gran died, he was that upset. And drinking always makes him snore. I got heartily sick of it to tell the truth.' She stopped and gave a sigh.

Georgie glanced at Swift. 'Top that,' she said, 'for something that smacks of the truth. And I've got it all on tape.'

'Yes, I'm aware,' he said, glancing at the small bulge in the pocket of her jacket.

'So! I think we've proved our point,' Georgie said. 'And it's high time you let

271

justice take its course and released Shaun Busfield.'

'Yeah, let him go, please!' Tina was suddenly overcome, tears spilling over her lashes. Poor Shaun; she hadn't stood by him like she should have. She'd been blown about by her doubts, thinking it might be good to be as free as the air and manage on her own without having to rely on a bloke. It just showed how much she knew about herself.

'We demand that you release an innocent man,' Georgie said, planning to write verbatim whatever response the DCI managed to come up with.

'He's already been released,' Swift said. 'Half an hour ago.'

14

'So were you blown away by the force of the wind rushing out of her sails?' Laura asked, as she and Swift drove to Sylvia Farrell's house. The image of her boss being confronted by the foxy Georgie and the doll-like Tina was very much to her liking.

He smiled. 'I managed to stand my ground.'

They were met at the door by Jayne Arnold. 'Hello!' she said, smiling at Laura.

'This is Detective Chief Inspector Swift,' Laura told her.

'Please come in.' Jayne led the way into the sitting-room. She was wearing a bright red knitted wool dress over black leggings and clumpy high-heeled patent shoes. In Laura's view she looked as though she had just stepped out of the fashion pages of one of the quality newspapers. Feeling rather lumpy in her last year's tweed coat and grey ribbed tights from Marks & Spencer, Laura made a note to make time to look in the funky fashion shops when she had her next day off.

'My mother's out at the moment,' Jayne said, 'but she should be back soon. Is there anything I can help you with?'

'We came to tell your mother that the suspect we've been holding regarding Moira Farrell's death has been released,' Swift said.

Jayne's smile faded. 'Oh, I see.' She spent a few moments in contemplation. 'I think my mother will be sorry to hear that. She's been hoping that there'd be some early resolution to Moira's death. Some sort of closure, I suppose.'

'I understand,' Swift said. 'Basically, the evidence our scene of crime officers found on the premises was not enough to enable us to bring a charge.'

'I see.' She dipped her head then looked across at Swift. 'I don't suppose you're at liberty to say what kind of evidence was found?'

'Not at present.'

'So — we're back to square one.'

'Not entirely,' Swift said. 'We've gathered quite a lot of useful information.'

Conversation ceased as there was the sound of the front door opening and closing, quickly followed by Sylvia Farrell's appearance in the drawing room. 'Oh!' she exclaimed, on seeing the visitors. 'The police again.'

Jayne made introductions between Swift and Sylvia. She did it in a skilled and soothing manner, as though underlying the necessity of her mother's need to be shielded from any further distress. 'Would you like me to make some tea, darling?' she asked her parent.

Sylvia shook her head. She sat down. She had a copy of the latest *Echo* in her hand and she laid it on carefully on the table. 'I expect you've come to tell me about this,' she said, pointing to the blaring headline and the winsome photograph of Tina Frazer.

'Don't get upset,' Jayne told her. 'The police are doing everything they can to find out who killed Moira.'

'I'm glad to hear it,' said Sylvia, looking sceptical.

Jayne gave her mother a brief and entirely accurate account of what had been said prior to Sylvia's arrival. 'Chief Inspector Swift says they've gathered quite a lot of useful information,' she concluded.

'Good,' said Sylvia, still unconvinced.

Jayne turned to Swift. 'Have you another suspect?'

'We're following some promising leads,' Swift said.

She gave a twitch of a smile. 'That sounds suitably noncommittal, Chief Inspector.'

'I gather you were out of the country at the time Moira was killed,' Swift said. 'It must have come as a shock to hear the news when you got home.'

'Terrible,' Jayne agreed. She looked kindly at her parent. 'It was worse for Mother, of course. As I told Constable Ferguson, Moira and I weren't very close. Different ages, different life-styles.'

'How is Rajesh bearing up?' Sylvia asked. 'I keep meaning to get in touch with him, but . . . it's just all so horribly difficult. I expect I'm a terrible coward. I keep thinking of the past, remembering some of the times we all used to get together — myself and Anthony, Moira and Rajesh. There are some good memories.'

'Is there anything further you can remember concerning Mrs Farrell's death?' Laura interposed gently.

Sylvia turned to her, askance. 'Good heavens, no! This murder was some dreadful random act, I'm convinced of it. I know absolutely nothing about it.'

Laura looked at Jayne, who gave a regretful smile and a little shrug. Me neither.

★　★　★

'So,' Swift said, on the way back to the station, 'do we know much more about Sylvia and Jayne than we did before?'

'I don't think we do.' Laura looked out of the window admiring the way the sun, which had not been seen for days, had suddenly made an appearance around midday and turned the countryside surrounding Bradford into a place of brilliant light and shade topped by a stunning cobalt blue sky. Just now it was setting, rolling down behind the hills like a huge glowing pumpkin.

'What we do know, is that Sylvia Farrell had no alibi for the time Moira was murdered; that she didn't seem to be on very good terms with Rajesh or Moira. Neither of which means very much at all. Not at present, anyway.'

'And Jayne does have an alibi, but as far as we can tell she didn't have any close connection with Moira — different age group, different life-style.' He drew the car to a halt at traffic lights.

'I checked the booking list for flights from Prague in the days around the time of Moira's death,' Laura said. 'Jayne cancelled her original flight back and booked an earlier one setting off around lunchtime, a few hours after the murder.'

'Did you check the boarding lists?' Swift asked, letting out the clutch and easing the car across the junction.

Laura felt a prickle run down her spine.

'No.' Colour climbed into her cheeks as she glanced at his face. He didn't respond for a few moments, throwing her into silent torment.

'Don't beat yourself up about it,' he said. 'But check when we get back to base.'

A sensation of horror seized Laura as she imagined the scenario in Finch's office if her omission had come to light there. His icy derision, the awful humiliation. She looked across at the DCI and blessed him for his humanity.

★ ★ ★

Georgie drove Tina back to the house she shared with Shaun. As they turned off the main road running centrally through the estate and into one of the network of smaller roads Tina's agitation accelerated.

'You'll come in with me, won't you?' she said to Georgie. 'If he's there.'

'Sure. Try and stop me, I want to talk to him.' She pulled up in front of the house, looking around and feeling faintly disappointed not to see a crowd of photographers and hungry newshounds swarming around the front door.

'Come on!' she said to Tina, who was huddled in her seat looking as though she might refuse to get out of the car.

'He'll be mad at me,' Tina whined.

'Of course he won't. Why should he?'

'I didn't go and see him. I didn't do anything to help him.'

'You didn't shop him, though, did you? That must count for something.' Georgie hoped she wouldn't need to spend much more time with Tina, the girl was getting on her nerves.

Georgie hopped out of the car, leading the way to the front door, then braving the gloom and damp of the hall. Going into the living-room she saw that Shaun was sitting slumped on the sofa staring blankly at the flicker of the television. 'Hi!' she said cheerily.

Shaun turned and leapt to his feet. 'Who the fuck are you?'

Georgie held up her hands in surrender. She handed him her business card.

His eyes were shifting all over the place, fear emanating from him like smoke. Georgie could tell that the arrest and questioning of Moira Farrell's murder had shaken him badly.

Tina came slinking into the room looking as though she wished she were invisible.

Shaun took his attention away from Georgie and looked at his girlfriend, his suspicion little diminished at the sight of her.

He grunted some form of acknowledgement of her presence.

'Are you all right?' Tina said, hardly allowing her lips to part to let out the words.

'What do you think?' His voice was angry and sullen, and his eyes bored into Tina's face.

She blinked. 'I'll go make us a cup of tea,' she said, hurrying to the kitchen.

'Don't you remember me, Shaun?' Georgie asked, in no way disconcerted by the viciousness of his mood, which she considered entirely understandable.

He looked at her and frowned. 'You what?'

'We went to the same school — Ravenscar First.'

'That shit-hole,' he said.

'Quite,' Georgie agreed. 'Anyway I remember you, you were quite a livewire. Now listen, Shaun, I'm after clearing your name regarding this arrest for murder.'

His eyes were slits of distrust. He squared his shoulders. 'How do you know I didn't do it?' The question had a chill to it, but Georgie liked a challenge.

'Well, of course, I don't. But I'm inclined to believe Tina when she says you couldn't have done it because you were tucked up in bed with her at the time of the killing.'

Shaun pursed his lips and took some time

to think about what he might have to say on that score. 'Aye, she stuck by me, didn't she? She could have dropped me right in it if she'd wanted.'

Georgie was not much concerned regarding the ins and outs of Tina and Shaun's relationship, although her gut feeling was that it was fragile and rocky, subject to as many shifts and changes as the surface of sand under an ebbing tide. And that strangely enough it could be one of those pairings that lasted.

'I've thought of a way we can prove you didn't kill Moira Farrell,' she told him.

Shaun's frown was still in place, but he was interested now.

'If you'd agree to take a lie detector test, I'd make sure the results were splashed all over the papers and everyone would know you're an innocent guy who's been shamefully treated by the police.'

He took his time in thinking about it. 'Do they really work, these lie detectors?' he asked.

'From what I've been told, yes. If they're administered properly and interpreted by someone who knows what they're doing.' Georgie watched him, knowing that if he was guilty he'd be backing out fast. And that she'd be without her next big story.

Tina came in with the tea. She seemed to have been listening, and cheering up. 'That's a good idea. Don't you think so, Shaunie?'

He took the mug she held out. Georgie held her breath.

'I'm not sure what I think,' He eyeballed Georgie. 'Are you going to get it all sorted out, then?'

'Yeah. I've already been in contact with someone who'll be able to do the test.'

'Who'll pay?' Shaun asked.

'My newspaper.' Georgie was filled with bravado now things were going well.

'And what'll I have to do?'

'You'll have some sensors put on your fingers, then you'll be linked up to a monitor which would chart electrical responses from your skin.'

'I'll not have any electric currents passed through me.'

'No, you won't have. And it's all quite painless,' she hastened to assure him.

'It had better be,' he growled. 'I've had enough grief this past week to last me a very long time.'

'Sure,' Georgie agreed. 'Then you'd have to answer some simple questions. You won't have to make any speeches, just answer yes or no.'

Doubt was creeping into his face. 'What

sort of questions?'

'Some general questions about yourself and your work, that kind of thing. Then mixed in with those there'd be questions about the time of Moira's murder and what you were doing and so on.'

Shaun's face was closing down, becoming fixed and stony. He took a long drink of his tea. 'I'll need to have a good long think about this,' he said.

'Don't wait too long,' Georgie warned. 'I've got someone lined up who can get it all done for us later today. We don't want to hang around, Shaun.' Watching him as she finished her tea, she began to wonder just what had happened on that morning Moira Farrell met her death. But if he agreed to take the test she'd get fantastic copy whatever the outcome. Guilty or not guilty, it didn't really matter.

* * *

Swift was summoned to Finch's office.

'Ed! Come in!' There was the merest suggestion of excitement in the superintendent's voice. 'We've got results from forensics on the earth found in the van Busfield used during the autumn.'

'It matches the earth found on Busfield's

trainers?' Swift suggested.

'Stealing my thunder,' Finch commented without rancour. 'It does indeed. Which does suggest that at some point Busfield has been in Moira Farrell's garden.'

'And also suggests he must have met her outside the confines of the hospital. And most likely at her home.'

'Maybe he was doing a bit of gardening to earn extra cash,' Finch said. 'But whatever he was up to he was lying about only having met Moira at the hospital.'

'Do you want us to pick him up?' Swift asked.

Finch did a little pacing. Although he had only occupied the office for two months he was already wearing a small, narrow track in the carpet behind his desk. 'It's tricky,' he said. 'We don't want to look as though we're playing some kind of cat and mouse game with him. This is interesting evidence, but still not enough for us to bring a charge.'

'No,' Swift agreed. 'But on the other hand it would be even more tricky if he went to ground again.'

'And that teenage journalist penned another of her pieces of fiction.'

'I'll go talk to him,' Swift said. 'I'll take a backup team with me.'

Laura sat at her desk staring at the phone. She had just spoken to flight officials at British Airways. The flight manifests including the boarding lists showed that Jayne Arnold had not taken a flight from Prague on the afternoon of Moira's death. She had, in fact, boarded a plane from Prague to Gatwick on the day before Moira Farrell was killed. Officials at Leeds-Bradford Airport were able to provide further information that Jayne Arnold had boarded the last evening flight from Heathrow to Leeds-Bradford and come through passport check at around 9.30 p.m. She could easily have been home 10.30 on the evening before Moira's death.

The information had made Laura's pulse speed up and her heart start pounding. She knew Swift would carry the can for her omission to check out Jayne's alibi in sufficient detail. But that didn't make her feel any less guilty and inadequate. Shame swarmed through her veins. What made things even worse was that there was no one available whom she could tell. Well, no one she felt she could bear to give the news to. The thought of a meeting with Ice Man Finch in his office made her feel slightly sick. She headed to the ladies' loo, locked herself in the nearest cubicle and tried to steady the violent workings of her autonomic nervous system.

*   *   *

Swift found Busfield's house empty. He went straight to Tina's place of work and without preamble knocked smartly on the door the receptionist had pointed out to him. Tina opened it, her face already pinched with anxiety. Behind, a woman lay stretched out on what looked like a doctor's couch. She had white paste all over her face and slices of cucumber covering her eyes.

'Where's Shaun?' Swift asked.

'He's with that journalist, Georgie.'

'At the newspaper offices?'

'I think so.'

'Thank you.' He turned away.

'He's not in trouble again?' Tina called after him.

He did not turn back. He raised a hand in farewell.

*   *   *

Sitting in a tiny office adjacent to the main news room at the *Echo* Shaun was in the mood for giving everyone in his orbit a hard time. Having grudgingly agreed to go ahead with the lie detector test he was now sulky and uncooperative, like a truculent 4-year-old who couldn't make up his mind what he wanted.

The polygraphist whom Georgie had hired from a privately run security service was a young man with round-framed glasses and a serious demeanour. He appeared unruffled by Shaun's brooding hostility and patiently explained the procedure to him, encouraging him to handle the sensors that were to be attached to his fingers and the cuff that would be placed around his upper arm.

'There ain't no electric currents going through there, are there?' Shaun demanded.

'No. What we're doing is simply recording your body's reaction to the questions we're going to ask.' He indicated a small winking monitor which he'd set on the desk. 'The results will appear up there, like a chart.'

Shaun sat silent and glowering.

'It's a process involving bio-feedback,' the polygraphist elaborated.

'Talk English,' Shaun grunted.

'We're measuring the reactions of your autonomic nervous system,' the polygraphist told him. 'Which basically means we're recording the reactions in your nerve fibres when we ask these questions. Reactions that are automatic reflexes, things neither you nor I have any control over.'

'Like if you hit my kneecap with a little rubber hammer, my leg'd shoot out in front of me, even if I tried to stop it.'

'That's exactly it.' The young man permitted himself a smile. 'You've obviously experienced that.'

'Oh, aye,' Shaun agreed. 'I've had a few quacks going over me in my time.'

'Right. Now, Miss Tyson and I have drawn up a set of ten simple questions to ask you. Some are just general questions with no relevance to Mrs Farrell's murder — '

'And the others aren't?'

'Correct. All you have to do, Shaun, is listen to each question, think about it and then answer yes, or no.'

Shaun's face creased with conflict. He levelled a beady glance at Georgie. 'Tell me this isn't going to land me in the shit again.'

'I'm on your side, Shaun,' she said.

He was not reassured. He looked at the polygraphist and the equipment he had brought with him. He looked again at Georgie. 'I don't know, I just don't know.'

'If you're innocent of Moira Farrell's murder,' Georgie said quietly, 'this test will prove it once and for all. And I'll make sure that proof is in every newspaper across Britain.'

Shaun beat a tattoo on the desk. 'All right, then,' he said, addressing the polygraphist. 'Let's get it over with.'

The technician stepped forward and placed two flat discs on Shaun's fingers. He bent down, checking that the placing was accurate. 'Relax,' he told Shaun. 'I promise you this is not going to be painful. No electric currents, no shocks.' He bound a grey cuff around Shaun's upper arm and checked the attachments to the monitor. His movements were unhurried and confident. Eventually he was satisfied that everything was in place. He looked down at Shaun. 'Are you comfortable?'

There was something about the other man's air of quiet competence that soothed and reassured Shaun, gave him a renewed belief in the possibility that other people might just wish to help rather than harm him. He felt himself move towards a decision. He swallowed. He glanced towards Georgie, edgy again and mutinous. 'I'm not doing it while you're here,' he told her. 'I just want him. You wait outside.'

Georgie shrugged. 'That's fine.' She got up. 'See you later.'

Shaun waited until the door closed behind

her. 'Go on then,' he told the polygraphist, who had been waiting patiently. The sheet of questions lay beside him on the desk. He pulled it towards him.

The first question was easy. It was to confirm Shaun's name and his age. There was no difficulty in saying yes. And the second was laughably simple too. 'Does milk come from cows?'

And then things got a bit nearer the bone.

★ ★ ★

Doug settled himself into an armchair in Pat Bainbridge's sitting-room. She made him hot strong coffee and offered a variety of small iced cakes.

Her sitting-room was small and cosily warm. It was furnished with plump chairs filled with brightly coloured cushions. Two fluffy white dogs slept by the gas fire. Doug noticed that all of the fabric surfaces in the room were covered in white hairs. Maybe Pat was so fed up with cleaning other folks' houses, she had little inclination to bother with her own.

'So, how can I help you?' she asked, her face curious but also guarded.

'We're just going over old ground,' he said. 'It can happen as time goes by that things you didn't think of before come to mind. Human memory's an amazing thing.'

Pat did not disagree. 'This chap you've had in for questioning,' she said. 'Shaun Busfield.'

Doug put down the piece of cake he was about to put in his mouth. 'Yes?' he said encouragingly.

'I think I might have seen him at Mrs Farrell's house.'

Doug abandoned all thoughts of the cake. 'When was this, Mrs Bainbridge?'

'Quite a few weeks back. Maybe October last. I'm not absolutely sure it was him, don't run away with that idea.' She reached for her cup of tea, frowning in concentration. 'When I saw the pictures of him on the TV a few days ago, I had a vague feeling I might have seen him before. But — well, basically I forgot all about it, because I've been having a lot of trouble to do with my daughter. Well, to be honest it's her husband who's causing the problems. He's a right cheating bastard.' She seemed on the point of elaborating.

'To get back to Shaun Busfield,' Doug prompted gently, 'if we assume it was him you saw at Mrs Farrell's house, can you remember what he was doing there?'

'I think he was doing something in the garden. Well, whoever it was, this guy was putting in some rose trees. In the back garden. That was definitely what he was doing. Digging a new bed at one end of the lawn and planting rose bushes. But I'm not one hundred per cent sure it was the man you were questioning.'

'Can you remember what he looked like? I'm talking about what he looked like in the flesh. Try to forget the picture they showed on TV.'

'Let me think.' She pressed her lips tightly together. 'He was medium height, on the skinny side. But he was pretty handy with a spade. Strong and sinewy. Some smaller men are like that, aren't they, much tougher than the big bulky ones?'

'Can you remember his face?'

She considered, then shook her head. 'No, I didn't really see him close up. What I'm remembering is the picture on the TV. Which isn't really much good to you, is it?'

'Anything you can tell us is useful, Mrs Bainbridge,' Doug said encouragingly. 'Did he have a vehicle?'

She shook her head and looked regretful. 'Sorry, can't help there. If he had a car or a van and he'd parked it around the side of the house like we do, I wouldn't have seen it from the kitchen. And that's where I saw him, from the kitchen window.'

'Did you ever see him with Mrs Farrell?'

'No, I don't think so.' She pondered. 'No. Sorry.' She looked at him curiously. 'You let him go though. So presumably you don't think he did it.'

'We have to work on evidence, Mrs Bainbridge. Facts. And if we don't have enough of those, we can't go ahead with a charge.'

'Yes, I see. Right.' Her eyes gleamed with speculation. 'So basically you might have released a murderer into the community,' she commented, before biting into the bright pink icing of a little round cake.

Doug didn't reply. 'Is there anything else you remember, that you didn't mention when we spoke to you before?'

She gave herself time to swallow her chunk of cake. 'No, I don't think so. But there's something I'd like to ask you.'

'Go ahead.'

'Was Mrs Farrell pregnant?'

'We can't give out detailed information until the body is released to Professor Patel,' Doug told her, switching into formal non-disclosure mode.

'Which means she was,' Pat said with satisfaction. 'I told Meg. I told her Mrs F was expecting. I've got a nose for that kind of thing.' She patted her stomach. 'A gut feeling.'

It struck Doug that Pat Bainbridge was like someone in a soap opera, with a tendency to fill their lives with drama. 'You've been very helpful, Mrs Bainbridge,' he told her dutifully, rising to his feet.

She followed him to the door and opened it to let him through. 'Whoever that bloke was who was putting in the roses,' she said in thoughtful tones, 'he left his trainers in the utility room. They could only have been his. They were there after he finished the job, and they stayed there for weeks.'

Doug swivelled around, giving her his full attention. 'And?'

'Well, they're not there now.'

'Do you know when they were moved?'

'I'd say sometime around the time Mrs Farrell was killed. But I couldn't be more specific than that. Meg and I were so upset by what happened, we were all at sea. Well, I still feel pretty shocked when I think about it.'

'Mrs Bainbridge,' he said with some urgency, 'was there anyone else in or around the house and garden on the day Mrs Farrell was killed? Did you see anyone or anything unusual?'

'No,' she said firmly. 'Like I said before, we didn't see anyone. Until all you lot arrived.'

15

By the time Swift entered the premises of the *Echo*, accompanied by a back-up of three uniforms, Shaun had completed his test. He was still sitting in the little office close to the newsroom and was drinking the tea Georgie had rustled up for him. The polygraphist had printed out the responses from the monitor and been through them with Shaun, explaining the implications of the answers he had given. And then he had packed up his equipment and left.

Shaun had felt sick. He cursed himself for being persuaded to take place in this charade. He knew the police would get to see the results of the test. He didn't know how much trust they put in lie detectors, but he knew that, for him, the results were not nearly as clear as he had hoped. If only he'd kept his mouth shut, or simply kept on saying no to Georgie's mad idea. She had said the test had gone fine. But then she would, wouldn't she? She'd got her story and she was just saying anything she thought he wanted to hear. She was the sort of person who'd fall in the shit and come up with a ten pound note. Whereas he'd just sink deeper and deeper.

He'd thought of making a run for it before the police caught up with him again. But then he'd just be digging himself into an even deeper hole, making himself look more and more guilty. He folded his arms on the desk and laid his head on them.

The door opened and DCI Swift walked in. 'Hello, Shaun.'

Shaun looked up. He felt a sense of relief. Anything was better than just waiting. 'I suppose you've come to take me in again.'

Swift sat down. He could see that Shaun Busfield was exhausted, that the spirit was slowly seeping out of him. 'I'd like to ask you some more questions. And I'd prefer to do it at the station. But I'm not arresting you.'

'What? You're having me on.' He glanced furtively around him, his eyes coming to rest on the door of the office. 'Are you on your own?'

'I've got a backup team with me. But I won't be asking them to do anything.'

Shaun got to his feet: he knew when he was beaten. 'What choice have I got?' He paused at the door. 'Is she coming with us? That journalist.'

'I've had a talk with her about the lie detector test. And I've suggested she stays away from the station for the time being.'

'Will she do as she's told?'

'Oh, yes.'

Shaun had the feeling the DCI meant what he said.

At the station Swift took Shaun into interview-room two. Doug joined them, bringing Busfield's steadily fattening file of notes and tape transcripts with him.

'You're not under caution,' Swift told him. 'But we will be taping the interview. Do you want your solicitor?'

'No.' Shaun went so far as to offer a tight smile. 'Give the lad the night off.'

'I've been talking to Mrs Pat Bainbridge,' Doug said.

Shaun shrugged. 'Don't know her.'

'She works as a cleaner at Moira Farrell's house.'

Shaun shifted from side to side on his chair. 'I said already — I don't know her.'

'You probably don't,' Doug agreed. 'But she reports that she saw you in the grounds of the house. That you were doing some gardening for Mrs Farrell. Sometime last autumn.'

'I'll kill that bloody Georgie Tyson,' Shaun exclaimed. 'If it hadn't been for that lie detector test — '

'I'm not interested in what's emerged from a lie detector test commissioned and set up by an amateur,' Swift told him. 'The evidence we're questioning you about came to our notice through Mrs Bainbridge in conversation with Constable Wilson.'

'Was it you, Shaun?' Doug asked. 'At Mrs Farrell's house?'

Shaun closed his eyes for a few moments. 'Yes. All right, yes it was me. I did a bit of gardening for her.'

'And you lied to us about not knowing her.'

'Wouldn't you have?' Shaun demanded. 'If you'd been me, under arrest and told your trainers had been dug up from the victim's garden. With her blood on them. Well, wouldn't you?'

Swift leaned forward. 'Shaun, there's a lot to be said for the truth.'

Shaun leaned his chin on his hands and closed his eyes.

'When did you first meet Moira Farrell?' Doug asked.

'Back in October, last year. I delivered a new pump for the boiler to her house. She was in the garden as I came down the drive. Digging away, she was. She came to meet me to show me where to put the pump. We kind of got talking about the garden. She mentioned that their gardener was off sick and that digging was back-breaking work, and I said I'd help out with the roses, if she liked.'

'OK. And how many times did you help out?'

'A couple of Sundays. It brought in a nice bit of extra money.' He paused. 'And I enjoyed the work. She was good to work for. Friendly, but didn't interfere.'

'Did you meet her husband?'

'No. I never saw him.'

'Tell us about the trainers.' Doug said. 'The ones with the mud and Mrs Farrell's blood on them.'

Shaun winced. 'I must have left them there, after I finished the job.'

'Come on, you can do better than that,' Swift said. 'You must have been thinking about it, Shaun. Crucial evidence that could have got you charged, maybe convicted.'

'Yeah, yeah. I've thought about it. I remember changing out of them, before I got in to drive the van on the last day I was there. I'd worn them to drive in before and the mud got all over the place.'

'So what happened to them, Shaun?'

'I just don't remember. Maybe I put them on the roof whilst I put the other trainers on, and they dropped off when I set off. Or maybe I left them on the drive.'

'So what happened to them after that?'

'Dunno.'

'What's your guess?'

'Someone must have found them and picked them up, I suppose.'

'Who?'

'Well, Mrs Farrell, most likely. She'd have gone out to look at the work I'd done after I'd gone, the punters always do that. She'd have seen them, wouldn't she?'

'And what would have happened then?'

'I'm not a bloody psychic,' Shaun snapped, becoming rattled and irritated.

'If Mrs Farrell had found your trainers,' Swift persisted, 'what would she have done with them?'

Shaun frowned, looking cornered and edgy. Imagination wasn't his strong point.

'Would she have left them on the drive?' Swift asked.

'No.'

'Why not?'

'She seemed like a careful sort.'

'So?' Swift wasn't letting him off the hook.

'She'd have picked them up and put them somewhere safe.'

'Like where?'

'Somewhere inside where they wouldn't get wet.'

'Did you go inside the house?'

'No.' The answer came without hesitation. Shaun recalled that it was one of the questions he had been given in the lie detector test. One of the easier ones.

Swift leaned back, letting his arms hang loosely by his side. 'That's fine, Shaun.'

Shaun frowned. 'What?'

'You're free to go.'

'Is that it?' Disbelief blazed from his eyes.

'For now, yes.'

'Right.' He stood up, a pale, insignificant-looking man, stooping as though he had the world on his shoulders. He started to head for the door.

'Stay around where we can contact you, Shaun,' Swift said.

Shaun grimaced. 'Don't worry, once I get my head down on the pillow I won't be going anywhere at all.'

'Well, well,' Doug said, as the door closed behind their former prime suspect.

'What are you thinking?' Swift asked, gathering up his notes.

'I'm thinking, do we have anyone in the frame at all now? I'm thinking, what will Ice Man say when he hears what's been going on today. And I'm wondering what you're thinking.' Doug thought some more. 'And by the way, am I right in thinking you put some store by the information from the lie detector?'

'From what I've gathered, respondents can't fool the lie detector as it were. But they can block it by deliberately creating some kind of pseudo-emotional response to each question.'

'Like?'

'Like clenching toes or anal muscles.'

Doug made a grimace of distaste.

'They could create the same effect by clenching something more obviously visible, but that would rather give the game away,' Swift elaborated. 'The main thing is that by creating tension in the body they can cause a measurable response to show on the monitor. And if it they do that in response to every question then no differences will be registered between any of the responses. That would suggest that the respondents are either equally upset by all the questions — which is unlikely, given that a proportion of them are in no way contentious — or they're lying every time.'

'So basically the test would be invalid.'

'That's right. Now, on Shaun's response sheet, the detector shows very little nervous activity for any of the questions except that of ever having visited Moira Farrell's premises, and of previously knowing her prior to the meeting in the hospital. Both of which he had previously lied about. But when asked directly if he had killed her his answer was given instantly and the line on the monitor remained steady, no jumps or even a tremor.'

'You're convinced?' Doug asked. 'Convinced Busfield isn't our man?'

Swift squared the collected papers and aligned them against the desk top. 'Convinced is one of those worrying words like never.'

'Almost convinced,' Doug said, holding the door open for his boss.

'That's probably more like it. Although I should be praying I'm right, because by the time the *Echo* next goes to press the rest of the county and probably far beyond are going to believe that Shaun Busfield is innocent.'

'And we could be looking pretty red-faced to have let him go for a second time.' Doug closed the door with a gentle click.

★ ★ ★

Laura pulled her car up at the address printed on Jayne Arnold's business card. Her home turned out to be an apartment on the second floor of a high Georgian house just a stone's throw from the town centre of Ilkley. From the large windows facing the street there were glimpses over the tree tops to the sky above. Like Laura's own flat the main room combined kitchen and sitting/dining areas, but the proportions of the room were twice those of Laura's and the décor had a style and individuality which had Laura drawing in a tiny breath of envy. Cylindrical cushions with tassels, Buddha sculptures, a round mirror with a huge gilded sunburst frame.

'I like to mix periods and style,' Jayne said, bringing mugs of tea from the kitchen and observing Laura's interested inspection of her pad.

She sat down and smiled at Laura. Today she was wearing a tiny grey skirt and a chunky grey cardigan with black leather trimming. Her legs and feet were bare, tanned to a gentle gold which Laura guessed had not come from the Yorkshire winter sun. 'What do you want to know?' she asked pleasantly.

Laura snapped herself back into full detective mode. 'I'd like to check on the time of your flight from Prague on the day Moira died.' She consulted her notebook. 'On the first occasion I spoke with you and your mother you said that you got a flight as soon as your mother telephoned with the news.'

'Yes,' Jayne said slowly.

'When did your mother phone with the news?'

'Mid morning. Shortly after the police had visited to tell her about Moira's death.'

'The airline's records show that you cancelled your original booking to return the following day, and booked a flight for that afternoon.'

Jayne moved her hips slightly and then crossed her legs. She nodded agreement.

'But the boarding list in the flight manifests doesn't show you on that flight,' Laura said. 'Although if we go back to the day before, January 15th, your name does appear on the boarding list for the afternoon flight. And we know that you went through passport control at Leeds-Bradford in the evening. The day before Moira died.'

'Oh dear.' Jayne said, her expression one of wistful remorse. She looked across at Laura. 'Don't look so forbidding.'

'Why did you need to lie, Jayne?'

'It was actually my mother who told you I was in Prague when Moira died,' Jayne pointed out politely.

'She did. But you freely confirmed that later on when we were talking on our own outside.'

Jayne sighed. 'I'm really sorry about this. Let me explain. I was on a hot weekend with a boyfriend whilst I was in Prague. My mother really liked this guy and she thought things might be getting serious between us. Unfortunately he and I had a big row and I decided to come home early. I didn't contact my mother or tell her about the break-up, and then when Moira was killed, it just didn't seem important to tell her . . . '

'So your mother was under the impression that you didn't come back to England until later on in the day when Moira died.'

'That's right.'

'And is she still under that illusion?'

'Yes. I know it's not very good to keep things from her, but I'll get around to telling her when the time's right. She's still very upset about Moira.'

'Will your boyfriend corroborate what you've told me?' Laura asked.

'Oh, yes, of course.' She picked up a notepad from the coffee table and wrote on it briefly. 'There, that's the number of his firm.'

In her car Laura called the number Jayne had given her.

There was an instant and crisp response, 'Lamming and Strong.'

Having verified that Liam Strong was in his office Laura drove around to his premises on the east side of the town. The board outside told Laura that Lamming and Strong were a firm of accountants. From his prominent place on the list of personnel she assumed Liam must be a partner.

He met her at the door of his office, a man

in his thirties with sandy-coloured hair and craggy features. On a scale of 1 to 10, Laura gave him an 8 for good looks. He gave her ID a cursory glance, smiled at her and invited her to sit down.

Laura explained that her team were investigating the murder of Mrs Moira Farrell. That she wanted to ask him some routine questions.

He seemed unperturbed. 'Fire away.'

'I believe you're a friend of Jayne Arnold,' Laura said.

His pale-blue eyes sharpened with interest. 'Friend,' he said. 'I'm not sure friendship describes what Jayne and I had together. But whatever it was we had, it's over. She dumped me.' He gave a rueful smile: desolation at the end of the relationship did not seem to be on his agenda.

'Were you with Jayne in Prague recently?'

'Yep. We went for a long weekend, but she got in a strop and walked out on me.'

'Do you know what she was in a strop about?'

He blew out a sighing breath through his lips. 'To be honest, no, I don't.'

'There must have been something that happened to make her leave suddenly,' Laura suggested.

'Well, for the record this is what happened.

We were having pre-dinner drinks at the bar in our hotel. She'd been moody ever since we arrived, not wanting to get up in the mornings, not really interested in any of the sightseeing we'd planned. Not really interested in me. I wondered if it was woman-type problems, PMT or whatever. To tell the truth I was getting a bit sick of the way she was carrying on; it was like being on holiday with a difficult teenager. So, while we were having our drinks, I tried to find out what was wrong. She just flipped. Said she never wanted to see me again and stormed out of the bar. Next thing I knew she was pulling her case across the foyer, heading for the waiting taxi outside.' He spread his hands. 'End of story.'

'Have you been in contact with her since?'

'No. And I don't think I will be in the future. No point flogging a dead horse.' He looked hard at Laura. 'Is Jayne a suspect — in your murder enquiry?'

'We have to investigate all possible leads in a murder enquiry,' Laura said.

'Oh, come on! Take the plum out of your mouth. She's a suspect, isn't she? Did she know this woman, Moira Farrell?'

'Yes, she did. Did she ever mention her name to you?'

'Not that I can remember.' His eyes were

now gleaming with speculation. 'When did the murder take place?'

'The morning of January 16th.'

'So Jayne could have been back in England in time to do the deed.' He took a little time to process the idea and his face began to darken with concern.

Laura stood up. 'So could a lot of other people,' she said. 'Thank you for your time, Mr Strong. You've been very helpful.'

Driving back to the station, Laura was unsure what to conclude from the interview with Jayne. She felt that Jayne's account of her deception had been plausible; moreover the reason for her leaving Prague had been spontaneously corroborated by Liam Strong. As she contemplated Laura recognized that on a personal level she really wanted to believe Jayne had been telling the truth. She wanted her to be blameless and innocent, in order that her own lack of thoroughness would not become general knowledge and be further compounded by having held up the investigation and the apprehension of Moira's killer. She recognized that the lead she had followed at the hospital from Cavanagh through to Anderson had been a false trail, and that Cavanagh was no more than a sleek, slippery red herring as far as Moira Farrell's death was concerned.

She knew she had to talk to the team about all this. She would even offer to lay her omission at the feet of Damian Finch. The latter thought and the prospect of its reality was so alarming that she distracted herself for the rest of the journey by wondering if a constable's salary would run to Buddha sculptures and a heavenly in-your-face mirror in a sunburst frame.

16

Swift phoned through to Damian Finch's office and requested his presence at a case review. He suggested that his advice as a senior officer would be valued. Though he seldom offered it to others, Finch was not averse to flattery. He requested the team's attendance in his office pronto. Swift smiled to himself, guessing that the superintendent felt more confident when fighting on his home patch.

Listening to Swift's account of what had been happening in the last few hours, Finch's facial expressions underwent a number of transformations, few of which were encouraging.

'I believe it's still January,' he commented as Swift finished speaking. 'Not April the first.'

No member of the team made a comment.

'So,' Finch continued, looking thunderous, 'it's not a joke that you want me to rejoice in hearing that we have dismissed our prime suspect for the second time. That a journalist has jumped the gun on us and taken it upon herself to set up a lie detector test whose results will entirely convince the gullible public. That you want me to fritter away our scant resources on a search of the victim's half-sister's flat in the face of virtually no hard evidence against her.' He stopped, stunned into silence by the staggering incompetence of his underlings.

'That was my suggestion, sir,' Laura said, aware of an annoying nerve flickering beneath her eye.

Finch rounded on her. 'Well, don't stop there, Constable. Defend yourself and your suggestion.'

'I'm very sorry, sir, about my failure to check Jayne Arnold's alibi as thoroughly as I should.' Laura braced herself.

'I'm glad to hear it,' Finch said.

'But having thought things through after my interview with Liam Strong, my opinion is that Jayne Arnold was in a highly emotional state during her visit in Prague. It was that high level of emotion that caused her to walk out on Strong and fly back to Britain.' She stopped, conscious of weaknesses in the argument she was trying to put forward.

'All very interesting,' Finch said. 'And I'm aware that modern training methods for our service include a certain amount of psychology.' He spoke the last word with transparent scorn. 'But how does all this navel-gazing connect up with Jayne Arnold's possible wish to kill her half-sister?'

'We don't know, sir. That's why we think a search of her flat would be useful. At least to eliminate her from our enquiries.'

'Which you would very much like, Constable, so as to feel exonerated from your initial sloppiness in checking out Jayne Arnold's alibi.'

Swift was about to intervene, but Laura, now she was in the thick of it, was gathering confidence. 'That is quite true, sir,' she said. 'But my main reason for suggesting a search is a genuine belief that Jayne Arnold might be a possible suspect. She lied about her flight from Prague. She lied about her whereabouts at the time of the murder. She was in a disturbed state just prior to the murder. She would have not have had to break in to the house, because she was known to Moira and Professor Patel.'

Finch pursed his lips and paid his constable the compliment of appearing to make a serious consideration of her points. 'I'm not sure it's enough,' he said eventually. He turned to Swift. 'What do you think, Ed?'

'On balance I think we should pursue Jayne Arnold further.'

Finch nodded, somewhat mollified by Swift's carefully considered approach. 'What had you in mind?'

'Another interview with Sylvia Farrell, with a view to discovering what had been bothering Jayne prior to Moira's death.'

'I see the sense in that. Entirely,' Finch said.

'And then I think a search should be carried out, with a view to finding the murder weapon, or any other evidence which could be relevant.'

'I think I could manage to summon up a little happiness regarding that strategy,' Finch said. He turned to Doug who had been sitting in attentive silence. 'And have you nothing to say, Constable Wilson?'

'I'm a man of few words, sir,' Doug said. 'I've agreed with all that's been said, so I didn't feel a need to speak.'

Swift gave an internal smile, experiencing a stab of satisfaction at the way his team had responded to the superintendent's barbs. Maybe Finch had got where he was because interview boards judged he would provide a good training ground for young officers learning how to handle irascible and self-important witnesses and suspects.

* * *

After the session with Finch, Swift sent his team home, then got into his car and drove to Sylvia Farrell's home. Walking up the drive towards the house he saw that the lights were on in the hallway and two cars parked close to the front door.

Sylvia Farrell did not appear pleased to see him. 'I have some of my family here for supper,' she said. 'This is not a good time.'

'I do need to speak to you,' he said. 'It won't take long.' The first true, the second open to doubt, he thought as he followed Sylvia down the hall and through into a small room furnished sparely with two armchairs, a desk and a small television. The room was obviously not often used; the central heating radiator was off and an unwelcoming chill hung in the atmosphere.

Sylvia waved him to a chair, but remained standing herself, as though poised for flight any moment.

'I'd like you to sit down,' Swift told her.

She looked at him for a moment and then sat. 'Well?'

'Mrs Farrell, we've been told by your daughter that she flew home earlier than we were initially informed.'

'I beg your pardon! Are you joking? I would have expected you to come here with news of my stepdaughter's murderer being apprehended. Not comments on my own daughter.'

'Your daughter lied to us, Mrs Farrell. She led us to believe that she was in Prague at the time of Moira's murder.'

'So?' The tone was pure ice.

'Whereas in fact she was at home and in the vicinity of Moira's house at the time Moira was killed.'

Sylvia closed her eyes. 'Oh, for goodness sake. You're not suggesting Jayne killed Moira? That is preposterous. And, frankly I'm not even going to waste time considering it.' She started to get up.

'Sit down, Mrs Farrell,' Swift told her. 'I'm not suggesting anything at this point. I'm simply aiming to gain further information in the light of what Jayne has told us.'

He knew she would not believe that. She would assume that they were treating Jayne as a suspect. His hope was that in getting her rattled she might make an attempt to defend her daughter and thus offer information which would not be forthcoming through direct questioning.

She replaced herself on the chair. 'Well, why don't you ask Jayne?'

'We have spoken to Jayne. She has no alibi for the time Moira was murdered.'

'Neither do the majority of the law-abiding people in this county,' Sylvia pointed out. 'A lack of alibi hardly brands Jayne as a murderess.'

'The majority of law-abiding people hasn't deliberately lied to the police in a murder investigation,' Swift pointed out. 'Nor have those people any known connection with Moira Farrell.'

'Very well,' Sylvia said with heavy resignation. 'I accept that you have a job to do. I also know that my daughter is not capable of killing anyone. Let alone her half-sister, for whom she had a good deal of respect and affection.' She breathed in deeply.

Swift waited.

'I must insist that you don't hound Jayne about this dreadful murder. Her health has not been good during the last year.'

Swift preserved a neutral expression, which made it clear to Sylvia that he was not impressed by ill health as an excuse for deception.

Sylvia began to elaborate. 'She had a miscarriage in the spring and then in August she had to have surgery because of persistent endometriosis. I don't know if you're aware of that condition, but it's a very distressing and painful one. Jayne has suffered with it for years, and eventually she decided that she couldn't take any more. So she had a hysterectomy which, as you will appreciate, is a tragedy for a young woman who might one day want a family.'

'I'm very sorry,' Swift said.

'Yes.' She turned wary eyes on him. 'Do you have children?' she asked.

'One daughter.'

She looked hard at him. 'It's not easy, is it?' she said softly. She raised her head and squared her shoulders. 'I think you should go now, Chief Inspector, and leave us in peace.'

Swift nodded and stood up. 'Did Moira offer Jayne any advice about her condition?' he asked. 'Medical advice?'

'It's possible. Jayne used to visit Moira occasionally. As I said, she had a great respect for her.' Sylvia was at the door now, holding it open. 'I hope I've been of help to you,' she said. 'Please feel free to let yourself out.'

Swift sat in his car, reviewing his shorthand in the notebook. He thought about conception and birth and death and began to see a link between Jayne and Moira's situations. He wondered whether to contact Finch and insist on a search warrant being issued for Jayne's flat. But then if they didn't find anything they could simply succeed in frightening her off. As it was she could be shaken when her mother telephoned her. Which she was probably doing right now. He sat in the darkness, drumming his fingers on the wheel. Above him the cold cloud-filled sky was blank and empty of moon and stars.

★　★　★

A few hours earlier, as Laura headed for the council car park in the market square so she could pop into the shops for something to eat, she had spotted Saul running down the steps from his office. Her heart gave a jolt of panic, and once again the fear of the consequences of her one night stand with him gripped her innards. Taking a breath to steady herself she swung the car into a space and went to the machine to get a short stay ticket, knowing from experience that it was not a good idea to risk getting on the wrong side of the traffic wardens.

A woman parked near the ticket machine was struggling to lift a number of bulging supermarket bags into the back of her Range Rover. She was hugely pregnant, hardly able to bend to pick up the bags.

Laura stepped forward. 'Hello! Let me help.'

'Oh, thanks!' The woman smiled gratefully. She had a pretty, delicate face which contrasted sharply with the waddling clumsiness of her swollen body.

Swivelling around from the Range Rover to reach another bag, Laura was suddenly aware of Saul loping into the park, his stride long and rangy.

As he registered her presence she saw his face freeze.

The pregnant woman turned and grinned at him with delight and relief. 'Hi, babe! You're late! As usual.'

A cannonball of feeling rolled through Laura's insides. She lifted the last bag into the car and smiled at the pregnant woman, glancing meaningfully at her enormous bump. 'Good luck!'

The woman smiled back. 'Thanks, and bless you!'

Without a glimmer Laura walked past the stunned-looking Saul. There was no curse bad enough for him.

In the car she struggled to steady the shocked thumping of her heart. Then after a few moments she fired the engine and eased the car out of its space then waited to turn into the traffic.

In her flat she went to the bathroom, feeling a sudden familiar grinding starting up deep inside her. Reaching between her legs with a tissue revealed firm evidence that she was not pregnant. She leaned back against the toilet seat, her nerves singing with relief.

Later on she cooked herself a mushroom omelette and poured a glass of wine. 'Time to grow up, Laura,' she told herself, speaking the words out loud. And very clear.

★　★　★

Swift drove to Jayne Arnold's flat. It was in darkness and there was no reply to his repeated ringing of the entry buzzer. He called the station for back-up, indicating that he was concerned about Jayne Arnold's state of mind and her situation. A female and a male uniform appeared within minutes. The female officer was able to manipulate the lock with a device which looked like a credit card. Swift had not seen this technique before but asked no questions.

As they entered the flat the intruder alarm went off, a piercing, relentless whine. 'Can you do something about that?' he asked the female officer.

Swift and the male officer went through the flat, calling out Jayne's name. There was no response. The flat was empty.

'Damn!' Swift murmured to himself, guessing the bird had got wind of trouble and flown. 'Might as well have a look around while we're here,' he told the male officer.

Their ears ringing with the shrill throb of the alarm, they began to open drawers and cupboards. After several ear-shattering minutes, a blissful silence fell. The female officer appeared at Swift's side. 'Need any help, sir?'

'Are you the station's technology wizard?' he asked her, as she started methodically going through the items in Jayne's delicate mahogany table on which the house phone stood.

'I've been on one or two courses,' she said.

'I didn't know our training division were up to such devious tricks.'

She glanced at him with a small smile.

'Times change,' he commented, reflecting on how old he must appear to twenty-something officers.

Their search continued but after an hour they had come up with nothing of interest or relevance.

'Should we start pulling up the floorboards?' the male officer asked.

'No.' Swift was mindful that they hadn't got a search warrant and were not acting within strictly laid-down guidelines. 'We'll leave it at that, for now anyway.'

'Do you think the suspect's removed anything likely to cause trouble, sir?'

'It's possible. It's also possible she's not in

possession of anything that might cause her trouble.'

As they closed up the flat and walked down the stairs to the street, he had a sudden bad feeling about the case, a sense of his own helplessness in moving it forward. He looked at his watch. It was coming up for 11 p.m. He'd had hardly anything to eat during the day. Not the best recipe for maintaining a positive outlook. He called in at a late-opening Chinese takeaway and purchased twice as much food as was his usual habit.

★ ★ ★

The phone woke him at 6 a.m. Pulling himself out of sleep, he pressed the receive button.

'Dad?'

He shot up into sitting position.

'It's OK, I'm not ill or anything. Sorry to wake you so early, but is it all right if I come home for a day or two?'

'Of course.' He waited.

'I've broken up with Jasper. It's difficult.' Her voice was shaky with feeling, she was on the verge of tears.

He took in a breath. 'Do you want me to come and fetch you?'

'Oh God, no! I'll get the train.'

'Get a taxi from the station. I'll pay.'

'I'll be fine, Dad. Don't worry.'

He offered no comment on the latter issue. 'Are you planning on coming this morning?'

'Yes. Can you leave a house key for me? I seem to have lost mine.'

'Naomi! Not again.'

'Sorry. Just leave a spare somewhere safe where I can find it.'

'Nowhere outside is safe,' he said patiently. 'I'll leave it buried in the earth by the rose tree nearest the front door.'

'Cunning,' she said.

'So is your average housebreaker.'

'How's your current case going?'

'Could be better.'

'I think I've heard that before,' she said. 'And by the way, Cat sends her love.'

He got up and went into the kitchen. As he filled and switched on the kettle, his thoughts were occupied with Naomi, and then moving on to Cat. And soon after that moving on to the dead Moira Farrell and her half-sister Jayne. It came to him that it would be pretty useful to have the skill of divination and find out just what Jayne Arnold was doing at this moment. He would try to talk to her this morning, get some sort of handle on what game she had been playing. Or maybe it had been nothing like a game.

Sitting in the train, Naomi watched the countryside roll by, the landscape a dull winter-grey, the vegetation sleeping until spring. Being dumped was the same as a physical assault, it made you feel as though you'd been thumped in the stomach. And being dumped by someone whom you were crazy about and at the same time knew was badly flawed, seemed especially desperate and horribly humiliating. He'd simply told her he didn't love her any more — just like that, no warning. He'd played it very gently and with a degree of pity which had scratched at her nerves. She knew she would cope; she wasn't a person who thought that love was forever — that was a lesson she'd learned when her mother had been snatched away by an act of fate. Time would go by and her hurting and humiliation would heal. But for now the shock of the break-up was scouring her stomach and churning in her guts. She needed to touch base. She needed her father.

Arriving home, she located the rose tree closest to the front door and found the key to the apartment wrapped in foil tucked close beside the stem at the point where it sank into the earth. There was something about this small success which made her smile. She was still smiling as she turned the key in the lock.

★ ★ ★

Swift had spent the last hour dealing with Sylvia Farrell's anxiety regarding the whereabouts of her daughter. She had telephoned him just after nine, her voice shaky with anxiety. 'Jayne's not at the flat,' she told him without preamble. 'And she's not answering her mobile.'

'When did you last see her?' Swift asked.

'Yesterday morning. She brought some items she'd got at the delicatessen. She stayed for coffee and left around eleven-thirty.'

'And when did you last speak to her on the phone?'

There was a pause. 'Yesterday evening.'

'Soon after I left your house?'

'Yes.'

'Did you tell her what we had talked about?'

'Of course!'

'Do you know where she was when she took the call?'

'No. She never bothers with her land line now, always uses her mobile. She could have been at home, I just don't know.'

Swift considered the new freedoms people

326

had been offered when mobile phones became more or less universal. Husbands and wives could be constantly contactable, and at the same time cheating. Sons and daughters likewise. And so on. Jayne could have been anywhere when Sylvia made her call.

'Did she give any indication of plans for visiting friends, or travelling?'

'No. In fact she said she'd be seeing me sometime today. She'd call to let me know what her plans were. What we might do together.'

'There's still time for her to do that,' Swift pointed out.

'Yes.' That one syllable was loaded with doubt and anxiety. 'Can't you do something about this?' Her tone had turned to challenge with a dash of reproach, which Swift guessed was related to the verbal exchanges they had had the previous evening.

'She doesn't qualify as a missing person. Not yet.'

'No, I understand.'

'Keep trying her phone,' Swift suggested.

'Yes.' There was a long pause.

'I'll get someone to go round to her flat,' Swift said. 'Check on the situation.'

'Oh!'

He could tell she was thinking that that might not be such good news as it sounded.

'Right. Well, thank you.' Another pause. 'I'm really very worried,' she burst out, and then the line clicked off.

Swift laid his phone on the desk. She was not the only one.

He went into the incident-room and updated the team on Sylvia's message. Doug and Laura were sent to visit the flat. Finch was apprised of the latest developments. He took a remarkably sanguine view. 'She's probably just off somewhere on a shopping spree,' he said. 'Or having her hair done, and whatever else modern young women spend their time and money on.'

Swift did not disagree.

'We've nothing on her, Ed,' Finch pointed out. 'Nothing of substance. Nothing to make me think I need to use precious funds to alert the nation's traffic teams, or have all the ports and trains and airports on alert.' He made it all sound faintly ridiculous.

Swift made his apologies and slipped away before the superintendent got into full flow about the scarcity of resources and the impossibility of his job.

★ ★ ★

'Dad?' Naomi's voice sounded odd. Just that one word and its trembling, questioning note made Swift's mouth go dry.

'Where are you?'

'At home.'

'You had a good journey?'

'Yes.'

'Is there a problem?' he asked.

'Yes.'

Things suddenly fell into place. 'Someone's there with you — a woman?'

'Yes.'

'I'm on my way.'

'You have to come on your own,' Naomi said ominously. 'Please don't — ' And then the connection was suddenly dead.

★　★　★

Swift drove through the morning traffic, his mind humming with a myriad of imagined horrors. He didn't think he was much good at speeding in traffic. He'd been on pursuits plenty of times, but in recent years he'd never been the one at the wheel. Going at fifty miles an hour on busy built-up streets with horizontal sleet pounding the windscreen was no joke.

Would Jayne Arnold hurt Naomi? Why should she do that? Whatever the answers to those questions he needed to call the station and alert them to what was happening. He drew the car to a halt on double yellow lines and took out his phone. Afterwards, as he nudged the car back into the traffic, he saw the blue and green stripes of a patrol car his rear-view mirror. Further on a second striped car pulled out in front of him. Traffic patrol working in tandem. He ground to a halt and punched the steering wheel with frustration.

A constable got out of the second car and took his time to stroll to Swift's window. He had his ID already pressed to the glass, but the constable was not for playing ball. He made a lazy gesture of winding with his forefinger. Swift took in a deep breath and pressed the switch to lower the window. 'DCI Swift,' he announced crisply.

The constable was not impressed. Swift reminded himself of the deep-rooted antipathy between uniform and plain clothes. Between anyone in the world and Traffic.

'Fifty miles an hour, sir,' the constable said with smug satisfaction. 'In bad weather conditions. Not a very good idea.'

'I'm in pursuit of a murder suspect,' Swift said flatly, trying to keep his temper.

'You were driving like a maniac,' the constable said. 'Sir.'

Swift got out of the car. 'And you're behaving like a pompous twit.' His fury was only just held in check.

The constable made a meal out of looking offended. He peered at Swift through narrowed eyes. 'I hope you haven't been drinking, sir.'

Swift reached out, grabbed the constable's jacket and rammed him hard against the car. As the man's cap tumbled into the grey sleet of the roadside, his partner began to get out of the car.

'I'm a DCI,' Swift shouted through the sleet. 'Just get back in the car.'

The officer speedily did as he was told and Swift turned to his captive who was now beginning to look alarmed. 'Listen hard, Constable, I'm getting back in my car and going on my way, and if you so much as twitch a muscle to try and stop me, you'll find yourself back pounding the streets on foot for the rest of your time in the police.'

The constable flinched and nodded.

Swift pulled out into the traffic, pressing his accelerator foot to the floor.

On reaching his apartment he pulled the car to a screeching halt and leapt out. The front door swung back and opened as he placed his key in the latch. Stepping inside he saw the hallway stretching out before him in half darkness.

Any consideration about his own safety in walking in blind was totally outweighed by his fear for Naomi. He tried to reassure himself that Jayne Arnold was unlikely to indulge in random violence. Her killing of Moira had surely been a spur of the moment surge of anger against someone who had been inflicting some sort of mental torture on her. He stood still for a few seconds, conscious of the dead silence around him. He moved forward, sick with apprehension at what he was going to find.

There were no lights on in the living-room. But in the gloom of a cloudy winter day he could see the scene with perfect clarity. Naomi, sitting in a straight-backed dining chair, trussed up like a dead bird, her eyes wide open with helplessness and fear. Jayne Arnold standing behind her, holding a pair of surgical scissors, their elongated points pressing into the skin of Naomi's throat.

'Hello, Dad,' Naomi said, raising a small but heroic smile.

'Hello,' He raised a smile back.

Jayne watched him with the still concentration of a cat.

'Jayne?' He offered her a welcome. He saw an evil demon of light in her eyes and understood that she was probably more mad than bad. His mind hurtled through what was to come; the endless questions to be asked, the gnarled cluster of motivation and psychiatric disturbance to be painstakingly unravelled. But now, there was this horrifying impasse to resolve.

'You seem to know quite a lot about me and my daughter,' he remarked, keeping his voice low and calm.

She neither confirmed nor contradicted him.

'If you used a private investigator they must have been very discreet.'

Jayne waited for a few seconds and then said, 'They've been watching you since you were assigned to Moira's case.'

'I see.' He kept quite still, kept his voice steady and soft. 'What is it you want, Jayne?' He gestured towards his daughter and then to her captor, to the whole grotesque tableau which Jayne had created. 'What is the point of this?'

Jayne drew in long breath and held it before she spoke. 'Haven't you worked it out yet, Detective Chief Inspector Swift?'

'Worked what out, Jayne?'

'What this is all about.'

'I talked to your mother yesterday evening,' he said, forcing his brain to work, move on from his initial theories, expand and develop them. And keep Jayne talking.

'Yes, she told me. I thought you were on to me.' The irises of her eyes swivelled. 'Maybe I was wrong. But most of the clues were there.'

'Put the scissors down, Jayne,' he said, 'and then we can talk.'

Jayne smiled at him in regretful disbelief. 'As if.' The point of the scissors pressed a little harder on Naomi's skin.

'You're hurting me, Jayne,' Naomi said.

Jayne relaxed the tension on the scissor points, just a fraction. 'I'm sorry. You're not the one I want to hurt,' she said.

'Who do you want to hurt?' Swift asked.

'You,' she said. 'Just at this moment, it's you I want to hurt. And the most effective way to do it, is to threaten your child.'

He was working things out. He came back at her without hesitation. 'Because the idea of a child is the most important thing in the world for you, isn't it, Jayne? The child you can't have.'

She listened and then she rounded on him. 'Christ! You're just like all the doctors and do-gooders — the GPs and the gynaecologists and the shrinks. You deal in ideas and motives and prognoses. You're all so sweetly understanding and dripping with sympathy. You all pity me for being barren. And in your hearts you despise me. You look down on me because you think I'm only half a woman.'

'Barren,' said Naomi. 'That's a good old-fashioned word.'

Jayne made a slight adjustment to the points of the scissors. 'Don't get clever with me, Naomi. You won't get round me that way.'

'Jayne,' Swift said, 'just tell me what you want, and we'll try to work something out.'

'What I want! What I *want*!' Her eyes flamed with rage. 'I want a baby. I want a baby of my own. A baby that has been conceived inside me, grown inside me, kicked inside me, made me blow up like a huge balloon. Made my breasts heavy and sore with milk.' She was screaming now, her face blotchy and livid as though she had been drinking. 'But I can never have that. Never, never, never!'

Naomi flinched. Swift saw her mouth frame the words, Oh, God. He tried to pull his gaze away from Jayne's fingers, holding the shiny steel, poising it to pierce Naomi's skin. For him at that moment Jayne was as lethal and unpredictable as a cobra.

It was vital to keep her talking. 'If you can't have a child of your own, there are children to adopt,' he said quietly, aiming to develop a dialogue on the only subject he guessed would appeal to her. But it was also a subject burning into her emotions, making her unstable and irrational. Talking to Jayne about babies and children was playing with live explosive.

'You got one of your own, didn't you?' she spat at him. 'Or rather your wife did. Did she have to go through years of pain and disappointment before she got pregnant?'

'No,' he said.

'You can't imagine how I feel,' she told him. 'You haven't a clue.'

'No,' he agreed.

'But you're suffering now,' she said, stroking a finger over Naomi's hair.

'Yes.' And how. He threw Naomi a quick glance, a look to assure her that everything would be all right. His innards heaved with anxiety.

Jayne gave him an appraisal through narrowed eyes. 'I've nothing against you,' she told him, 'as a person. But you're involved in my life now. You've almost worked out what happened that morning Moira was killed.' She waited. 'Haven't you?'

He said nothing for a few moments. 'Is that what you'd like to talk about, Jayne? Moira? Is talking about what happened to Moira one of the things you want?'

'Too easy,' she told him. 'I'm not so stupid as to fall for that. Once I've talked about what happened to Moira, I'll have lost my bargaining power.'

'What do you want to bargain for?' His mind raced. No arrest, no charge. Freedom

336

to hide out wherever she wanted. Would he set it up — in return for Naomi's safety? There was no doubt, no beat of hesitation.

'I'm not up for bargaining,' Jayne said. 'I'm enjoying this too much.' She seized a few strands of Naomi's hair and jerked her head back slightly. With her other hand she made sure the points of the scissors were still pressed against Naomi's throat. 'Power,' she said. 'Power takes away the pain.'

Naomi gave a tiny yelp of shock. She looked at her father and gave a brief, grim smile.

Jayne's expression had become glazed and fixed. 'Murder is easy,' she murmured dreamily, 'once you've done it the first time.'

Despite his anxiety for Naomi, Swift found himself seizing eagerly on the juicy morsel Jayne had just thrown him. His mind began to fit things together. He steadied himself. 'Did you ask Moira to give you one of her babies?' he asked in conversational tones.

'The white one,' Jayne said, with a devious glint. 'We'd done all our homework and got it all arranged. Moira would have the babies in a Swiss clinic, then on the way back to Britain she'd give the spare twin to me. She knew people who would do the necessary paperwork so the baby would appear to be mine — she was a clever and resourceful woman, my stepsister. And she'd take her little brown baby home to Rajesh, and he'd never know she'd been playing hooky with the hunky registrar on the gynaecology team.'

'And where would you and the baby go?'

'France or Spain. I've lots of friends in Europe.'

As Jayne spoke, Naomi's mouth had dropped open slightly, as she realized the level of psychological disturbance in this woman who had her in her power.

'And Rajesh would never guess what had been planned between you?' Swift asked, injecting a degree of disbelief into his voice.

'Rajesh was always working, or walking up mountains. He lived in his own private world,' Jayne said. 'He knew nothing of our little plot. Moira and me, having girlie chat sessions, putting our heads together and planning the most wicked and delicious adventure.'

Naomi made a little noise in her throat. 'What went wrong?' she croaked, her voice strangled by the pressure on her throat.

Jayne frowned. 'She changed her mind.' Her face crumpled. 'She decided she wasn't interested in our adventure any more. She wanted both her babies. She was going to tell Rajesh everything. She was going to *have* everything.'

There was long dead silence.

'She was pissing me about,' Jayne said with quiet venom. 'There were some scissors on Moira's desk. It only took one stab. It was so easy.' She glanced down at the scissors threatening Naomi's life. 'I've kept them with me ever since, just in case I should need them.'

Swift stood frozen and useless as the seconds passed. He estimated how long it would take to move forward and spring on Jayne. Too long to be confident that she would not have the opportunity to make a response.

Then, suddenly, there were footsteps in the hall. A woman's voice. 'Jayne? Are you in there? Are you all right? What's happening?'

Swift listened. So the station had managed to pass on his message for Sylvia. He had no idea what Jayne would do now her mother was here. But at least the present deadlock would be broken, the dynamics in the room would change in some way. 'In here,' he called out.

Sylvia appeared in the doorway. The blood left her face. 'Jayne!' she whispered. 'Jayne, what are you doing?'

'Go away, Mum!' Jayne shouted. 'Leave this to me. Just for once, leave things to me!'

Sylvia moved forward.

'Mum, stay back, I'm warning you.'

'Darling,' Sylvia said softly.

'No. I'm not your darling!' Jayne protested.

'Of course you are, and you always will be.'

'I'm not one of the two babies you lost,' Jayne spat back at her. 'They were your real darlings. I was just the replacement.'

'That's nonsense,' Sylvia said, as though crooning to a fractious infant. 'I always loved you just as much as the other babies.'

'They were the ones who lived inside you,' Jayne protested, tears glistening on her eyelashes. 'Flesh of your flesh. Blood babies — '

'I love you, Jayne,' Sylvia said. 'I could never have wished for a better daughter than you.'

'People say it doesn't matter,' Jayne said, impatiently. 'That blood connections aren't important. But those are the people who have blood connections with their parents, who know where they came from. They take it for granted. They pretend it doesn't matter, but it does.'

Sylvia's face was contorted with pain. 'I have never stopped you from finding your birth parents, Jayne.'

'But I couldn't find them! They were both dead by the time I started looking.' She was shaking with despair.

Sylvia started to speak again.

'Don't!' Jayne shrieked, beside herself. 'You know nothing of what I'm going through. You knew what it was like to have babies and to give birth. But I could never have that, the one thing that could have compensated for never knowing my blood parents. I couldn't have a blood child of my own, I could only have Moira's spare, her little cast off. And even that was taken away from me.' Her hand was trembling, pressing the points of the scissors harder against Naomi's skin. Her eyes turned to dark slits. 'The bitch, she deserved to die.'

Suddenly Naomi screamed: a shrill cry for her life. Its raw power ripped through the room like an electric charge. And then the air was filled with sounds and movement. Sylvia darted forward, calling out Jayne's name with the firm maternal authority of a mother instructing a young child to obey her. Jayne responded with the instant obedience of a scared kid, taking her hands off Naomi, letting the scissors drop to the floor.

Swift ran to Naomi, encircling her in his arms, dropping down beside her, imprisoning the scissors with his knee. Jayne sprang away from her parent, and raced for the door.

Swift was tempted to let her go. But no, that would be too easy for her. Moreover

Jayne was dangerous. As Sylvia Farrell moved forward and began struggling to free Naomi from the blue nylon rope which still bound her, he pursued Jayne out of the apartment and down the drive. She was a quick mover, and he was hard pressed to gain on her. On reaching her car which was parked in the road outside, she began fumbling with the lock, her desperation making her frantic and clumsy. He saw that she had no keys on her, that her means of a getaway were no more than a fantasy.

She sank down to her knees, defeated, all the rage temporarily knocked out of her.

Swift telephoned for back-up, whilst Jayne turned to look at him, her arms slowly raising in surrender.

17

Late afternoon sun slanted into Damian Finch's office. On his desk lay a word-processed statement.

Jayne Arnold had become quiet and rational on reaching the station. She had freely agreed to making a confession under caution. She had seen the forensic physician. Psychological and psychiatric reports had been requested.

'I'd feared we might find ourselves in a situation where a good lawyer might have persuaded her to retract,' Finch had told the team, prowling as ever behind his desk. He glanced up for a response, but no one spoke. 'I know,' he continued, 'ever the pessimist, that's what my wife calls me. Don't think I'm not aware of my failings.' He pondered for a moment. 'Can anyone please explain to me how a woman like Moira Farrell would agree to give up a baby to another woman?'

There was a short silence.

'Raging hormones, sir?' Laura suggested with perfect seriousness.

Finch blinked and cleared his throat. 'Really.' He sat down heavily at his desk and plucked at the sheaf of papers lying on its top.

Swift glanced at his colleagues who took the hint and followed him as he went quietly through the door.

'I wonder how long she'll go down for,' Doug said, in the more relaxed atmosphere of the CID room. 'I've seen it so many times before. These shrink guys know how to paint a villain as mad rather than bad.'

He and Laura looked towards Swift for a response. The DCI was staring into space, his face grey with fatigue. Privately he was reflecting on the way his skin had crawled as Jayne sat talking to him in the interview room, repeating her story in almost exactly the same phrases which she had screamed at him earlier. But this time her voice had been low and steady, her eyes cold and pitiless.

'Do you think Jayne Arnold's mad, sir?' Doug prompted gently.

'I'm not a psychologist,' Swift said diplomatically. 'But for what it's worth I think she's made up her mind that she'd like us to think she is. She's sharp enough to know a psychiatric diagnosis would get her a more lenient sentence.'

'Diminished responsibility,' Laura commented.

Swift nodded. 'But mad or bad, she'll be put behind bars.'

The three of them sat in solemn contemplation for a few moments. The room had an air of quiet desertion: with the news of the confession and the bringing of a charge the place had emptied as the rest of the staff removed themselves to the pub. But Swift had been reluctant to join the celebrations and his companion officers were reluctant to leave him on his own.

'You were a hero this morning, sir,' Laura told Swift.

'Seconded,' Doug said.

Swift looked from one to the other. 'So would you have been,' he said. 'If you'd been there at the time.'

'Is your daughter all right, boss?' Doug asked.

'She's doesn't crumble easily. She'll get through this.' He glanced at his watch and stood up abruptly. 'She's still at the hospital having a check over. I need to collect her.' There was a brief farewell nod, and then he was gone.

Laura watched him disappear through the door. 'Will *he* get through it, though?'

Doug gave a smile based on long experience. 'You've done enough fretting and pondering for the time being, Detective Constable Ferguson from Glasgow. I'm taking you for a drink.'

* ★ ★

The next day, reassured that Naomi was quite capable of pottering around the apartment on her own for the morning, Swift went into work and was surprised to see there had been a message left for him by Serena Fox, asking him if he would call to see her at his earliest convenience.

She answered the door before he had even rung the bell. Her welcome was unsmiling but she instantly invited him in. 'I need to talk to you,' she said tersely. Today her dress was a swirl of dark-blue cotton printed with vivid yellow parrots. Long silver ear-rings dangled from her ears almost brushing her shoulders and swinging slightly as she preceded him down the hallway and into her study.

'Sylvia Farrell came see me last night,' she said, swinging around to face him.

Swift had hardly had time to get through the doorway. Thick bands of winter sunshine flooded the room and pale dust particles swirled in the draughts from the tall sash windows. 'So, you're in the picture of what has been happening?'

'I'm in the picture according to Sylvia,' Serena Fox said drily. 'Which is probably more reliable than the picture according to Jayne Arnold.'

'You know that Jayne has been charged with Moira Farrell's murder?'

'Yes. And I know what happened yesterday at your house — the threats to your daughter. It must have been a traumatic experience.'

'Naomi's strong,' he said firmly. 'Tell me about Sylvia.'

Serena pulled thoughtfully on one of her long ear-rings. 'I've known Sylvia Farrell for some time. She first came to see me about eight years ago, ostensibly for a problem of her own, but it soon turned out that the focus of her anxiety was her daughter Jayne.'

Swift stopped her there. 'So — at that time Jayne would have been in her late teens.'

'She was eighteen, about to go to college to study interior design.'

'And Sylvia was at that time planning to marry Farrell?'

'That's right. They'd just got engaged. And Jayne had been extremely reluctant to accept the marriage. She became very hostile and abusive to her mother. She refused to go to college and then ran off to Spain with one of her dead father's married friends, leaving Sylvia with just a scribbled note to say she was going abroad. Not exactly an uncommon kind of story, but it was all very upsetting.'

'How long was she away?'

'No more than ten days. Jayne is volatile

and unstable, she finds it hard to make commitments.'

'That fits.'

'There was some kind of reconciliation with Sylvia and Jayne agreed to come for sessions with me.' She stopped.

'Medical confidentiality?' Swift suggested drily.

Serena gave a tight smile. 'The focus was on her feelings of being an adopted child. And the distress of finding out that she was suffering from severe endometriosis. I'm assuming you already know about this as I gather Sylvia gave you quite a bit of information.'

'That's correct.' Swift looked across to her. 'Why are you telling me all this, Serena?'

There was a beat of silence. 'Because I want to clear any stain on Moira's memory. For her sake, for Rajesh, for you, for anyone who knew her.'

'Go on.'

'When I was treating Jayne I had access to reports from a child psychiatrist who had seen her at the age of fourteen. There had been difficulties at her school for some time. She was known to be a persistent liar — or fantasist as we in the psychological business prefer to call it. In other words she found it hard to distinguish between reality and invention, always producing the version of an event which suited her own purposes. Clearly this had a significant effect on relationships she made with both male and female friends, and inevitably led to rejections. The money she inherited from her grandparents made her independent and meant she had no need to work, which I believe made her life devoid of purpose.'

'Thus the need for a child became overwhelming.'

'Yes. But thank God she never had one,' Serena Fox said with a rare display of feeling.

Swift raised his eyebrows.

'She's a narcissist. She thinks only of herself. I doubt she could ever meet the demands of a baby — either physical and psychological. In fact . . . '

Swift felt himself stiffen.

'In fact I would have been very worried for any child she had the care of. When she was thirteen she killed a Siamese kitten she had begged her mother to buy for her. It had put its claws through a new cashmere sweater so she stabbed it with an old razor she found in her father's bathroom cupboard. The matter was all hushed up, but Sylvia eventually told the story to Jayne's child psychiatrist as she was so worried about Jayne's development.'

'Where is the link with any stain on

Moira's memory?' Swift asked.

'As you know Jayne is superlatively skilled at putting on a good front when it pleases her. She's convinced a good many quite perceptive people with her lies. When I heard Sylvia's version of what Jayne had said regarding the plans which Moira and she were alleged to have cooked up together I was horrified. Moira would never have agreed to give away either of her babies.'

'Did Moira talk to you about this?' Swift interposed sharply.

Serena did not flinch. 'No. And that is the truth. She talked to me about her work.' She hesitated. 'There were concerns about a colleague — it was all rather sensitive.'

'We know about those concerns,' Swift told her.

'Right.' She frowned and put her hand up to stroke an ear-ring. 'She told me nothing of having an affair. She simply said she was having twins. She seemed secure and happy about the future and the pregnancy seemed to be going well.'

Swift wondered if Dr Fox was lying to defend her dead friend. Or maybe it had been Moira who had been the manipulator, concealing the truth from Serena. Or perhaps Serena Fox, despite her professional experience, was being surprisingly naïve. It struck him that her profession, like his, was heavily based on making decisions about the likely truth of what they were told. They were all capable of getting things wrong, even the most canny and experienced. 'Why did you ask me to come here this morning?' he asked.

She hesitated. 'It's Rajesh I'm worried about. I don't ever want him to hear the story Jayne fabricated about Moira's plans to give a baby away. He would torture himself for the rest of his life wondering whether it was true or not.'

'But we don't know the whole truth about that, do we? And maybe we never will.'

'No.' Serena frowned impatiently and he could tell she didn't welcome being challenged. 'But I have no hesitation in saying that I believe Jayne's version to be a fabrication. Moira never gave any intimation to me about some sort of deal with Jayne.'

Swift said nothing, but his sceptical expression spurred Serena on.

'Moira and I were close friends,' she protested. 'It was not in her nature or her personality to make such an arrangement. Let alone renege on it. And, besides, she was well aware of Jayne's disturbed personality. She would never have given her the care of a child.'

'It's possible that your conviction on the issue might well be coloured by your friendship with Moira,' Swift reminded her. 'You said yourself when we first spoke that you had reservations about taking her on in a clinical capacity.'

Serena's eyes became steely. 'In my view, and I'm speaking professionally now, Jayne displays all the classic signs of a sociopath, someone quite capable of killing her stepsister on impulse simply through jealousy of her happiness in expecting not one child but two.'

'Did you invite me here and tell me all this in the hope that I would act as a messenger between you and Rajesh?' Swift asked.

Serena pressed her lips together.

'If you want to talk to Rajesh in the capacity of a friend,' he said, 'that is up to you, Dr Fox.'

'Are you advising me to leave well alone?' she asked.

'It's not my job to advise you,' he said evenly.

She considered. She closed her eyes briefly. 'No, you're right.' As she put up a hand once more to stroke one of her ear-rings he saw that her fingers trembled with apprehension.

★ ★ ★

When Swift called to speak to Rajesh Patel later on, he found the house in darkness. For a moment he was gripped with a surge of anxiety, concerned that Patel had decided against serving his life sentence of loss and horror following his wife's murder, that he had taken himself for a long walk up one of the Yorkshire peaks, deliberately straying from the charted trails and simply losing himself.

In answer to his ring at the front door, there was a long delay and then a light went on in the hall. Rajesh appeared, blinking in the brightness, as though he had just wakened from sleep. 'Chief Inspector. Come in.'

'I'm sorry if I disturbed you,' Swift said.

'No need to apologize.' He led the way into the darkness of the kitchen and turned on the lights.

Swift noticed that although Rajesh Patel looked drowsy and relaxed, he was still fully dressed, so maybe he had not been to bed, merely taking a nap. 'Would you like a drink?' Patel asked courteously.

Swift shook his head. 'There are some further issues connected with Jayne's confession that I need to talk to you about,' he said gently.

Rajesh remained perfectly calm. 'She was here quite a lot, you know, at the house. Visiting Moira. They seemed to have become quite good friends,' he said, surprising Swift and throwing him temporarily off track.

'When was this?' he asked.

'Oh, in the last few weeks.'

Swift wondered if he had failed in appreciating what a complex man Rajesh was. 'You never mentioned that in your various statements,' he pointed out.

Rajesh gave a weary smile. 'Why should I? Jayne was part of our family.' He bowed his head for a few moments. 'I had a visit from Sylvia earlier on today. She told me some rather disturbing things. She told me she would rather tell me herself than have me find out some other way. She's a very brave woman.'

Swift said nothing, deciding that nothing Rajesh would tell him could any longer surprise him.

'Jayne incriminated that poor man Busfield,' Rajesh reflected. 'She put Moira's blood on his shoes and then she planted them in the garden.'

'Yes. She admitted to it in questioning.'

Rajesh shook his head in sorrow. Silence filled the room and stretched on.

'Moira would have known, you see,' Rajesh said reflectively. 'She would have known the possibilities of two of her eggs being fertilized by different sperms. She would have known that during the short space of time in which her ova were released and were then no longer viable, it was quite possible for the two of them to be fertilized by sperm from different men.'

Swift found it disturbing to watch this contained man rubbing the salt into his already agonizing wounds, mutely considering the image of Moira sleeping with her husband and another man in a very short space of time.

'She would have been aware that the babies would be of different ethnic groups,' Rajesh said. 'That does rather limit the chances of passing off another man's child as one belonging to your husband.'

Swift made no comment.

'So she found an escape route in Jayne. And presumably a wonderful way of making her happy. That is very like Moira. But then to decide to disappoint her . . . '

'And thus to end all deception regarding yourself,' Swift said, regretting the clumsy inadequacy of the words as he uttered them.

'Yes. Honesty was typical of Moira too. But in this particular matter she seems to have been acting out of character in respect of both honesty and trust. And simple kindness.'

'She was facing some very hard decisions,' Swift said.

'Indeed.' He looked gravely into Swift's face. 'And later on I had a visit from Serena

Fox. And I heard an account that was rather different.' There was a silence. 'So now — I have to choose what to believe.'

Swift watched the other man's face, at a loss to find words to convey his sympathy for this man who faced an eternity of unanswered questions.

Rajesh sighed. 'There is no way of making this tragedy smell sweet,' he said.

'No.'

Rajesh rose slowly to his feet. 'I appreciate your coming,' he told Swift. 'And your openness and humanity. But now I'd like you to leave. I shall be quite all right on my own. I've braced myself for the years ahead. I shall not shun my life sentence through suicide. You can depend on me, I'm as immovable as the rock within the Dales hills as far as stoicism is concerned.' He gave a faint, wry smile. 'Stoicism used to be highly thought of,' he commented. 'Once.'

18

It was some weeks later and Cat Fallon had come down from Durham for her interview with North Yorkshire Police. She decided to stay over for the weekend and on the Friday evening Swift took her and Naomi to one of Bradford's family run Kashmiri restaurants which had earned itself a national reputation over the years. Once a tiny shop-like café, it had expanded and cloaked itself in an aura of glamour which managed to embrace both eastern and western cultures.

'Flash place, this,' Cat commented, looking around at the marble flooring and the vivid-coloured leather sofas which stood against the walls.

'Wait 'til you taste the food,' Naomi told her. I'm having lamb karahi bouna. And nan bread. You should see those nans, they're the size of Scotland.'

As they ate, Cat fed them little bites of information about her interview earlier in the day. It appeared that Damian Finch had been on the interview panel. 'Interesting guy,' she commented. 'It was quite a relief when he was doing the questioning.'

Swift took a sip his cranberry juice. 'Really — how come?'

'He'd ask a question and then seem happy to do most of the answering himself.'

Swift smiled. 'That sounds like Damian.'

'Very keen on budgets,' Cat reflected.

Swift was still smiling. 'Sounds as though he was running true to form.'

'I've got a feeling I might get offered this job,' Cat said.

Naomi replaced her glass on the table; she was on pomegranate juice. 'A detective's hunch?' she queried. 'They're often right,' she said, glancing at her father.

'Yeah,' Cat agreed. 'Let's hope so.'

'You'll be needing a place around here,' Naomi said. 'We'll help you find somewhere.' She slid one of her spiky glances at her parent.

Cat noticed and threw him a glance of her own.

Swift knew that he was under some sort of siege. His feelings for Cat had been steadily growing over the last few weeks. He had found himself recalling the way she had helped him through those difficult days when Naomi had slipped off the rails, Cat's instinctive warmth, coupled with a fine appreciation of how to keep her distance. He recalled too the warmth of her greeting when she arrived in Yorkshire the previous evening, the slight pressure of her lips, slightly opening as she kissed him. And he knew that keeping a distance was no longer what he wanted as far as Cat was concerned.

As for Naomi, she was clearly a driving force behind any womanly plot to capture his heart. Not that he thought for a moment that Cat had been plotting. He loaded his fork with aubergine curry, devoting himself to the pleasure of the food for a few moments, trying to forget the feelings of terror during those hellish minutes when Naomi had been in horrifying danger from Jayne Arnold. She had emerged unscathed physically, but he knew that the incident had left mental scars. She had started coming home quite frequently at the weekends, seeking the comfort and refuge of home, and presumably his company, support and protection.

She was young, he told himself. She would, as the psychologists say, work through it and achieve closure. And he suspected Cat would be there alongside him to help along the way. With that thought came a gentle glow of inner warmth which did not spring from the spiciness of the lamb. So now, there was just the question of the job to consider. There was a post coming up in research and policy development. A desk job — and he was wondering about it.

A shadow fell across the table. 'DCI Swift! Hi! How're tricks?'

He looked up and saw the foxy face of Georgie Tyson. She was with her friend Barbara who stood a pace or two behind her, assuming a tactfully disinterested expression regarding whatever verbal interchange was about to take place.

Swift stood up and introduced his companions, to whom Georgie threw a brief nod, before turning back to Swift. 'So you got your man,' she said. 'Or woman rather.'

'We did.'

She waited, her eyes hungry for any morsel he might toss her. 'Your press officer was rather minimal with details.'

'We have procedures to follow,' he said.

'Yeah, yeah. But I guess there's a whole lot more to what murderer Jayne and victim Moira got up to than the line we've been fed.'

'I guess,' he agreed.

'We're going to have wait until the court case apparently.' She shook her head in mock despair. 'But, of course, if she's decided to plead guilty, then there'll just be the sentencing to consider.'

'Quite,' he agreed.

'Whatever, it's going to make good copy,' she said, ever optimistic.

'Do you really expect me to say something off the cuff?' he asked.

Georgie grinned. 'It's always worth a try.'

'Go and fish somewhere else,' Swift told her amiably. 'I'm sure you know plenty of other ponds where there's mud to stir.'

'I surrender.' She grinned broadly. 'I'm pretty skilled at getting blood out of stones, but you're more like bloody Stonehenge. Ah well — I'm sure we'll be doing further business together in the future, Chief Inspector. Have a nice evening.' With a wink and a coy tilt of her head she turned away and she and Barbara moved off.

'Nice girl!' Cat said.

'I don't know how you do it, Dad?' Naomi commented.

'What?'

'Put on that inscrutable act as if you're one of the guardsmen on sentry duty in Horse Guards Parade.'

'Now, maybe that's a job that would suit me,' he said.

Naomi and Cat smiled at him with knowing fondness.

He smiled back. I might surprise them, he thought.

I might surprise myself.

★ ★ ★

Rajesh Patel parked his car in the lower park at the foot of Skiddaw. In the low-lying fields surrounding the mountain tiny remnants of crusty-looking snow clung to those crevices in the walls where the sun could never penetrate. On the drive up from Yorkshire he had seen the crocuses at the roadsides of the villages dying back and the daffodils beginning. The air smelled of damp earth and a mingle of prickling scents which heralded the imminent regeneration of spring.

He had climbed six peaks since Moira's death, one each weekend. Skiddaw, today, would provide a good stretch of the legs, even though he intended to go easy on himself this morning, and take the unchallenging tourist route up the mountain. The weeks of grief had taught him humility: the ability to come to terms with the pointlessness of constantly pushing himself to the limit.

In the future there was the challenge of meeting with Moira's family again to face. Of confronting Sylvia's own life-sentence of distress, maybe even seeing Jayne and trying to make sense of what had been driving her. They were both victims, rather like him. But not like Moira. Oh, Moira! He paused in his walk to the foot of the mountain, closing his eyes at the thought of her punishing fate: the ultimate price.

Bringing himself back to the here and now he began moving forward again, his gaze moving upwards to the massive flank of the mountain and its as yet hidden summit.

We do hope that you have enjoyed reading this large print book.

Did you know that all of our titles are available for purchase?

We publish a wide range of high quality large print books including:
Romances, Mysteries, Classics
General Fiction
Non Fiction and Westerns

Special interest titles available in large print are:
The Little Oxford Dictionary
Music Book
Song Book
Hymn Book
Service Book

Also available from us courtesy of Oxford University Press:
Young Readers' Dictionary
(large print edition)
Young Readers' Thesaurus
(large print edition)

For further information or a free brochure, please contact us at:
Ulverscroft Large Print Books Ltd.,
The Green, Bradgate Road, Anstey,
Leicester, LE7 7FU, England.
Tel: (00 44) **0116 236 4325**
Fax: (00 44) **0116 234 0205**

RETRIBUTION

Angela Dracup

When businessman Jack Wells is found battered to death in his workshop, skeletons begin to rattle in the family cupboard as DCI Ed Swift investigates. Jack's widow Sheila, however, points the finger of suspicion at Tamzin Crowther, a self-styled white witch. Whilst Swift must act on the strength of the forensic evidence mounting against Tamzin, he senses that the real killer is still free. Things take a sinister turn when Swift is assaulted outside his home — an attack that sounds a warning against his continued probing into the dead man's family — and the chilling and unexpected motive is revealed.

WHERE DARKNESS BEGINS

Angela Dracup

When the body of a teenage girl is found in a Yorkshire quarry, evidence points to the senile old farmer who discovered her. But DCI Ed Swift is not convinced . . . His superintendent is desperate to get the case sewn up and Swift is in a race against time to find the real killer. His investigation points to the possible guilt of three people and Swift faces a tangle of lies and deceit to uncover an act of evil which has destroyed the life of more than one young person. And then he must find the proof . . .

A KIND OF JUSTICE

Angela Dracup

Josie Parker is found drowned in the bath on her wedding night. The circumstances indicate murder and DCI Ed Swift is forced to regard the distraught bride-groom, Jamie, as chief suspect. But Jamie claims to have lost all recall of the time leading up to his bride's death. When Swift investigates the family dynamics of the newlyweds he uncovers a shocking trail of deceit and treachery. Then Swift takes Jamie back to the scene of the crime and the young widower recaptures his buried memories. Swift must reveal the truth behind Josie's killing if justice is, finally, to be done.

THE ULTIMATE GIFT

Angela Dracup

Following a heart transplant, Kay becomes disturbed by a menacing and recurring dream. Convinced that her new heart is carrying messages from its previous owner, she determines to discover the truth about his death. When she finally meets the donor's family, Kay is horrified to find herself triggering off further heartbreak in their lives. However, the charismatic family head, Majid, agrees to help her unearth the dark secret that marked the end of his cousin's life. But as she discovers the shocking truth, Kay finds herself in terrifying danger. Will the donor's killer seek to put a final end to the heart that survived?

DYING TO KNOW YOU

John Paxton Sheriff

When freelance photographer Penny Lane discovers a dead body on Hoylake beach she makes a terrible error of judgement. Now she must put matters right. Her overnight transformation from photographer to amateur private eye is easy, but the body count increases frighteningly, and tracking down the killer is difficult. Encouraged by her crime writer husband Josh, she finds herself at odds with the police, and rubs shoulders with villains in seedy Liverpool nightclubs. As Penny follows a trail that rakes up the past and shows her a menacing future, she's led to an unexpected and shockingly brutal success.

CHEATED HEARTS

Jane McLoughlin

Lucy Drake and Sue Stockland know nothing of each other's existence, yet both are in love with Paul Meyer. However, when Paul is found dead from a heroin overdose in a Soho alley, his connections to gang boss Big Saul Kramer cause Police Inspector Guy Dugdale to suspect murder. Lucy and Sue find out about their lover's double life and both tell Dugdale that the other is Paul's killer — then find themselves romantically drawn to the policeman. But Paul's estranged wife Vita Virgo has a motive for murder . . . Can it all be disentangled before there is further violence . . . ?

APL		CCS	
Cen		Ear	
Mob		Cou	
ALL		Jub	
WH		CHE	
'd		Bel	
'in		Fol	
Con		STO	
Til		HCL	